AF414655

# STARLITE PULP REVIEW #5

## Pulp done right.

**FEATURING:**

Charles Ardai ✦ Robert J. Binney ✦ Connor Boyle ✦ Chris Brady ✦ Colin Brightwell ✦ Ron Clyburn ✦ P. N. Harrison ✦ Karen Harrington ✦ Gabriel Hart ✦ David Scott Hay ✦ Paige Johnson ✦ Andrew Miller ✦ Eric O'Neal ✦ Frank Reardon

Starlite Pulp

Starlite Pulp Review #5 Copyright © 2024 by Starlite Pulp

Cover art is 'Union Station' by Tim Townsley



These stories are works of fiction. Names, characters, businesses, organizations, places, events and incidents are either the product of the author's imagination or are used fictitiously. Any resemblance to actual persons, living or dead, events, or locales is entirely coincidental.

These stories were chosen by the editors at Starlite Pulp through submissions sent to our Submittable page.

For information, contact : editor@starlitepulp.com
Site : www.starlitepulp.com          Instagram : @starlite_pulp
Youtube channel : youtube.com/@starlitepulp

Book and Cover design by Tristan and BT
Executive Editor : Brian Townsley
Associate Editor : Jake Naturman

ISBN: 979-8-218-56118-5

First Edition: December 2024

"What we refuse defines us."

Charles Wright


"Years of love have been forgot/in the hatred of a minute."

*Edgar Allen Poe*


"Go bring me my shotgun/You know I got to start shooting again/
You know I'm gonna shoot my woman/'cause she's foolin' around with
too many men."
*Bring Me my Shotgun*, Lightnin' Hopkins

# STARLITE PULP REVIEW #5

# *LINER NOTES*

I know I say this with virtually every issue, but this Review was just so *different* from an editing perspective, in all the right ways.

'Beter Not Cry' by Robert J. Binney starts this collection off, as it was the first story chosen as well. It's got a holiday theme to it, which is not something we generally do, but trust me, it fits. Let's call it a Santa noirish comedy.  The second story in here is by Edgar and Shamus award-winning writer Charles Ardai, and was, coincidentally, the last story to join the collection. It's short, eloquent, and finely crafted—as one would expect from the editor at Hard Case Crime.

Ever heard of pulp in ancient Rome? I hadn't either—that is, until 'Necropolis' showed up.  You can thank Chris Brady for that.  Andrew Miller brings us back to the post-covid present with an LAPD tale of immigration and corruption in 'Red Swarm.'  Next, Connor Boyle takes us behind the curtain with a hybrid 'story cloaked in another story' where the Old West meets horror. Or Sci Fi. You choose.

'Jailbait Birthday' is next, by Paige Johnson from Outcast Press, and she delivers some gritty neo-noir, as you'd expect.  'Anthropodermic' follows, and it's just your average, every day story about books made with human skin. As a side note, I don't have any of those.  'BRUTAL LOVE...' by Frank Reardon follows, and it has a sort of Thompsonesque feel to it, and manages to combine armed robbery with hippies in Alabama in the late 60's. 'The Return of the Grievous Angel' is next up, and continues the theme of 'never a normal Western' in these pages, as you'll find out.

'Domesticated' is next on the bill, and if you had told me we'd be publishing a story about a down-on-his-luck PI that speaks with animals, well, I'd have probably thrown something at you. But here it is. And man, is it fun. 'The Fisherman' by Gabriel Hart follows, with a creepy yarn about The Salton Sea—if you're familiar with that body of water and its maladies, Gabe doesn't pull any punches here. I loved 'It Felt Like a Kiss' the first time I read it, as it wonderfully combines the femme fatale archetype with the often abusive lyrics of the girl bands of the 50s and 60s into one fun read. 'The Recluse' by Karen Harrington is next, and I believe this is the first time we at Starlite have published a story with a writer as protagonist, though it is a well-used trope by King and many others. The story is a polished gem. We finish the volume with 'Clicker Hill' by Eric O'Neal, who was in the 1st Review as well. It is a Sci Fi story masked as a Western. Maybe. You be the judge.

So, another issue in the books, and I certainly hope you enjoy reading it as much as we enjoyed putting it together. Until next time, here's to the blank page.

BT, Starlite Pulp, Winter 2024

# BETTER NOT CRY
## BY ROBERT J. BINNEY

They don't tell you how many kids piss on Santa's lap.

His first day on the job, Nick Dettmer hadn't known any better and sure as hell didn't bring an extra pair of red pants. Full disclosure: He thought he'd pissed himself. He hadn't done that in a while, but he also hadn't been up and functioning during daylight in a while, either.

The folks downstairs wouldn't issue a second costume, so he blew the last of his pre-first-paycheck cash at the Dress for Less on five pairs of red sweats. He'd figure some way to get even with his new employer, Langstrom's Department Store, even if it meant swiping $39.89 worth of fancy chocolates from that pop-up display on Level Four. *"Level Four,"* crap, now he's starting to sound like them.

Some of the moms thought he looked tacky, but who were they to talk, in their Lululemons, coddling mouthbreathers for so long that the mere sight of a man with a beard and rosy-as-hell cheeks undid years of potty training? Only thing for him was to remember to swap his 30-day chip on breaks.

The photographer couldn't care less if the kids flooded Nick's pants, as long as they smiled. He had all sorts of tricks – he'd wave puppets, make goofy faces – but that often scared the brats more.

Why couldn't they just be normal, sit on his lap, and ask for GI Joes and Barbies? He had this one kid this morning tried explaining crypto to him. Saw Christmas as an opportunity for "leveraged earnings." Another had an absolute tantrum that Nick didn't know what a 3D resin printer was; right before lunch, he had to explain to Whitney, who was "seven and five-sixths," that Santa wouldn't replace her servants this year. As if it couldn't be more galling, Whitney's visit was chaperoned by a woman from the West Indies that Nick was sure wasn't a blood relative.

And that elf Rudy, always with the "oopsies:" "Did someone have an oopsie?", "Looks like someone oopsied!" Singing carols like he was in some goddamned Hallmark musical. "Rudy Toot-Toot," Nick called him, and that is what landed him in today's "Diversity and Inclusion" lecture down in the Personnel office.

Nick had hoped to use his lunch break to sneak into Accounting and rummage through their archives, not getting lectured by some college graduate with a bullring in "their" nose about "respecting the struggle" and making sure that Santa's Workshop was a "safe space."

He'd figured that since it was Accounting's holiday luncheon, he could bash in, toss out some "Ho Ho Ho"s and disappear into the file room. Full disclosure, he had no idea what he was looking for, but he was running out of options and the statute of limitations was close to expiring.

"You done learnin' to be respectful, Santa?" Christy, one of the broads from Personnel, had been sent to lock up the room. So much for sneaking a drink before heading out. Nick's first reaction was to give her the finger, but then he decided to grab his crotch and let fly a "respect this" or something, but then he decided to leave everything be. So it all ended up looking like some spastic shrug.

"I hope you're more enthusiastic with the children!" The twinkle in her eye and slight smirk led him to believe she wasn't busting his balls as bad as he first supposed.

She had one of those key rings that looked like an old phone cord wrapped around her elbow. He hadn't thought about that, that the file room would be bolted shut, even during the day. It had been a long time since he'd had to pick a lock. He'd gotten used to bashing doors in – or, more often, getting other guys to do the bashing.

He looked at his Timex, then down the hall. Damn near out of time.

"Goin' to the Accountin' party?" He placed her accent as Texas, but her frosted bob and floral dress – definitely not from Level Four, or if it was, she used her Langstrom's employee discount during the H.W. Bush years – seemed more hillbilly-in-the-city. Pennsyltucky. Probably first in her family with teeth.

Christy looped her arm around Nick's elbow. "Won't I be the belle of the ball, showin' up at the Christmas party with Santa!"

"Really, that's okay, I can make it—"

"Nonsense!" She leaned into him, pressing her chest into his bicep. He felt the industrial-strength nylon of her bra straining against its contents, her perfume starting to get to him. Fruity, all-encompassing without being overbearing. Maggie used to call it "rose water."

Hell. Maggie.

"So what does Santa do when he ain't Clausin'?"

Resent his fall from grace. Drink to forget about the resentment. Think about how to turn the tables on the brass that framed him. Drink some more to bury his inability to find a solution. Drink even more to forget what a pathetic loser he'd become.

He didn't think he'd ever walked so slowly in his life, Christy dictating pace like it was the damned Langstrom's parade, her white flats scuffing along the stained industrial linoleum.

"Really, I need to get back upstairs to the North Pole and, you know, spread joy and all."

"You get lonely in that Workshop all night?"

So help him God, Nick could picture himself unhooking that bra. Could sense the relief they'd both feel as she spilled out of it, straddling him. But then he remembered where he lived. Definitely not a panty dropper. Hallway innuendo aside, even this 50-ish jowly matron in control-tops was out of his league. But she did have those keys.

She threw the door open to Accounting, announced Santa's arrival, and he made it past the build-your-own cookie buffet.

❄❄❄

"The hell you been?!?"

"Language!"

Just like a wife, nagging before he's even in the door. Nick had barely set foot "backstage" of the Santa's Workshop set – a fire trap of black polyester curtains and space heaters – and already they were starting on him. First out of the gate was his Mrs. Claus –real name Didi, or Dierdre, or something – and the censoring admonishment was from his twinkle-toed elf.

"I was learning how to meet Prancer over here 'where he is'," Nick looked over at Rudy Toot-Toot, whose face modeled a caricature of hurt feelings, "No disrespect."

The elf put his hands on his hips and pouted, assorted bells on his costume jingling, then with mechanical precision lit up with a festive, "Who's ready to make merry?" He leaned in and sniffed both Clauses.

Back on that first day, Nick made the mistake of sneaking a Camel Light in uniform. The loading dock supervisor snitched him out to Christy – she let him go with a "verbal warning" but Rudy Toot-Toot has not let him forget that the kiddies don't want their Santa to smell like desperation and hopelessness.

With a quick nod of approval, Rudy Toot-Toot threw open the workshop door – its cheap plywood construction rattling on undersized bought-in-bulk hinges – and, in his singsong tenor, proclaimed the arrival of Father Christmas.

The screeches of excitement from the children was a potato peeler to Nick's spine as he made his way to the big chair. There were a hundred, maybe more, critters sucking on Go-Gurts and bin candy waiting to negotiate with a strange man for toys they'd play with, at most, twice.

And the lights were hot. Place was lit like a TV studio. Rudy Toot-Toot says it's to capture a larger-than-life color palette, but they can't put a flash on the camera? You got your filters that make you look like a cat, or everything look like an old-timey tintype – they couldn't adjust for light?

Mrs. Claus stepped into position, the light catching her earrings. Moonbeams reflecting off a river. Nick couldn't figure why she'd work here if she had that kind of money. Maybe one of those bored wives of hedge fund bros, but that didn't square with the dark rings under her eyes battling the drugstore-brand concealer, or the self-taught angles of her manicure and bangs.

Then it was time for the kiddies. One after another. And the crap they asked for. He knew Langstrom's catered to an expensive sort, but the way these brats wanted – no, demanded – specifics felt like order-taking. It wasn't Tommys asking for Xboxes –extravagant enough – but Galens asking for Xbox Pros with multi-core processers and Acro-Slam Pack Vibrating Console Chairs. The Sonic Sailor version not the Captain Universe version, of course. Some six-year-old – her name was Allegra, like the cold pills – actually asked Nick for a more humane way to pull his sleigh. Cruelty-free or some shit. When he said he'd use a snowmobile instead, she started crying and blubbering about fossil fuels and what future was she leaving for *her* children?

Say this for Mrs. Claus, she could read the room and knew when it was time to move on. Rudy Toot-Toot would let each kid talk to his heart's content, but when she saw Nick was done, he was done. Yes, that was a genuine twinkle in his eye when he thanked her for shooing the booger-eating eco-warrior back to her soccer mommy.

If he was a betting man – and he wasn't, not anymore – Nick would have laid down a tenspot that Mrs. Claus wasn't wearing those earrings before lunch.

Mouth-breathers and lap-pissers populated the afternoon. The worst were entire families doing Christmas card pictures; it always had to be just right. But Mom always blinks then Junior cries and Dad snaps and... After the Himebaughs – all nine of them, each somehow heavier than the last – had their portrait shot, Nick was ready for a break. He needed a smoke and he needed pants that didn't smell like a Philadelphia phone booth, but Rudy Toot-Toot promised one more.

When Nick first started, he kinda expected to see guys from the job bring their kids and grandkids in. But long gone were the days where a jake could afford to live on this side of town; Nick could barely afford it even when he did live here. Most folks resented commuting for their paycheck; they weren't going to spend their off days on the goddamned subway, not to shop at a place where a pair of jeans ran more than a week's groceries.

Scratch what he said before. The worst were actually boys alone with their dads, because it was usually a Custody Day thing, and it was always steeped in resentment.

This one took more coaxing than usual; it had been easier to convince Nick to stay than to get the brat to come forward. He was petrified. Maybe five, or a neglected six, a lousy bowl cut, his mouth candy-cane-sticky and eyes wide with terror. Nick could see why: his dad was literally pushing him, sneering at him, to "talk to Santa." Nick used to run across guys like that, who thought because they were a "job creator" or a "friend of the councilman" they belonged in a wider seat on the airline of life. Full disclosure, they were just assholes. Like this guy. Yelling into his phone and at his son – "Jimbo" - simultaneously.

Against his better judgment, Nick felt for the kid. He'd made his career roughing up bullies – street level and C-suite level – and this twerp was clearly bullied. His dad was a bully.

Rudy Toot-Toot took Jimbo's hand and led him to Santa. The poor kid's efforts to climb into Nick's lap reminded him of the one time he tried to get on horseback; once Jimbo was settled, he wrapped his hands around the big man's neck like a long-lost lover.

"Ho ho ho, what's your name? Is it Jimbo?"

The kid didn't speak so his father did. "Answer his questions, Jimbo! Otherwise you're getting shit for Christmas!" He turned to the other parents in line with a shrug: What're ya gonna do?

Nick spoke with his Victim Voice. "It's okay, why don't you tell me what you'd like for Christmas, Jimbo?"

Even with the kid's breath steaming inside Nick's ear, he could barely make out the whisper. "It's James."

"What's that, little friend?"

"My name is James."

His dad stepped forward, hand-muting his phone. "Can we move it along, Santa?"

Nick bounced the kid once on his knee. He could feel the tell-tale warmth of a faulty bladder, but it wasn't Santa that the boy feared. It was everything else. "Go ahead and tell Santa. Do you want a video game? Or maybe a chemistry kit?"

James snapped his head toward his father, then buried his face in Nick's neck again. Nick wasn't sure he heard what the boy said, so he asked him again.

"I want dad to stop hurting my mommy." He said it like it was a question, not believing in its potential.

"Do you... do you mean hurting her feelings?"

The kid sniffled. Barely a whisper: "He hits her."

In this job, Nick had grown used to bawling kids, faces full of snot; this was a quiet, syncopated sniffle. He recognized pain.

"Come on, Jimbo. We gonna do this picture or not?"

Rudy counted to three, the happy moment memorialized. The plywood-and-artificial turf platform shook under dad's march to collect his son. "You got elves or fairies working for you?"

"That'll get you on Santa's naughty list," Nick let James down and stood. "You shouldn't talk about Santa's helpers like that."

The dad waved Santa off as he shoved James' arms into a puffy coat.

Nick put his hand on the man's shoulder and squeezed. Hard. He winced and turned, looking for a fight.

With his other hand, Nick extended a candy cane. The confused man took it, and Nick gave him a warm smile. "Better watch out!"

Nick and Rudy walked off to finally take their break, his hand resting on the elf's shoulder. "Only I can talk about Santa's helpers like that."

❄❄❄

The rest of the shift passed with the comfort and joy of a tequila hangover. The last Saturday before Christmas, Langstrom's should charge more; demand pricing, like the airlines.

The Security line at the employee exit was longer than usual. The guards were ransacking everyone's bags, making them turn out their pockets, wanding them.

Ordinarily the subcontracted force was as diligent as an arthritic basset hound; today, even shift supervisor Cedric Warren was on his feet inspecting. He and Nick had gone through Academy together and had passed on the street once or twice since, but that was all a long time ago. For Nick, thirty-five pounds and a scraggly white beard ago.

Cedric did not recognize him. Asked him to take off his watch cap. Made Nick wonder who would ever attend a "dog and pony show" in the first place. He started to ask what the hubbub was and thought better of it: He needed a drink and to practice his lockpicking.

Nick took his coat back from the guard, who barely hid his look of disgust, when he felt an arm grab his elbow. That's it, he thought. Jig's up.

"Buy a gal a drink?"

It was Mrs. Claus, skipping the line and pissing everyone else off in the process. She wore gold hoops in her ears.

"Something wrong with your mouth? You sound funny."

She shrugged. Cedric shrugged. What the hell.

❄❄❄

Nick's cousin was a park ranger in center city Philadelphia, of all places, and he used to talk about a bar across from the Liberty Bell that, after all the day's sightseeing tours wrapped, filled with dozens of Ben Franklins and Betsy Rosses getting their loads on.

That story came back to Nick, sitting here in Glider's Pub. Two blocks off the retail core, half its clientele either had genuine long white beards, or was still picking at the gum that held on fake ones all day. A room of retail Santas chewing the ice out of bottom-shelf spirits. Ho ho ho.

Tonight, "half the clientele" meant three people. Nick wasn't good at math, but he knew liquor receipts alone wouldn't cover the owner's nut on the place. Whatever other business went on in the back, it didn't matter. Glider's was one of the last places in the city that didn't have SportsCenter blasting all day and still picked through your change for the next round.

Dee – Nick decided to call her just "Dee" – was the only Mrs. Claus there. He spun his 30-day chip on its edge while they knocked back shots of

Crown.

"You, ah, supposed to be drinkin' with one a' those?"

Nick didn't look up. "Not that kind of deal."

"What kinda deal is it?"

The kind where you go thirty days not showing up drunk to work. Thirty days of not topping off your coffee or having a midmorning pick-me-up. Thirty days of sober work for the first time since he and the rest of the varsity team lugged irrigation equipment across Coach Watson's cabbage fields.

"Nice sparklers you had on earlier."

Dee instinctively reached towards her left ear, then paused. Busted.

"Funny how you weren't wearing them when we left Security. Where'd you hide them?"

She paused, then flashed a toothy grin.

"Bold move, making a pull during a shift. How'd you make the slip?" He signaled for two more shots.

"What are you, some kinda detective?"

"Not anymore."

Her eyes flashed in momentary panic.

"Relax, Dee. Long time ago. Tonight I just want to have a drink and get on with things."

"Those things involve getting home to Wifey and the little ones?"

"Also a long time ago."

"She didn't like being married to a cop?"

"It was complicated."

Full disclosure, Maggie hadn't minded being married to a cop. Not at first. With his pension and health insurance, both felt a security neither had grown up with. When he made detective, they indulged with the apartment on Astoria Avenue, in the precinct and in the shadow of the truly successful. Barely five blocks from where he sat right now, but a world away.

They'd see neighbors heading out in tuxedos and low-cut gowns turn up on Page Six days later. Neighbors from the higher floors, of course. The top two floors – you needed the doorman to turn the elevator key to get there – belonged to Arvid Langstrom II. Rumors were he had a lap pool, a bowling alley, a private elevator inside his apartment. Not that a guy like Arvid Langstrom II bowled, but to be rich enough to soundproof that big a space – to waste that much space – is something. Nick and Maggie felt like millionaires just being that close to such luxury.

It's not fair to say Mags grew resentful, but when she learned Nick's gold-shield salary bump was likely his last, that they were as rich as they were ever going to be, something changed. Not resentful, but disappointed. Like someone took away her plate before she finished.

Then one foggy Christmas Eve, Nico was born. That didn't help financially, but he was pure sunshine and infused their tiny apartment with a joy they'd never imagined. They even learned to love each other again. Nick took extra shifts doing private security –insurance work, or providing "protection" for stripclub-hopping linebackers – and things were good again.

Until Nico started having headaches. No one could find anything wrong with him, but everyone agreed a four-year-old shouldn't be balled up in the dark, squeezing his skull and moaning. No family was ever more grateful for a civil servant's health plan. By the time the specialist found the tumor, they had only a few days to show him a lifetime of love before they abandoned him in that little pine box.

They both dealt with Nico's death by not dealing with it. Maggie replaced her devotion to him with an equal affection for vodka; Nick took undercover work. Just to get out of that goddamned apartment. At first he'd be gone – on loan to other precincts – for just a day or two, but turned out he was good at it. And he had nothing to come home to. So the assignments got longer, the covers deeper.

He was posing as a mid-level dealer in some pharmaceutical scam when he first noticed a real change in Mags. When he'd left, she was in one of her Tito's Handmade blackouts, sprawled on Nico's bed, kitchen sink filled with dirty pots and its white tiled walls splattered with store-brand sauce.

But this time, after closing the case, he walked in, the place was spotless. The satellite radio was tuned to "Pop Hits" and Nico's room had been converted to a cozy parlor. Just a small couch and two comfortable-looking chairs. Full disclosure: Nick was pissed off she'd tossed away their boy's stuff, erased his existence, without discussing it. But he figured if this was her upswing, he'd take it. She was still drinking, it seemed, but she had energy and life.

Every day, people lied to Nick; he knew this too was an all an act. She wasn't ready to be a loving wife, that even though she'd amputated the vestiges of their son, phantom pain lingered.

Over the next three months, he went home only twice. His latest case was a ballbreaker, sapping whatever humanity he had left. And each time he came back to Astoria Avenue, it was different: a leather couch, a fully-stocked bar cart (clear and brown liquor), three kinds of crackers in the pantry. He didn't know their credit card's interest rate, but he didn't ask questions.

One night he came in unannounced, hoping he'd catch her in bed – either alone or with someone, it didn't matter, he'd at least put his imagination to rest either way. Instead he walked in on a party. An actual goddamn cocktail party, with about a dozen well-dressed people laughing and talking and patting each other's forearms and honest-to-God smooth jazz playing on the wireless speakers he knows he didn't buy.

Maggie was momentarily taken aback before hugging him and introducing him around. She was wearing a stunning black halter-cut, looking like he'd never seen – the precision of her eyeliner, the casually-engineered perfection of her hair – and framed in the center of her pushed-up bust was a gold necklace filled with enough rubies to eat up a year's worth of his salary. He was so enraged he wasn't even impressed when one of the swells introduced him to Arvid Langstrom II himself, a remarkably-preserved sixty who smelled of Clubman talc and single malt older than Nick.

He wanted to fire a round into the ceiling and throw everyone off the balcony. They wouldn't have fallen far. But he hadn't seen Mags that happy since Nico's last birthday, and, what the hell, he'd always been a go-along to get-along guy.

By the end of the night, he figured he wouldn't have to worry about his credit card balance. It was clear that Langstrom was writing some checks. Maybe not for the booze and veggie plates, but her dress, that necklace, her newfound attempts to embrace enthusiasm. In that moment right before a party begins to wane, Nick spotted them in conversation, her head tilted the way it was back when he described his earliest cases. And she laughed at everything the old man said. And he was the only guest she walked out. Nick knew the elevators could be slow, but they were gone a long time. Instead of saying something he'd regret, he just left.

He never saw his wife alive again.

To this day, what he regrets is not waiting to say goodnight.

The day after the party, Nick stormed Langstrom's office – the one on Level Six of the very store where he now works – waving his badge and acting exactly how a man whose life is falling apart acts: Like a raging asshole. For his part, the executive denied having an affair with Maggie, even called her a "slut" and "gold digger" who was "too much drama." Nick, drunk with both rage and Dewar's, was dragged out by Security. Now he sees that same guard in the break room every morning. He doesn't remember leaving Langstrom a voice mail that night, but from the excerpts they played for him later in the interrogation room, it was a corker.

Maggie had been concussed by a scotch bottle with Nick's fingerprints on it. It was his apartment, his scotch, but he never once put so much as a finger on that woman. Ballistics matched the kill shot back to his service revolver, which he had locked in the gun safe in his nightstand before leaving on assignment. And was mysteriously missing during the investigation.

One reason he wasn't in prison right now was his airtight alibi – he was undercover at the Port Authority with Spider Corcoran, recruiting teenage junkies for Spider's backroom casinos.

Nick knew, he was positive, it was Arvid Langstrom II who beat the love of his life and shot her point-blank. But to push that idea, to make any of it public – and "Retail Titan Bludgeons Mistress in Love Nest" would become public – would put Nick in the spotlight, too. At best, the Corcoran investigation would collapse, years of task force work wasted; at worst, he'd be at the bottom of the river.

So it was ruled suicide. Self-inflicted shot to the back of the head. They still took Nick's badge and his pension. In one fell swoop, his son, his wife, his job, his savings – all his reasons for living – gone.

They never found that necklace, and, full disclosure, Nick had forgotten about it until a few weeks ago – late October – when he found himself in the old neighborhood staring at Langstrom's display windows. At the larger-than-life photo of one of TV's "real" housewives wearing identical goddamn rubies.

Back in his new apartment – a fourth-floor walkup with a leaky radiator and creepy-crawlies the size of Halloween candy – he curled up with a bottle of Quixote Gold (four dollars a fifth) and re-read the autopsy. No necklace.

Somewhere in his agave-and-grain addled mind, he was convinced he could find proof that Langstrom had given it to Maggie and had now regifted it to his latest squeeze.

Nick hadn't shaved or exercised since the firing, and knew he was in no shape to strongarm an investigation, but he could clear his head enough to make it through the seasonal Santa hiring process. He traded the tequila for Clorox, combing it into his beard until he thought his face would burn off, and here he was.

Mostly sober, and staring down the deadlines of his admittedly ramshackle investigation, he didn't even know what he was looking for. But he knew he'd find *something*. Guys like Langstrom weren't smart, they were just bullies with resources. On a good day, Nick was smart. And on a bad day, he was violent.

"Hello? Earth to Santa Claus?"

Martini the bartender stood there with their Crown shots on a mildewy tray, refusing to set them down til he saw cash. Nick couldn't run a tab here even when he was on the job.

Dee looked at him with, what he guessed, concern. "You okay?"

"Yeah. Just was thinking about..."

He was holding a photo from that last Christmas with Nico. The three of them in matching peppermint-striped jammies. Waiting at the window for Santa Claus. Nick didn't remember pulling it out of his wallet.

Not one year after that picture was taken, Nick was begging doctors he didn't trust and a God he didn't believe in to make his kid's headaches go away. But that night, right after the picture was taken, Nico told them he had asked Santa for the three of them to always be that happy. For every day to feel like Christmas.

Out of the mouths of fucking babes.

"This should be the best time of year for a kid," Nick yelled at Dee.

"They say it's the hap, happiest time of— Hey! Where ya going?"

He stood, pulled on his coat, and threw some bills on the table. "I have to..."

"Aintcha gonna drink your shot?"

❄❄❄

Cedric was still working the desk at the Employee Entrance.

"Store's closed, Santa."

Nick raised his palms, complacent. "I know, I got all the way home and remembered I left my uniform here and it's laundry night, so..."

"Guess you're wearing dirty tomorrow."

"It's not just dirt, it's... Look." And Nick explained the piss and the five pairs of sweats and the smell of Philadelphia phone booths and tried to convince Cedric to give him one of those phone-cord keyrings.

Cedric wasn't happy, but he gave in. Kind of. "With that nonsense in the Jewelry Department this morning, I gotta walk you back to your locker."

Nick pretended like he didn't know what the nonsense was, while trying to figure out how to get what he needed with this off-duty flatfoot tailing him.

The whole walk to Santa's Workshop, Cedric would not shut up about how much his kids used to love getting their picture taken with Santa, and now his grandkids, and did Nick have kids? And what a great feeling it must be to spread so much happiness and see their faces light up and on and on and on until Nick finally saw an opening. His chance to get a moment alone.

"Why don't you go on and have a seat right here in the big chair? See how it feels while I root through my locker?" He pulled the curtain open as invitation. Also to confirm that what he was looking for wasn't out on the set; he hoped Rudy Toot-Toot stored it in his locker.

"Aw, I couldn't do that. That would be disrespectful."

Shit.

Nick popped his locker open and reached through the dirty clothes until he found a bottle of schnapps he'd been saving in case of emergency. This qualified. "You want to share in a little yuletide spirit?"

Cedric took one look at the bottle and Nick feared that his gamble was about to go balls up. Then his face glowed and Nick could absolutely picture how stupid his children and grandchildren must look in their matching sweaters on Christmas day in the morning. "Let me go to the cafeteria and get some cups!"

That was what Nick was banking on. He'd never seen a rent-a-cop move so quickly; he thought he actually saw Cedric's tongue hanging out the side of his mouth as he took off.

Before the door was even closed, Nick was prying Rudy Toot-Toot's locker. Who needs skill when even the tiniest amount of brute force will pop the lock?

In the top cubby, Nick got his hands on the prize. The laptop. He powered it up – of course it needed a password. Brute force won't work this time, and no way he could guess what went through that man's head. He pushed aside about a dozen different after-shaves, expensive skin toner, a vape pen that smelled suspiciously like cannabis – you naughty little elf! - and found what he'd hoped. A post-it note with both user name and password. It never fails.

Nick pulled up the transaction ledger. Something simple, like a list of kids' names and addresses, was clearly too much to hope for. No, this was a not-totally-inscrutable table but did include last name and credit card billing zip code. And a blue underlined transaction number that Nick hoped was in chronological order.

The one he was looking for should be forty or fifty from the end. Hoping for a Christmas miracle, he clicked on the transaction. Yes! A small picture popped up on screen, a proof copy of the photo with Santa. It was just a thumbnail – Nick had to squint – but he remembered that bratty little girl. Wanted a new phone for Christmas. Who the hell is a six-year-old calling? Anyway, she was about half an hour later than the one he was looking for.

A little trial and error, and the third time was the charm. "Viola!" he said, out loud; Maggie used to tease him for that. It wasn't much, but it was hopefully enough to go on. An Adamson Heights address, of course.

Nick got everything locked back up just in time to enjoy a toast with Cedric. He stuffed a sack with his official uniform – pants and all – and begged off a second round. The library closed in 25 minutes, and he had research to do.

❆❆❆

In his civvies, Nick fit right in with the homeless guys surfing softcore porn on the public computers. It was amazing what SimplePeopleFinder.com turned up: In less than five minutes, he found an address and photos confirming that the people he was looking for lived there. When he was on the job, an official records search, done through proper channels, would have taken hours and probably been wrong. Jack Frost nipped his nose while he bound down the library steps, but he didn't care. He was on a mission. He tipped his cap to the lion statues and double-timed to the bus stop.

Patience and fortitude indeed.

❆❆❆

The subways don't run to Adamson Heights. If they made it easy for people of limited means to get to the nice neighborhoods, just imagine what might happen? Nick caught a case out here once, and the pearl-clutching at the mere thought of *those* people and the crime they brought had stuck in his head. You can't afford a mortgage on a place like this by following the rules, but out here was different. Out here was white-collar crime. Emphasis on the white.

He transferred to a number 36 bus, which still dumped him six blocks from his goal. He had changed into his Santa outfit, earning a few smiles from

24

the polyester-formalwear clad folks waiting to board. He figured they had been working neighborhood Christmas parties; he imagined every morning, troops of domestic help marching away from this very corner, fanning out to make an honest living.

The air had the wet bite that made everything feel colder than it was; it smelled like the season's first snow was on its way. But it was the faintest trace of misgivings that gave Nick shivers. What if he was at the wrong house? What if the situation wasn't what he thought it was? What if *they* were having a big party?

He dismissed the first and last concerns, knowing he could pivot if needed on the other.

The neighborhood got ritzier, the cars in the driveways nicer – Benzes, Escalades, nameless blocks of plastic saving the environment by sharing a 220 outlet with the hot tub – before descending back into the mere lower-upper class. Middle management, at least. Basketball nets, yards decorated by dads and not services.

Finally, Nick found the address he'd written on his hand. A two-story colonial, the porch done up with whatever was on sale at the craft store. Tastefully festive and definitely a woman's touch. Lights from the back rooms – kitchen probably, and maybe a widescreen on the opposite side of the house – cast shadows against the sheer nylon curtains in the front living room. Either the angle was funny, or the Christmas tree in there was leaning against the side wall. Could be sitting in one of those piece-of-shit tree stands, he rationalized. More likely, someone had knocked it over.

One light upstairs. Back bedroom. Probably a night light. Nick checked his watch. He didn't know what time kids went to bed these days, but he hoped his timing was right.

He stood at the door, adjusted his uniform. He'd traded blue for red, there was nothing hanging on his belt save for a bowlful of jelly, but it felt good to be back at it. Knocking on doors. Restoring his sense of purpose.

His leather-gloved hand hovered over the brass ring. Maybe this would go easy. Maybe just a friendly chat. And maybe the 36 bus back downtown will be pulled by eight reindeer.

He heard angry voices inside. Who wouldn't be riled up at such a clatter at this time of night. The footsteps approaching on the other side were not friendly. Moment of truth time.

The door opened. Bingo. James' dad.

Nick forced his best eye-twinkle and ho-ho-ho's.

"Hell do you want!"

It was not going to be a friendly chat.

Nick forced his way inside, smiling, shouting up the stairs that he hoped that little James was nestled all snug in his bed upstairs. Mostly as a warning.

The man laid hands on Santa; Nick didn't retaliate, being an illegal B and E and all, but with a quick squeeze and twist of his finger, let him know that all touches from here on out were bad touches.

The living room, save for the leaning tree and broken ornaments on the floor, was immaculate. Evidence that a lovely table had once been set in the dining room – candlesticks, dessert forks, China coffee service – was belied by the indications that whoever sat at the head did not like his meal.

The kitchen was a disaster. Broken glasses, smashed plates, lasagna smeared across the floor. A woman at the sink, white-knuckling the counter, concentrating on the dishwater.

The man yelled at Nick to get out, threatening him. Largely background noise until he pulled on Nick's arm. The intruder spun, popped the man in the face with a closed fist, feeling that satisfying crunch of cartilage turning to jelly. The man howled, spun away, buying Nick a few seconds at least.

Nick approached the woman, tried speaking softly. To cut through the chaos. He put his hand – lightly, so so gently – on her shoulder. She flinched.

This could go one of two ways, he knew. She could turn on Nick, protect her house, her life here; she could have a meat cleaver under the sudsy water. He stood next to her, palms on the counter. Caught their reflection in the window over the sink, a ridiculous tableau. He'd forgotten what he was wearing. But there was nothing cute or charming about her bruises, obvious even in the darkened glass. Their eyes met.

"Let me help you," Nick whispered.

"It's my fault."

He let that hang.

She sucked some snot up her nose before continuing. "I know he likes green peppers in his sauce... I forgot to pick them up. I knew better."

"Would you like some help?"

Nothing.

"For James?"

She closed her eyes. A tear rolled down her nose and hung on the tip.

Dime-sized snowflakes fell outside. It should have been beautiful.

"Leave my wife alone!"

Nick caught the flash of metal in the window and twisted, taking the fire poker on his shoulder instead of his skull. He turned. He was glad he didn't have his weapon.

❄❄❄

Nick walked to the stairway. The man was curled up in a ball next to the tree, soaked in his own blood and urine – oopsie – and moaning about missing teeth. Nick reminded him they weren't missing, he could get them in the morning if he was careful about flushing. Mom stood in the door frame, holding a wet dish towel. Full disclosure: Nick would have bet a tenspot she was seconds away from kneeling over her husband to daub his wounds. People were funny. Always with the goodwill toward the wrong men.

He peeled off his bloody gloves and shoved them in his pocket on top of his 30-day chip. This will be a hell of a share at the next meeting.

James had slept through the whole thing. Probably learned to tune out slaps and shrieks and tears way too long ago. Nick kneeled next to his bed, adjusted his sheets. "It would have been easier if you'd asked for an Xbox."

The boy was wearing peppermint-striped pajamas.

❄❄❄

Nick's boots crunched in the snow walking back to the bus stop. He owed Rudy an apology for breaking into his locker. He figured the little fruitcake would understand.

Tomorrow he would confront Arvid Langstrom II. He'd find an angle. Might ask Christy out for a drink.

Right. Maybe after that, peace on Earth. But for now, to all, a good night.

# STAGES

## BY CHARLES ARDAI

Tipsy already with only one drink in him, Carroll Starlight fumbled with the stage door, trying to get it open. His key didn't seem to fit the lock, try as he might to make the match. He was on the point of calling for help when the door swung open and a stagehand helped him through.

"Heard you out there, Mr. S," the man said. "Too cold a night to leave you fumbling with your keys."

"I wasn't fumbling," Carroll Starlight said.

"Don't exactly know why you had to go out," the stagehand went on, helping Starlight off with his overcoat and scarf. "Nothing you couldn't have had here. Except cold air and a chance to slip and break your neck, which wouldn't have done us any good at all. Well."

He stood back to look at the thin old man before him.  Starlight was already dressed in his costume, a dandied-up suit of eveningwear with white spats and a stiff, high shirt collar.  The stagehand pulled a cane from a prop trunk, tore off the label that said "Starlight," and handed it to the old man, who took it in his hands gingerly.

"Off you go," the stagehand announced, waving Starlight upstairs to the dressing rooms.  "I'll call the ten and the five."

"Thank you," Starlight said, putting none of his weight on the cane as he climbed.

The stagehand slipped off to arrange props for the acts in the wings.  Carroll Starlight paused halfway up the stairs to catch his breath and get his bearings.  He held onto the narrow wood rail, worn shiny by a half-century of use, and let his eyes swim in his head.  Balance mocked him as he swayed on the twelfth step up.  How long since the last time he had climbed these stairs?  Thirty years?  He took a deep breath and made his way to the top step, slowly.

From the stage below came the sounds of a tumbling act.  The heavy, rhythmic thumps of bodies springing and landing and turning about.  And applause, polite for the lesser tricks, enthusiastic for the marvels.  As Carroll Starlight pushed the door to his dressing room open, he closed his eyes and smiled, brought back by the sound of applause to the days when he first trod the boards.  "A unique act," F.P.A. had written in <u>The Conning Tower</u>, "half dexterity, half nerve.  If an opening-night audience's applause is any indication, 'Carroll Starlight' (his mother called him Charlie Schearl) has many such nights ahead of him." Somewhere in his apartment, Starlight had a yellow, brittle copy of that review, pressed between sheets of cardboard.

Starlight pulled the door closed, shutting out the sound. He turned and sat at the mirror, unscrewed the caps from a half-dozen jars and started daubing his makeup on his cheeks. His fingers were still stiff from the cold and unsteady from the tall tumbler of scotch he had left unfinished at Parnell's down the block. He worked carefully, coating his face with even layers of foundation and white greasepaint, wiping his hands on his makeup rag when he finished. He paced the room, catching himself on the wall once when he thought he might fall, then sat and stretched out first his left leg, then his right. He spun the cane between his fingers and it fell to the floor with a clatter. He looked around, embarrassed, as though someone might have seen. When he bent to pick the cane up, he felt the strain in his back.

At the door, the stagehand's voice boomed: "Ten minutes. Mister S."

"Thank you," Starlight said.

#

When the stagehand called five, Carroll Starlight left his dressing room, made his way down the stairs, and hid in a corner of the wings.

From behind a painted prop tree, he watched the act on stage. A young juggler spun china plates through the air, catching each at the last possible instant before it would have smashed to the ground. The audience held its breath, laughing nervously as the juggler added flourishes: spinning in place, tossing the plates behind his back and under his legs, catching one plate with his foot.

Finally, all the plates were down, safe and steady on a metal stand, and the juggler bowed to a roar of applause. His long, curly hair hung down and as he stood up again it covered his face. He made a show of not being able to see, of stumbling about, until he bumped into the plate-stand and tipped it over. He lunged for the falling plates, catching them literally as they touched the stage. The applause was an explosion this time.

Starlight stepped into the juggler's path as the gangly young man left the stage. He put a hand on the juggler's shoulder. "That was marvelous," he said.

"Really?" the juggler said. He was trembling; sweat glistened on his bare arms. "You don't know what it means to me to hear that from you, Mr. Starlight. I grew up watching you."

Carroll Starlight smiled. "What's your name, young man?"

"Jeremy Tarbell."

"You are very talented, Jeremy. You can tell people I said that."

The audience grew quiet then and Carroll Starlight heard himself being announced: the great, the incomparable, the world-famous Carroll Starlight. Let's have a big hand for Carroll Starlight.

A young woman appeared, took Starlight by the hand and led him to the stage. His apparatus was laid out in order. The audience was hushed and nervous, wondering, Starlight knew, whether he could still perform.

He stepped out into their sight, striding across the stage. The applause began, an eruption that rolled over Starlight like a wave, genuine, enthusiastic and true.

Then, as he pressed the tip of his cane against the stage: silence.

\#

The stagehand helped Starlight on with his coat. Jeremy Tarbell watched from a corner of the room as Starlight walked through the door and climbed gingerly down the three steps to the street. The wind had picked up; it whipped Starlight's scarf into his face. "Take care," the stagehand called after him. "Go easy on that leg."
Starlight didn't answer.

As he swung the door shut, the stagehand saw Tarbell watching, his own prop case balanced against one hip. "The poor guy," the stagehand said. "They should never have dragged him out of retirement. Seventy-five years old, you shouldn't try to perform like you were twenty-five."

"He was one of the greats," Tarbell said.

"Sure. But he should have known better than to come back now and try it again."

Tarbell set his case down. "I hope that fifty years from now I have the guts to come back here and try it again."

The stagehand shook his head. "What you do is different, it's juggling."

Tarbell flipped open his case and drew out a plate, white china with a blue border, which he spun high into the air. He stepped back. The stagehand looked up, startled, and reached for it too late.

They both looked away as the plate hit the floor and smashed to pieces. Shards shot across the floor like shrapnel.

"Why'd you do that?" the stagehand said. "Now I've got to clean it up."

"It'll give you some practice," Tarbell said. "Fifty years from now I'll probably break every last one of them."

"Listen, I didn't mean~"

"You meant," Tarbell said. He closed his case, hefted it, and, taking care not to slip, hurried through the door, down the steps, and after Starlight's distant, slowly diminishing figure. He left the door open behind him, bits of snow blowing in on the wind.

# NECROPOLIS

## BY CHRIS BRADY

Drusus's ass hurt from the wagon's hard wooden bench as it bounced across the ruts and gouges of the Appian Way, the highway to the world's most glorious city-state. Rome. Where patricians and politicians amassed power and wealth under the guise of a republic. But in the poor neighborhoods, plebes went hungry. Buildings collapsed while criminals kept law and order. Drusus loathed the city.

He raised a hand over his brow to shield his eyes from the dust and sun. His galea's hot bronze burned a knuckle. These helmets were a bitch to wear in the summer.

Through the dust that rose from the wake of the two chariots running point, he couldn't see much in the distance other than thirsty fields of millet and wheat whose stalks spangled different shades of yellow.

The handful of legionaries in the wagons behind him coughed and wheezed as the gritty dust cloud passed through their lungs.

Nothing to be done about that, Drusus thought. Pulling up the rear on convoy duty was full of disadvantages.

Then, without notice or comprehension, Drusus noticed that the surroundings had switched from grain fields to boneyards.

His eyes caught the sight of a cat darting out from a dirty roadside ribcage. It ran under the wagon, howling as it came out the other side.

The thick smell of death set in Drusus's nostrils like an invisible fog. He'd encountered this odor many times before in the eastern campaigns. But on a battlefield, the stench was purer. More honest. Out here, mourners and the outcasts who lived among the dead tried covering up the aroma with myrrh and cassia, creating a nauseating potpourri that layered sweetness on top of spoilage.

As the convoy drove deeper into the stench, more cats ran around the convoy, spooking the horses. Drusus's driver, Rufus, wrangled the reins to keep his team in check. As the wagon jostled, the heavy metal cargo hidden under sackcloth in the bed of the wagon rattled tempting chimes of wealth and riches. Drusus knew these seductive tones were tickling the ears of all the soldiers in the convoy. But to him, they meant nothing.

The cats were strong and well-fed, living off a steady diet of sweet meat from decomposing flesh. Generations of inbreeding had perverted their features into goblin-shaped eyes and sharp fangs. They were mean bastards, too, as their herds pushed out the gaunt wolves and dogs who tried scavenging off the remains of corpses. As such, they were among the caretakers of the mass graves where Rome flung her dead, unwanted, and disgraced.

Soon, makeshift lean-tos and small shanties appeared along the highway.

Drusus waited until the convoy was in the middle of this castaway community before hollering, "Halt!"

The convoy's chariots and wagons came to a full stop. A large gray cat with green eyes jumped up next to Drusus and hissed an evil greeting. Rufus punched it off the wagon with a meaty fist while calling it a nasty sonofabitch.

The shanties sat quiet. Surrounding these rickety structures loomed forgotten tombs. Faded graffiti on their marble and stone exteriors mocked the sacred intentions of the burial grounds. Behind them, a forsaken field of bones stretched out to the horizon and beyond.

From the periphery, Drusus spotted a bronzed, shapely leg dangle out from a darkened doorway. A high-pitched giggle floated through the filthy air.

Moments later, a small crowd of women scampered out of the run-down dwellings. They wore torn, ratty togas and tunics, dirtied with the dust of the dead. Some had necklaces made of finger bones that rattled as they shimmy-walked toward the soldiers. The mob of mangy cats rubbed their whiskers against the women's seductive ankles. A chorus of purring rose up as they surrounded the wagons.

Drusus counted eighteen women, matching the number of soldiers in his convoy.

"Centurion," the bustiest among them called to Drusus. Her black hair was thick with Medusa curls. Her voice rang with authority. Yet, if you were to snatch her vocal notes out of the air, string them together and ring them out, steamy puddles of sex would pool around your feet.

Drusus knew her name to be Karolina. She was of Macedonian descent and oversaw this band of prostitutes long exiled out of Rome. Even though prostitution was encouraged and legitimized inside the city-state, these women were accused of conducting business in ways that went against the virtues of the republic. Whatever the hell that meant.

"Are you in need of the Army's assistance?" he answered.

"By the looks of your men, it is you who are in need." She strode closer to one of the point chariots. Her fingers walked up the bicep of the legionnaire who held its reins. "Still an hour's ride to Rome. The road gets easier after you've rested with some fine company who can relieve you of any unnecessary burdens you may be carrying."

"I assure you, our wagons are up to the task of hauling our freight."

Karolina's hand floated under the soldier's tunic. "I'm more concerned about the other goods your men hold."

The soldier's knees buckled. He grasped the front of the chariot and turned to look back at Drusus with pain tormented eyes.

"Come on, sir," he begged with quivering lips. "I'd just as soon be drug through the streets of Rome under the accusations of being a coward over being denied of this woman's helping hand."

Drusus was keenly aware that men fresh from combat duty felt a fever in their balls once the fighting was over. The closer they got to home, the hotter it got.

"I'm hurtin'," the soldier pleaded.

Drusus surveyed the pathetic looks on the soldier's faces.

"Alright," Drusus barked. "Any man wants to take care of his necessaries has my permission to do so. Any services you procure will be paid out of your own pockets or personal bullshit bargains. Understand?"

The soldiers stomped their feet and grunted in unison. Drusus ordered them to disperse.

It didn't take long for the women to pair up with the soldiers. Then they disappeared into the huts and shacks, out of the sun and out of sight.

The road was all but deserted except for the wagons, chariots, and the damn cats. Rufus stayed seated on the wagon. He spit onto the dry ground and rubbed sweat off his forehead.

"I'm not gonna wait all day," Drusus told him. "You better hurry on up and get you a piece before time runs out."

Rufus shook his head. "Think I'll pass. Stink out here is getting to me, done put me out of the mood."

"Smells worse inside Rome."

"Maybe. 'Sides, my preference is for Spanish pussy. Don't want to lose my honor to these graveyard whores."

Drusus nodded. "Suit yourself."

He stood up from the bench and pulled his gladius out from its sheath. The sword was short and sharp. Perfect for killing up close. His time in the Army had taught him how to use it effectively when a maniple came together and locked shields in phalanx formation. Any attacking barbarians who came up against the troop would tire themselves out, bashing endlessly against an armored shield wall. Then they would separate just enough for a soldier to throw a stab into an enemy's armpit or shin. One by one, adversaries were slaughtered by Roman steel. Bye, bye, bar bar.

Drusus moved behind Rufus and stood above him. He looked down at the driver's neck.

"This ain't gonna bring your family back," Rufus said without turning around.

"Probably not," Drusus agreed.

A drone of cicadas rose around them.

"Sandal's come undone."

Rufus chuckled. "Appreciate that, sir."

As Rufus bent down and pretended to reach for his foot, Drusus drove his gladius into the base of Rufus's neck where it met his spine. When he removed the short sword, blood spurted up onto Drusus's stomach and thighs. The dead driver slunk sideways off the wagon's bench and landed hard onto the dusty ground.

After sheathing his sword, Drusus grabbed handfuls of sackcloth and yanked it off the wagon's cargo.

Mithridatic gold, plunder from their campaign, shimmered in the sun's rays. Coins, necklaces, crowns, rings, bricks, rods, and baubles of every shape and size winked at him. This haul was intended to fill Rome's coffers, safely escorted into the city under the protection of the convoy. But Drusus had other ideas.

From inside the shacks, sounds of groans and gasps drifted into his ears. Anyone else would have figured his company was climaxing in concert, but he knew that Karolina's women were plunging hidden daggers into his men. Throats were slit, backs stabbed, sides punctured. He hoped a few were lucky enough to finish inside their killers before dropping into the fields of Elysium.

They were fine soldiers, but he couldn't depend on their loyalties to see his plan through. The temptation of skimming from the treasure pile rendered most of them untrustworthy. The rest held a foolish devotion to the serving the republic, an ideal that Drusus could no longer abide.

One by one, either fully nude or half-naked, Karolina's women stalked out into the air, away from remains of their sensualized bloodletting.

A woman with Egyptian features placed a galea on her head, taken from the soldier she had freshly murdered. She fastened its cheek plates and ran her fingers through its plume of red-dyed horsehair.

"We're rich, bitch!" she shouted at the sky. The others started laughing and danced around the wagons. Some had rubbed blood onto their faces and breasts.

Karolina walked over to Drusus, eyeing the wagon's contents with an ugly cat cradled in her arms.

"Where the fuck's he hiding?" Drusus asked her.

She let out a loud whistle between her teeth. A patter of steps scratched from behind one of the huts.

Just then, Senator Urban scurried out into the open from his hiding spot. The rotund patrician politician was draped in a spotless white toga as if he were ready to deliver a speech to the full Senate. Luxurious sandals covered his feet. As he came closer, Drusus noticed he had a deep sunburn peeling on his balding head and fat cheeks. Men like Urban didn't venture outside too often and were vulnerable to the elements outside of Rome.

"Ah, Centurion. Centurion," Urban cheered. "Let us take a moment to celebrate our successful stratagem." He pushed his way through the dancing women and reached his hands into the wagon bed, pulling up handfuls of gold. "It's ours now."

Karolina let the cat down to the ground and looked at the senator. "Suppose you want a fuck on top of the loot, don't you?"

"By the gods, madam." Urban's hands released their clutches, letting the treasure rain back down onto the pile, before grasping at the shoulders of his toga. "Nothing would please me more."

Drusus clasped a hard, calloused hand around the senator's squishy wrist. "You need to listen first."

"Of course, Drusus. Of course. Many details need fleshing out. How many men remain to sneak our treasure into Rome?"

"There's only us."

A worried look eclipsed the joy on Urban's face.

"All the legionnaires are dead? Who will protect our shipment into the city?"

"The gold's staying right here."

Urban shook his head in disbelief. "But...but. This is to help strengthen the republic against the ambitions of Consul Sulla. We had a plan. A deal."

"Sulla marches his army on Rome."

Horror flashed in Urban's eyes. "Blasphemy. He wouldn't dare seize power as tyrant."

"His army is in motion as we speak. Why this convoy was so light."

"To what ends does he seek the seat of dictator?"

"I don't give a peacock's pecker what his plans are. The gold will be kept out of Rome."

Urban leaned against the wagon. "You're right, Drusus. Of course. With Sulla out of his senses, the riches won't be safe inside the city walls. We'll need more co-conspirators. Though their intrigue will come at a high price. Let us bury our own shares out here amongst the dead to protect our interests."

"The dead are done with your filthy greed. You will not disturb them anymore."

Drusus grabbed Urban by the shoulders and flung him away from the wagon. The fat senator tripped and rolled on the ground before coming to a stop next to a pile of skulls. The cicadas stopped their droning performance.

"You dare betray me?" Urban whimpered. "A senator of the Republic? Man of the people?"

For the first time, Drusus saw dirt on Urban's toga.

"Tell me about your district, Senator."

"You know it well enough. You come from the neighborhood."

"How many apartment blocks have collapsed under your representation? Six or seven sound about right?"

"You exaggerate."

"Wouldn't be surprised if my count was light."

"I fight for construction improvements in the Senate chamber."

"And what will prevent further tragedy?"

"Access to gold from Asia. You know this better than I. The Army's victories bring needed funds, and its flow impregnates Rome with wealth and opportunity. But I am not the only politician requesting stimulus."

Drusus scoffed. "You make it sound orgasmic. We fight and our plunder gets ejaculated all over the city. But ropes of golden jism never find their way into Rome's most fertile areas. Like my fucking neighborhood where it's most needed. Instead, it dries up and crusts inside patrician homes. In the halls of the Senate."

"Do not speak to me in such a manner, you insolent piece of plebian shit."

There it is, Drusus thought. The contempt that lived under the senator's gilded speeches and gladhanding manner.

The gladius sang as Drusus pulled it from its sheath. He nodded at Urban's sandals.

"Your feet look mighty comfy. What is that? Lambskin? Embedded with jewels from Pontus no doubt."

Urban shook his head and held his arms out in a pathetic gesture of self-protection.

"Gifts they were" he cried. "Donations from the assembly to my campaigns."

"Think they could absorb the impact of a four-story drop?"

"I don't understand."

"My wife and daughter went barefoot. Our apartment was fourth floor, top of the block. Went down while I was at war."

"But I am neither architect nor contractor."

"To say the least, asshole. But you're their agent."

"A soldier cannot murder a senator. You are offending the gods."

"Shut up!" Drusus roared. "Shut the fuck up. I told you it was time to listen."

Urban looked around at Drusus and Karolina. Her legion of prostitutes had stopped their celebration. They stared back at the senator in silence.

"I hear nothing."

Drusus pointed his sword at the field of bones.

"Your constituents are speaking. Can't you hear their words?"

"What would they have to tell me?"

Karolina whistled. The women reached into the wagon, picking up the heaviest pieces of gold they could handle.

Drusus pointed his sword back at Urban.

"They say, 'Join us.'"

The Egyptian woman hurled a golden rod at Urban. It struck the center of his chest. He gasped for air while the others pelted him with Asian riches. He tried yelling stop it, stop it, stop it until a hefty ingot split his forehead.

When the women's hands were empty, blood ran down Senator Urban's face and neck, staining his toga. His limbs were broken and fractured, twisting his body into an insectile posture. A last breath blew a purple bubble from his mouth. It popped and sprayed a gory mist into the putrid air.

Drusus walked over to the politician's corpse and removed the fancy sandals from its feet. He handed them over to Karolina.

"Further thanks. Afraid you won't be able to salvage the rest of his garb."

She accepted the footwear and tossed them into the wagon.

"No need for Roman robes out here." She gestured at the gold. "What will you have us do with these spoils?"

"Whatever the hell you want. Start your own city-state. Trade it all for wine. Just don't let it fall into Roman hands."

She rested a palm on Drusus's cheek while he looked out at the field of bones.

"Are they out there?" he asked.

"Somewhere. Most get dumped by lot. It happens so often I can't give you a precise location."

"Then I'll go look for them."

She released her caress as Drusus took off his helmet and cloak. He unfastened his weapons belt that clinked onto the ground. He tossed his sandals, greaves, chest armor, and tunic into a pile before standing naked in the sun.

Then he walked off the Appian Way into the field of the dead. His heavy step snapped dried remains under his weight. At random, he picked up a skull, estimating its size by heft. Then he respectfully sat it back down as he continued his search. His search continued with a tormenting tenacity.

Karolina and the other women watched him until his silhouette was no longer in sight on the horizon.

By the time the sun went down, the gold was hidden in the shacks. The convoy's vehicles were dismantled with their wood being used for construction materials or burned for heat. Senator Urban and the legionnaires were placed naked among the forgotten souls who lay outside of Rome's walls. The stench of their decay fermented up into the foul fog of funk that hung over the people who dwelled in this city of the dead.

# RED SWARM

## BY ANDREW MILLER

On Tuesday night, December the 7th, 2021, a 911 call was patched

through to the detectives of the Northeast Division of the Los Angeles Police

Department. A guest had been murdered in the room of a motel on Glendale

Boulevard in Silver Lake called the Cosmopolitan, a place long known by the

department to be frequented by male prostitutes. Just a short walk from the

reservoir, the Cosmopolitan was a still-standing piece of sleazy L.A. history that

had miraculously survived the economic devastation of the virus.

Detective Shelby Jones and Detective Anthony Dobbs were personally

assigned to the case by their Captain, even though they weren't next in rotation.

Shelby figured the Higher Ups wanted to highlight their diversity, so they were

parading her, an African American, a woman, and a lesbian—someone seen as

high up on the ladder of victimhood in American culture these days, though not

as high up as she used to be.

Dobbs had been feeling sick all week with a lingering cough that he couldn't quite shake, something he assured all his fellow officers wasn't the virus. He took a home test he'd bought at a Namaste Mart Rx and claimed it came up negative. Everyone knew Dobbs had been shrugging the virus off for months now. He'd already gotten it twice.

On Glendale, they saw parked LAPD sirens flashing from the Cosmopolitan lot ahead. While holding back a sneeze, Dobbs parallel parked their department Crown Vic in front of the motel. The neon sign of the Cosmopolitan shone on the pavement that still glistened from the rain earlier in the night.

"Wasn't there a vehicular manslaughter over here this week?" Dobbs asked.

"Driver wasn't deemed at fault. Some broad on her way to the Red Lion couldn't get off TikTok and walked right into traffic."

"That's possibly the most Gen Z gentrifier death I've ever heard of."

Patrolman Chavez, a first responder, waited by the entrance. "This way," he said, leading them down to the end of the L-shaped succession of rooms. At 11, Chavez passed Shelby a clipboard and pen. She and Dobbs both scribbled down their names and went through the doorway, crossing under the tape.

There on the bed was a naked old man, dead from multiple stab wounds. He was wrapped in sheets and on his back. Black blood splatters coated the wall above the headboard. His arms were spread out like Jesus. He was physically fit.

Shelby recognized the guy. He was some old movie star. So *this* was why she'd been called in special. A diverse-looking detective investigating a Hollywood bigshot was good optics.

"It's Norman Sassoon," Dobbs said.

"I recognize his face, not his name."

"An unpleasant end for a legend of Hollywood style."

Sassoon's seemingly posed arms were covered in defensive slashes. Shelby had worked many stabbings. She caught a vicious one that came with media baggage just before the virus. It had inspired serious drama in her personal life.

"If we find out who Sasoon came here with, we've got the killer," Dobbs said nasally. "Since they came here, to the Cosmopolitan, does that mean we're looking for a member of the male sex? Is this our own Ramon Novarro? Shelby, you know how the silent film star Ramon Novarro died?"

"Some dude choked him to death with a dildo and robbed him."

Shelby sensed something off with this scene. She couldn't place it. A wallet and cell phone were on the table by the door. Tossed clothes were in the corner. Old SNL jokes from the '90s came back to her. Norm Macdonald clowning on Sassoon over something.

"Weren't there actual sex rumors about this dude? Like, from long ago?"

"Right," Dobbs said. "Something about a hamster…" Dobbs turned to Chavez. "Any male street walkers in the motel or nearby—we need to talk to them. Who knows about Norman Sassoon and this joint? They'll have a favor coming for hard facts."

A department photographer came in and started snapping. A stretched out N95 was under his chin. Two MEs arrived and got to work. The blade hadn't been recovered so far. Patrolman O'Neil, Chavez's partner, stuck his head through the door.

"Vic's wife's outside," O'Neil said.

The woman waited out in the parking lot, clutching a nervous Pomeranian. A KN95 covered her mouth and nose.

"Is it true?" she said, her voice muffled. "Is he really dead?"

"Who are you?"

"I'm Norman Sassoon's wife," she said. "I'm Clara Sassoon."

"I'm sorry to say yes. Norman's been killed."

She cried. Her Pomeranian started howling. Dobbs found her chair and got her a cup of water. Clara slid her mask down under her chin and drank it.

"Do you know why your husband was at this motel?" Dobbs asked.

"When he left home tonight, he said was doing work on his new project."

"Which project was that?"

She kept her mask under her chin. "*The Impact Zone* at Netflix. It's based on a huge video game. Norman's casting was a bit of a surprise. He was getting more attention than he had been for a while. You see, Norman supported the Dalai Lama."

"Buddhism?" Shelby didn't understand.

"He wasn't too popular in Hollywood lately," Dobbs said. "Low marketability."

Shelby still didn't understand.

Dobbs extended his hand to pet the Pomeranian. It yipped. "What work for *The Impact Zone* would Norman be doing here?" he asked.

Clara scanned the area. "I don't know."

Shelby and Dobbs looked at her.

"Norman wasn't gay, if that's what you mean."

"What makes you say that?"

"Because it seems like prostitutes hang out here. Norman always laughed off those rumors. He never found out who started them. Yes, he experimented with bisexuality when he was younger, so it wasn't some big threat to his masculinity. But trust me, Norman wasn't gay."

"So you've got no idea why he came here, or who with?" Shelby asked.

"None at all."

Chavez walked up, eager looking. They stepped aside to speak with him.

"A Filipino tourist saw someone leaving number 11, after Sassoon had checked in. He saw the car. Said it was a BMW. This motel's got cameras, and the manager showed us. We got it. It's queued up for you to watch, but the angle is pretty good. It's a brand-new BMW. You can't see the man well. He might have a pony tail, but I'm not sure. Here's the plates."

Chavez handed them a torn piece of paper form his notepad. Dobbs looked at it. "Did you run them?"

"Yeah. It's a Chinese consul plate."

*

Shelby and Dobbs waited at a table in the Gallery Bar inside the Biltmore Hotel downtown. It was one thirty and the bar was dead.

"What do you make of this consul plate thing?" Shelby asked Dobbs.

"I sure don't like that it's from a country we'll be at war with before long."

They waited on Daniel Magarian, an Armenian entertainment lawyer and Hollywood bagman. He was also one of Shelby's confidential informants. She'd maneuvered Magarian into his current position years back after he'd been arrested by some vice cops for soliciting and needed to beat the charge.

Shelby researched *The Impact Zone* deal online and saw Magarian's name mentioned by The Hollywood Reporter as an associate producer, so she called him up. Magarian said he was staying here at the Biltmore, even though he lived in Sherman Oaks. Shelby figured he must be here with another hooker.

"Hopefully Magarian can shed some light," she said.

Then Magarian, wearing a light blue surgical mask, walked in through the door from the hall and sat down beside Dobbs. He looked at the bartender and made a hand gesture that said 'the usual.'

"You been on your phone?" Shelby asked.

Magarian took his mask off and wrapped it around his wrist. "No. What?"

The bartender brought Magarian a chilled martini.

"We'll get to that," Shelby said. "Our questions are about Norman Sassoon."

Magarian took a sip. "I just spoke with him tonight."

"About what?" Shelby asked.

Magarian made sure his phone was turned off. "I tipped Norman that some people I know at Netflix might consider him for the father in *The Impact Zone*. I'm an AP on this thing, which is on track to do a limited series of special theatrical screenings in China. It'll likely make some money, since the Chinese are permitted to play that game, and are familiar with it. The rumor was that the Chinese were making revisions to their Hollywood blacklist again, so I figured I might be able to resolve that whole situation with Norman."

"How do you mean, 'resolve'?" Shelby asked.

"I know Tony Chan, one of the top guys at Willow Vision, the corporation that lists the top theatre chain in China as one of its assets. Chan's tight with all the important people in the film branch of the CCP. He says the CCP wants to switch up their image and make good with Norman. You know, show that all's forgiven from when Norman was a presenter at the '92 Oscars and his speech was about his fondness for the Dalai Lama and how fuckin' mistreated Tibet was, turning Free Tibet into the luxury cause in Hollywood. Before the Chinese officially took him off their list, one of Chan's guys wanted to meet with him and feel him out. Since I know both Chan and Norman, I set up their meet, which was tonight."

Dobbs asked, "Where?"

"Echo Park Lake, by the paddle boats. Chan wanted to go out on the water."

Echo Park Lake was just under two miles from The Cosmopolitan.

"Was Norman gay?" Shelby asked.

Magarian looked off-put by this curve ball. "I don't think so. He's married. Wasn't he into some kinky shit with a hamster?" He waited. "Was that Norman?"

"Norman got stabbed to death tonight at a motel in Silver Lake." Shelby said, withholding the ME's finding that he had not likely had sexual intercourse recently. "He was found in bed, naked, at a spot for gay hookers. We do know someone from the Chinese government was close. So far, their embassy hasn't been too cooperative."

His face dropped.

"Tell us what you're thinking," Shelby said to Magarian.

"Maybe Chan was running me." He shrugged nervously. "Maybe they weren't ready to make nice with Norman."

"Who did Sassoon go that hotel with?" Shelby asked.

He drained his martini. "How would I know? Yeah, I admit the guy I sent him to meet worked for a Chinese billionaire. You have to remember that people this powerful aren't going to get involved with this low level. Norman probably really was some kinky fuck." Magarian waited, then stood. "He probably got into trouble after the meet and got himself killed."

"I don't know where're you going," Shelby said. "We ain't done."

"We are for tonight."

"Sit back down"

"I'm going to my room. If you want to stop me, arrest me."

"Why the lake?" Dobbs asked. "A paddle boat ride with Chinese elites seems strange."

"They're a mysterious people. Ask anybody."

From his wallet, Magarian pulled out a twenty. Then he refitted his surgical mask back over his mouth and nose.

"Why'd you turn your phone off like that?" Shelby asked.

"They know who I am and they know what I did tonight. They could be listening. You never really know."

*

Dawn loomed back at Northeast Station. Shelby walked over to Captain Monica Thornton's office, which was now open. Shelby knocked lightly. Her KN95 dangled from her ear.

"You wanted to see me?"

The captain looked up. "You and Dobbs should take a few hours off. I know Anthony's walking around, pretending like he doesn't have Covid, just flouting his disrespect of CDC Guidelines." She shook her head and made a slight smile. The captain never bothered to wear a mask inside her own office unless the media was present. "Get some rest."

"Anything else?"

She shrugged. "The Higher Ups are now in the loop."

"Yeah?"

"They never just outright say it this way, but they're expecting no drama. How we solve it straight and achieve that is a mine field I don't know how to pass through quite yet, but you two should consider this a lull, and a chance to recharge. If nothing major breaks by tomorrow afternoon, visit Magarian again and play it tougher. He needs to talk."

"Why not brace him now? No time like the present."

Captain Thornton shook her head.

"What's going on with this case?"

"I'd bet a paycheck this Chinese stuff is a red herring. Hollywood people are degenerates. Wasn't this Sassoon a friend of Jeffery Epstein? I think Sassoon flew on that plane down to that pedophile island, didn't he? Norman was probably over the moon about getting a job, picked up some young ass and it all just went south."

Shelby went home to her apartment on DeLongpre in West Hollywood, where she lived alone. She got herself a cold canned Margarita, cracked it open, and flopped down on the couch to once again keep online tabs on Crockett, her ex-wife. Crockett had been through major changes since their divorce six months before the virus. There she was in an Instagram story wearing a hijab and ranting against Israel. Some of her rant was hard to hear, because she didn't take her KN95 off. Her full monologue was too long for an Instagram story, so Crockett got cut off mid-sentence. Shelby's next story was an ad for oat milk.

*

Going over ninety, Shelby tore across the 134 Freeway to Pasadena. The bubble siren on her roof blared. Traffic was congested over a Rose Bowl game. Shelby took the exit at Mountain and sped east across the surface streets, quickly arriving at the lot of the Namaste Mart Rx at the corner of Lake and Mountain. It was full squad cars from Pasadena PD, sheriffs, and a Pasadena city ambulance. Shelby saw Captain Thornton and raced toward her.

"I got here as fast as I could," Shelby said.

"I'm sorry, detective."

Dobbs lived close by. The house where he'd lived with his wife Letitia for many years was just around the corner, on El Molino. Shelby scanned the lot and saw Dobbs' old school white Cadillac. Its front door was open. Another ME was there, looking in, examining the interior. She saw the outline of her partner's dead body slumped over in the driver's seat.

"He's really dead?"

"Yes."

She couldn't believe it.

"How?"

"It looks medical. There's an open jar of pills in the driver's seat."

"What medication?"

"Some antibiotics for lung inflammation. I forget the name. The pharmacist said he'd just been in to pick it up. They've got him on camera, waiting in line. They said it takes longer to pull up the camera for the parking lot. Dobbs was sick." The captain waited. "Maybe sicker than we thought."

"He wouldn't have kept that from me." Shelby shook her head.

"I've got to go notify his wife. Their house is nearby. Maybe Letitia can extrapolate on his health issues. I was hoping you could go with me."

"I've been there before."

"He wouldn't have gotten that prescription unless his lungs really were in bad shape."

"Dobbs wasn't dying."

"I'm saying it looks like he had some sort of condition that was worse than he realized. That, or maybe he had a bad reaction to the antibiotics."

Shelby thought in silence. Then she said, "Call poison control."

"What?"

"Do it."

"Shelby, you're not serious."

"I sure as shit hope I'm fucking crazy."

The captain spoke softly, even though no one else was near them. "You're saying this is over Norman Sassoon?"

Both of them were thinking about the BMW from the Chinese consulate.

"I hope it's not airborne, getting inside us now."


*


Shelby sat in an interrogation box at New Parker Center, across from Palmer and Devery, two detectives from Robbery Homicide. A digital camera on a tripod recorded her.

All hell had broken loose. Dobbs' "medical issue" came back a homicide. The city coroner verified a nerve agent in his system, as Shelby predicted. Sheriff's Homicide, which usually handled murders within the Pasadena city limits, transferred the investigation to RHD, which was standard procedure for murders that came with political or media attachment. The FBI's Joint Terrorism Task Force was called in. So was the Department of Homeland Security.

The Namaste Mart Rx got shut down. Every individual who'd been anywhere near the pharmacy was checked for the substance and, so far, all were cleared. The FBI predicted that the nerve agent was likely in a family of Russian poisons called Novichok. At the moment, Palmer and Devery were taking her statement.

"And you just happened to know the lawyer and movie producer who hooked Sassoon up with the Chinese in the first place?" Devery asked. "How's that happen?"

"I keep good informants." Shelby removed her glasses and rubbed her nose. She was struggling to focus. "Magarian was plugged in. The wife told us about *The Impact Zone*, then I Googled it on my phone. Magarian's name came up, so I called him."

They had viewed the digital security footage from outside the Namaste Mart Rx: Dobbs walked to his Cadillac. A homeless-looking man in a full gas mask stumbled his way. A mask on any Angeleno wasn't unusual these days, but this mask was too nice for this particular guy. As he passed by Dobbs, he made a slight but perceptible gesture. He released whatever it was.

"We didn't get lucky," Palmer said. "Magarian's vanished. No one knows where he is. Think about this from our end. It would be nice if we could hear all of this from him."

Shelby visualized the Gallery Bar last night. She remembered those Eastern Europeans by the bar. They were a possible Russia connection. Shelby wondered if they were the key, the connection telling *them* that the LAPD was getting too close.

"Y'all just want me to say it?" She'd arrived at a more aggressive tone. "It seems like no one wants to talk about what's really going on."

"Explain it to us," Devery said.

"Last night, Dobbs and I caught Norman Sassoon. The scene was staged to look like 'Norman Sassoon, murdered at an LGBTQ motel.' In reality, Dobbs and Sassoon were both hits done by the Chinese government, out to further fuck with America, just to prove they can. They've had a beef with Norman about his high-profile support of the Dalai Lama and Tibet for decades, and these motherfuckers are intent on serving it up cold. Somehow, they learned that Dobbs and I were close, and the poison was them letting us know what they think of that."

Palmer cleared his throat. "You're saying the CCP has assets in L.A., killing Hollywood celebrities and cops?"

The location of the killer in the gas mask was unknown. They didn't know how much more of the nerve agent he had, or if he planned to use it on anyone else.

"Haven't the Russians been clipping people this way in other countries for years now? They already used this stuff in England. The Chinese must have someone to call in L.A."

Palmer and Devery kept poker faces. Shelby read their minds. They thought she was losing it because she just lost Dobbs. They wanted to be polite, so they didn't call her theory crazy, even though they thought it was.

*

Captain Thornton's door was closed this time. Shelby knocked and it opened quickly. A shabby and heavyset man wearing a beige Members Only jacket and with no mask covering his bearded face was on his way out. He passed by Shelby. The virus was no longer a threat to people with money or power and Shelby could tell this man had power.

"Take a seat."

Shelby shut the door and sat.

"I've had some talks with the Higher Ups today."

"I figured."

"You're off Sassoon."

"Who's on it?"

"Basically, the guy who just left. This thing is big. I'm not saying Sassoon's not important. It's just that this thing is bigger, so Sassoon's getting folded into his case. Palmer and Devery are playing ball. I told that man that you can be trusted too. He and his people will remember if they see you're on the team."

"What's his big case? Who is he?"

"His target is ... *our guys...* who, in part, made the virus, before it got out." The captain waited. "Understand?"

"I think."

Shelby didn't understand at all.

"It's complicated. It's going to take time, and the smarts to walk away."

"I've never been that smart."

"This time, you need to be. You're off until after Dobbs' funeral on Sunday. Stay home and rest. Prove that you can let this go."

*

Shelby's mandated leave began the next morning. With no intention of 'letting this go,' she set out for Silver Lake and the Cosmopolitan. On the way she kept an eye out for tails, making sure no one Chinese or Federal was keeping tabs. Her rearview looked clear.

A manager let her back into room 11, which was now vacant. She studied it. Nothing clicked. She canvassed the Cosmopolitan-adjacent businesses on Glendale and Silver Lake. Discarded masks littered the streets everywhere she walked. She canvassed Echo Park Lake. Nothing clicked.

That night, while drinking more canned Margaritas, Shelby researched the Chinese movie industry and its Hollywood partners. A Variety article listed Geoffrey Ziering-Campbell, a former development director at Disney, as the senior producer on *The Impact Zone* at Netflix. Variety said Ziering-Campbell knew Tony Chan, and that both were hosting a Chinese ambassador named Han Yong during his stay in L.A. this week. Han Yong was interested in seeing all the top tourist sites. Before his ambassador post, Yong had worked for years in the Chinese censorship bureau. Many in Hollywood knew him well.

The department cover story on Dobbs was released to the press. He'd died from anaphylaxis, caused by a bad reaction to antibiotics. Even Letitia was fed this fake news and while it was dutifully disseminated by a collaborating media, Dobbs had in fact tested positive, so anyone who bothered to formally look up his cause of death would of course see it listed as the virus. His funeral was on Sunday at Forest Lawn.

Shelby called all of her Beverly Hills informants. One was a pool boy at the Beverly Hills hotel who had a good tip. Ziering-Campbell was at the Polo Lounge. Shelby drove there fast. From across the room she watched him eating shrimp cocktails with Tony Chan.

She didn't see Han Yong, but knew he was close.

She went home and thought it all over. They'd killed her partner. Nothing was ever going to come out in court. Shelby was supposed to just let this pass.

"Fuck that," Shelby said, talking to herself.


*

Her pool boy tipped her off again the next afternoon.

When she got there, Shelby scoped Han Yong having lunch with Ziering-Campbell and three other lower-level Hollywood executives. A bodyguard was posted against the wall.

Shelby approached their table. The bodyguard saw her. Shelby flashed her detective's shield at Yong.

The bodyguard stepped closer. He and Shelby locked eyes. He had a ponytail. Shelby didn't notice it at first. She touched her holstered side arm.

She looked at Yong. "Sir, I need to speak with you."

Ziering-Campbell and the others froze. The rest of the restaurant hadn't picked up on the drama yet. Shelby didn't blink. Yong spoke in Chinese.

The bodyguard huffed and moved back to the wall. With a nod, Yong signaled for the table to leave. When they were gone, he gestured for Shelby to sit.

"A tad dramatic," Yong said. His Chinese accent was thick. His voice had a child-like timbre. He spooned the last bit of his tortilla soup into his mouth and pushed the cup and plate aside.

Shelby tilted her head toward the bodyguard. "Who's he?"

"That's Shen."

"Shen ever drive a BMW owned by the Chinese consulate?"

Yong shrugged.

For Shelby, it all crystallized at once: Shen had a ponytail. Shen was probably already familiar with the Cosmopolitan for some reason—maybe he went there himself with boys whenever he and his boss were in L.A.

Yong knew Magarian. Yong knew Magarian knew Tony Chan. Yong knew Chan's name could warrant a meeting with Norman Sassoon. Yong had Magarian set it up. Yong almost certainly had Shen show up to do the murder and stage it as a gay thing. An implicit direction for Shen's staging—don't make it too hard for the LAPD to know the truth. Show them their own helplessness. Clarify that the CCP now kills with impunity in Los Angeles County.

"I'm surprised you would have a gay man like Shen so close to you."

Yong chucked. "Your kind can spot each other so easily?"

"Yup."

"In our updated system, considerations are made for the good of the party. Even semi-capitalist and semi-western considerations. I don't permit homosexuals to work for me, but I don't ask questions about what Shen's up to during his free time here."

"Seems unprincipled, like your dedication to communism isn't strong."

"When *Thor* plays in China, Chinese audiences show an equal degree of admiration for Thor's cunning brother, Loki. China is a far older country than America."

Shelby looked over at Shen. She figured he must have been responsible for Dobbs, too. "So this is like a test run, leading up to when your country blockades Taiwan, and then who knows what else after that. You want to see how easily you can get away murder."

Yong leaned forward over the table. "Who got murdered?"

"Do I have to worry about keeling over from poison too?"

"What you think of me." He made a naughty smile. "What's this about poison?"

"My partner. Looks like you guys used something Russian on him."

"Sorry to hear that," Yong said. "But this has nothing to do with me. Russian poison? I'll have to remember this bizarre accusation of yours, officer."

"Sounds like a threat."

"It wasn't."

Shelby pointed toward the bar, at Ziering-Campbell and his toadies. They had no clue about the coming swarm. "I'm not an American grabbing bags full of money as our ship sinks. Come back here and the LAPD will be on your ass."

Yong took out his checkbook. "Is there any place I can make a donation for the fallen officer? Funerals can be expensive." His checkbook had a Mickey Mouse icon on it. Outside of his duties for the party, he was just as infantilized as an average American.

Shelby stood and walked away.

At home that night, Shelby invited Crockett to come pay her respects at Dobbs' funeral, which was tomorrow. Crockett and Dobbs had actually been friends once, long ago, before the virus. A face from the happier past was what she needed right now.

*

The rain fell hard. The department chaplain eulogized Dobbs. Shelby stood next to Letitia, steadying her as she grieved. The Chief of Police was on Letitia's other side. There was a 21-gun salute with rifles wrapped in plastic.

Crockett didn't come to the ceremony, or even bother to respond to Shelby's invite. This was no big surprise. Crockett was a revolutionary now, or at least committed to playing one online. No revolutionary could be seen at a policeman's funeral.

Yong and Shen had already flown home to Beijing. Shelby's scene with them at the Polo Lounge had become big department gossip. Her once bright and stable path—a succession of promotions up the chain of command—was off the table. The Higher Ups were pissed at her. Shelby was pretty sure she'd have already been fired if not for the LAPD's deep commitment to diversity, and the social capital her identity still held within that principle's framework.

The world would only remember the cynical headlines about Norman Sassoon, not the truth. Shen would get away with it. Shen would get away with Dobbs, too. An LAPD man. Who knew how much more of that poison was still out there, ready to be used again? In the long run, her bold stand at the Polo Lounge would make no difference.

Shelby thought about the coming swarm. The situation with China was already beyond repair. They'd infiltrated the very air we breathe.

Paradoxically, Shelby felt at peace. Even hopeful. There weren't any American laws against feeling hopeful. They would come for her one day, just like they came for Norman Sassoon. Until then, life would go on. Shelby pledged to honor all the sacrifices of the past by putting this great tragedy of the virus behind her, even if the rest of Los Angeles planned to live in fear of it forever. She would do her job and live her life and help keep alive some good in the world for as long as possible.

# THE ENTOMOLOGIST
## BY CONNOR BOYLE

That morning, like most mornings, the Trinidad General Store was quiet. The shopkeeper sat at his ledger and inspected the tallies from the night prior. Beside the cash register stood a young boy, his back straight and expression alert, as if waiting for a field marshal to arrive and inspect the line of his gig. On the counter beside the boy was a tall rectangular box, the front of it draped with a heavy black cloth.

The door bell sounded and a rangy man in dust-covered buckskins entered. The man, a cowboy by all outward appearances, made a quick survey of the store shelves, plucking out a selection of tinned goods, a bag of pinto beans, and a can of Arbuckle's Ariosa Blend coffee, then dumping the items on the counter.

"Excuse me, sir," said the boy. "Would you like to pay five cents to look at an assortment of arthropod specimens I've collected?"

"Arthro-what?"

"Arthropods," replied the boy. "Insects, bugs."

"Why the hell would I want to pay five cents to look at bugs? I got enough of them things in my bedroll."

The cowboy scratched vigorously at one sideburn and chuckled.

"And my hair."

The boy's expression remained resolute.

"These ones are better," he said, gesturing to the box. "I've collected specimens from Knoxville all the way to Denver. Concealed beneath this veil is the biggest and most diverse collection of insects in the United States, mayhaps the world."

"Diverse?" asked the cowboy.

"It means I have a lot of different specimens," replied the boy.

The cowboy permitted himself a thorough appraisal of the youngster, clocking the boy's inventory from head to toe. He'd been swindled by children before. It was their air of innocence that made them far more effective fraudsters than your average flimflam man or card sharp. Yet, there was something trustworthy, if not uniquely odd, about this one. He was neatly dressed in matching black slacks and jacket, although the clothes were slightly large for his size. His boots were worn and patched with cow glue, yet gleamed with fresh polish. "Quite the little salesman," the cowboy thought.

"How much did you want for a gander?"

The boy pointed to a short plank of lumber propped beside the display case. Across it was written in white oil paint:

*Jonah Hillum's World of Bugs*

Then, beneath that, in smaller type:

*An accretion of insect oddities*

*5 cents per peek*

"You Jonah?"

The boy nodded.

"What does accretion mean?"

"It means collection," said Jonah.

"Why doesn't it just say collection?"

Jonah shrugged.

"And what's an oddities?"

"Oddities is plural for oddity. An oddity is something strange."

"Why didn't you just write that, then? You're confusing your customers with all of this high-falutin jargon, son."

Jonah's eyes narrowed for a moment. He breathed deeply, and a moment later his stoic expression reasserted itself. The cowboy grinned.

"Well?" he prodded

Jonah spoke slowly.

"Perhaps I can revise my display so it is more appropriately phrased for the untaught wayfarer such as yourself. However, sir, I assure you that what is contained beneath that veil is far more interesting than the vocabulary on my signage. I can guarantee that you will not regret paying what is actually a quite modest fee to view what is a most extraordinary collection."

"I'll give you three."

"Five," Jonah replied flatly.

"I don't think a gander is worth five. I paid three to have a look at Smiling Bill Tipton's dead body in El Paso. You telling me this display of yours is more impressive than the corpse of the most dangerous outlaw in the West?"

"My collection is world class, sir," said Jonah. "As soon as I have enough money, I plan on traveling to Boston to have it displayed at Harvard College. I believe I could charge up to five dollars per gander in Boston society."

The shopkeeper looked up from his spot at the far edge of the counter.

"Sir, I suggest you discontinue conversating with the boy. He will not yield to any of your counteroffers or bargains. I have seen him hold steady as a boulder with many a persistent customer such as yourself, although your comment about his sign did appear to jostle him some."

"You his father?" asked the cowboy.

"No," replied the shopkeeper. "I allow the boy to display his collection at my store as a favor to his mother, who is a widower. As you have no doubt noticed, the boy is strange, most likely touched in his thinking parts by a heavenly angel. You would be doing him and his mother a favor with your patronage, although you are certainly under no obligation. Let me know when you are finished with your negotiations, then you and I will settle up on those tins."

The shopkeeper returned to his ledger, adjusting his thick lensed spectacles as he continued to tally the handwritten figures on the page before him. The cowboy watched the old man for a minute, noting the deliberate manner by which he conducted his calculations. The man was organized; disciplined in his business affairs. Probably didn't drink up all his profits or redistribute them to whores in the local brothel. Probably had a decent amount of cash on hand.

"That true?" said the cowboy, turning back to Jonah. "Your daddy's dead?"

"Yes, I believe so," said Jonah. "My father traveled to Boston when I was still a babe. My mother tells me that he was supposed to work on a whaling ship and earn money to send back to us here in Colorado. But after he left, we never heard from him again. We believe he died at sea."

"Your mama didn't remarry? She don't have no man in her life? Someone to look after you and her?"

"No, sir," Jonah replied solemnly.

The cowboy continued to stare.

The boy was certainly peculiar. An *oddity* in his own right. No father, no friends to help pass the time. It was no wonder he'd pick up such a strange hobby as bug collecting. Hell, what else was there for a boy to do in a town like Trinidad? The kid probably had all sorts of strange knowledge he'd *accreted* over the years. The cowboy had never been much for schooling. From an early age he had wanted to strike out on his own, and so he did. His formal education was in horse breaking and shooting. His classrooms were saloons and bunkhouses, where displays of intellectual curiosity were met by cruel rejoinders from hard men and unsympathetic women.

The cowboy smiled widely, revealing a pair of gold-capped cuspids.

"Hell," he said, removing a nickel from his pocket and slamming it on the counter. "Let's see what you got, kid."

Jonah collected the nickel and dropped it into his pocket. The coin clinked as it came to rest amongst other nickels and pennies there.

Jonah pulled the veil from the box, revealing a long, lacquered display case with a glass front. The polished oak sheened in the midday sun. Behind the transparent frontispiece were rows of segmented cubicles, each divided from the next by a thin sliver of wood.

The cowboy whistled.

"I sure can appreciate the craftsmanship. You build this yourself?"

"I did," said Jonah, a glint of pride in his eyes.

Inside the box was a variety of scorpions, spiders, beetles, locusts, mantids, ants, and other creatures the likes of which the cowboy had never seen. Red haired tarantulas with dozens of groping antennae. A bristly purple scorpion that sweated a glowing green liquid from the gaps in its carapace. A winged creature that looked to be a mix of cockroach and centipede. There had to be at least a hundred different bugs each in their own stall.

"That sure is something," the cowboy said, hunching to get a closer look. He could see Jonah's own entranced gaze reflected in the glass cover.

"I believe many of the specimens in my collection are previously unidentified species. I will be able to confirm that once I make it to Boston. There will be other scientists there. Experts whom I intend to study with."

"Some of these are poisonous, I reckon."

"Yes," replied Jonah.

"Dangerous handling that sort of thing."

"It can be," said Jonah. "But I have a way with these creatures."

"You ever been bitten?"

"Not once."

The cowboy flicked his middle finger against the glass. The insects inside responded with a frenzy of panicked activity. Those with wings buzzed and flapped against the glass front, others scampered back and forth between the walls of their compartment.

"Please don't do that," said Jonah.

"Hmm," remarked the cowboy. "I do reckon this... accretion is worth a good bit."

The cowboy hauled the case off the counter. He strolled up and down the aisles with it, regarding the contents with an expression of slack mouthed glee. The larger specimens intrigued him. He shook the case like he would a gold pan, studying the responses of the nasty looking bigguns inside. Some bared venom-dripping fangs, others gripped the sides of the box in distress. All the while, Jonah trailed him and pleaded, "Please, put it back!"

"I don't understand why a boy would be interested in something like this. Don't you have friends? Don't you like to play or nothing?"

"No, I don't have any friends. Please put it back! You are disturbing them!"

The cowboy continued his inspection, reveling in the boy's fretfulness. Finally, he returned to the front of the store and set the box down on the counter, resting an elbow atop it.

"I think this will fetch me at least a hundred dollars in San Francisco. They're not as educated as your Boston folk there, but I reckon I can find me a buyer."

"It's not for sale," said Jonah.

"You sure?" said the cowboy.

"Yes," said Jonah, his panicked gaze darting between the cowboy's face and the box. The front of the case was a prismatic blur of activity. The squealing and chittering of the insects formed a muffled chorus behind the glass.

"Regardless," continued the cowboy, "I'll take these here tins I've selected, this here bug box, a pouch of tobacco, and a bottle of whiskey."

"I said the box ain't for sale," said Jonah.

"I didn't say I was making a purchase," said the cowboy, tossing back the flap of his rawhide jacket to reveal a holstered .45 Peacemaker. "I'm taking them. You hear that, shopkeep?"

The shopkeeper put down his pencil and looked up from his work, squinting hard to see the cowboy.

"What did you say?" he asked.

"I said clean the god damn wax out of your ears and get your old ass over here. I'm robbing you, old timer. Now open the till and give me all the money."

The shopkeeper rose from his stool and made his way slowly to the cash register. He raised his hands and spoke in a quavering voice.

"I don't have much money, I'm afraid."

"Bullshit," said the cowboy, drawing the Peacemaker from its holster and leveling it at the shopkeeper's gut. "What are all those numbers you've got written down over there? You counting the clouds in the sky? I bet you got a safe back in the storeroom somewhere. And you,"

The cowboy turned his head to Jonah, his gun still trained on the shopkeeper

"Empty those pockets. I heard those coins jangling around in there."

Jonah stood firm.

"I will not be giving you my Boston money."

"Please, sir," said the shopkeeper. "Leave the boy alone. As I said, he's a simpleton. His mother-"

"Enough out of you," said the cowboy, cocking the revolver's hammer. "We'll be seeing to that safe in just a minute. Don't interrupt me when I'm talking to the boy."

Tears began to stream down Jonah's cheeks.

"I am not giving you my money," he repeated.

"Boy, I've killed children younger than yourself."

"This is uncivilized," said Jonah.

"Fine," said the cowboy. He reached out for Jonah, shoving one hand into the boy's pants pocket and groping for the coins there. As he did so, there came an explosion from the countertop. The front of the display case shattered outwards in a blitz of glass that entered the cowboy's shoulder like a round of buckshot. The cowboy screamed and reeled back. The manic screech of the insects filled the store as they surged forth in a river of carpaces, wings, feelers, and claws.

Jonah brightened to the noise, taking several steps backwards as the insects enshrouded the cowboy's head in a vibrating mass. The cowboy dropped his Peacemaker and pawed at his face rabidly. The creatures were as fickle as mercury, immediately replacing themselves as soon as the cowboy brushed a clump of them away. Punctuating this writhing insect mask were larger creatures whose bulk distinguished them from the rest. A scorpion clung to one eyelid, stabbing again and again at the cowboy's eyeball. An oversized roach nibbled at his lower lip, dangling like a loose bandage against the man's chin. A cluster of tarantulas took to feasting on his scalp, raking out large filets of head meat with their yellowed fangs.

The shopkeeper clutched the front of his shirt and uttered a brief prayer. It felt like his heart was twisting into a ribbon inside of his chest.

"Make them stop!" he bellowed.

The storm of insects continued their decimation of the cowboy's face, rearranging his previously handsome features into venom-saturated strips of flesh. A torn nostril here. A flap of cheek there. A piece of gum peeled back to reveal the white jaw bone underneath.

"I do not think my heart can bear to witness this much longer," the shopkeeper entreated. The boy waited a moment, then raised a hand. As if some magnetic force had been activated, the insects retreated to the box, each one settling into its cubicle and quietening.

The cowboy's body convulsed on the floor. A heavy stream of foam slid down the side of one cheek, and the front of his pants revealed a large patch of urine.

Jonah and the shopkeeper were quiet for several minutes. Jonah began to pick up the shards of glass from the box one by one. Finally, the shopkeeper, satisfied that his heart had settled, broke from his trance.

"How—" he started.

"I don't know," interrupted Jonah. "All I know is that I've been communicating with them longer than I have with human beings. My mother said I had a prolonged crawling period as a babe. Most children begin walking at the age of one. I did not take my first steps until three. My supposition is that individuals who spend their early childhood face down in the dirt nurture a special bond with the creatures who live there. However, your guess is just as good as mine."

The shopkeeper nodded solemnly. He kneeled down beside the cowboy and placed a hand atop his sternum.

"I believe I recognize his face from the newspaper, although it's terribly misshapen now."

He ran a thumb underneath the cowboy's top lip, inspecting his teeth.

"Yes," he said. "This is Smiling Bill Tipton. I can tell from the gold caps."

The cowboy suddenly came to life, his eyes darting open and his teeth clenching around the shopkeeper's thumb. The shopkeeper screamed and pulled back. The cowboy's teeth fastened deeper until the tip of the thumb dislodged in his mouth. The cowboy spat it out and rose to his feet, a look of insane anger and desperation glaring from beneath his swollen eyelids.

From an ankle sheath Tipton retrieved a stag handled Bowie knife. He charged Jonah with the blade, clutching it reverse-grip over his head. He moved like an injured deer, his knee collapsing inward with each step, his gait landing on his ankle rather than the flat of his booted foot. A shiver ran through his neck and shoulders, causing his head to flail back wildly like a sunflower in a heavy wind.

Jonah instinctively raised a hand to cover his face, while Tipton brought the blade down in a long arc. Jonah prepared himself for the impending pain. He hoped the knife would only slice through his hand and not cut his neck. He closed his eyes and brought up a shoulder, and as he did so, the cowboy tumbled awkwardly. A loud snap signaled the collapse of the wood floor beneath Tipton, and he found himself falling through the air, then landing with a loud *oompf* as he came to rest upon a mound of dirt.

He lay breathless, the shock of the fall nullifying the pain in his face for a few blessed seconds. He rolled over onto his shoulder and felt a sharp stab in the side of his chest. He was certain that a rib had broken there. If he wasn't careful, it would puncture a lung.

Tipton's mind began to clear. He steadied himself, raising up on an elbow and inspecting the den around him. He was beneath the store, he realized. Atop the foundation. His gaze soon fell upon a large burrow off to his right, inside of which a row of glistening black eyes, each as large as a cannonball, stared hungrily at him.

"Sweet lord!" Tipton yelled. His hands swept the dirt around him until he felt the grainy, striated texture of the Bowie's stag handle. He collected the knife and held it before him, stabbing defensively into the air between him and the black orbs. "Stay back" he hollered. The creature responded with a thick stream of silk that caught the cowboy's hand, pasting it behind his head to the den wall. A pair of segmented grabbers, each the length and width of a mare's foreleg, reached out from the darkness and hooked themselves above Tipton's shoulder. The silk shackle around his arm held firm, causing his hand to be separated at the wrist as the remainder of his body was dragged asunder. The sound of Tipton's cries lessened in volume and were soon no more than a dull moan as he was carried deep, deep into the earth.

Jonah dropped to his knees at the edge of the hole and peered down into the burrow, which was already beginning to fill itself in with dirt.

"Thank you!" he hollered.

From somewhere deep beneath the store came a high-pitched chirp.

After he repaired his display case, Jonah spent the next two days constructing a box for the hand of Smiling Bill Tipton. The box was similar to the one he'd made for his specimens, with a glass covered frontispiece and several small holes in the back to allow for the flow of air. The holes also allowed for the venting of noxious gases and fluids, ensuring that the hand decomposed as slowly as possible. When Jonah was finished, he placed the box on the counter at the Trinidad General Store, beside his *accretion of insect oddities*. He then threw a black veil over its front and placed a sign at its base, which read:

*Gunhand of Famous Outlaw Smiling Bill Tipton*

*Fired more bullets than Wild Bill*

*Three cents a gander*

*Non-negotiable*

From spring into summer, the box remained on the counter. Nearly every traveler who passed through Trinidad paid to view the hand of the legendary gunman. Jonah made a handsome bounty off of the spectacle. By winter, the hand had spoiled thoroughly and was little more than bones and a few sheaths of purple flesh. Jonah buried the hand in the plains outside of town, but by then he had enough money for passage to Boston.

# JAILBAIT BIRTHDAY
## BY PAIGE JOHNSON

"27 Club, woo!" I clink citrus shooters with my man, Olive Eyes. Gulping down that beloved burn, only dribbling a smidge onto our sandpapery motel sheets, I cheese more than him. "Smile, pretty boy. Who knows if we'll make 28?"

"That's sort of why I'm frowning, Cherry." Having to lay low from Miami heat after a sideways coke deal doesn't make him too sunshiney, but that's why I tell him now's the time for cloud-parting with one big wish.

"Don't be a wet blanket." I dab ours with the end of his tie. "Birthday boys have to be jolly, it's gospel."

He rolls back his dotted tie and tired eyes, unimpressed with my antics or the booze. "Isn't it a little early to be jubilant? What drug dealer do you know who's supposed to be up before noon?"

I glance at the alarm clock. "No, see, it's exactly the right time. 99-proof shots at 9:09 AM. It's like a Ke$ha song or something."

"I would actually prefer brain-rot pop to this goddamn jackhammering." His head leans toward the window. Beyond it, cancer-skinned constructioneers put up sheet metal for storage units so Macon, Georgia, can keep their broken two-strokes and Braves puffer coats safe until Christmastime.

Jackhammer. I smirk like a grade-schooler, imagining my head dangling by the dust ruffle, his frustration pummeled into the Eden between my knees. But it's the messiest time of the month and I like the bed runner the teal it is— not red. Besides, some guys aren't so easily drained of anxiety. Need stronger stress-relievers. Jailbait big.

I kiss his cheek and suggest we hit the streets, get some space powder to celebrate. I'm over the gak that got us in trouble. Sedatives are so in-season, the billboards for psychedelic therapy clinics around Northside say so.

***

We meet a plug with a surplus of 2-FDCK in a local cemetery because you're allowed to act weird there. Keep your nose to the ground-stone. Lay down for a good wallow. Even if it's obvious you're whacked off dissociatives, patrons will figure it's prescribed to deal with the grief.

In front of a Snapchat "gangster" with Urkel glasses and Steven Universe tatts, I say, "My treat," and wink at Olive Eyes. At this point, I don't have to ask his help transferring my old Only Fans funds into this dork's Ethereum vault.

Once the guy leaves, Olive Eyes laughs and pinches the cinch of my waist. "That was just moving my money with extra steps, Cherry."

"Probably, but it's the THOT that counts." We walk a wooden bridge that looks like it was built for a train during the Civil War. "You may've started my customer but look atcha now."

He nods, tipping his hat as we sit by a river with a name we can't pronounce. "Engaged to the very strange." He plucks a blossom off a tree and hands it to me. "Betrothed to the ghost of a bawdy chatroom host."

"Oh, working on your vows already?" I blow the little bud back at him. "Mom will be so proud when you bring that up."

He shrugs. "Still sounds better than saying, 'Going to marry my favorite berry, Cherry.'"

"Hahaha. That's okay. I like stupid. I live for stupid."

"You must love stupid." He gestures towards himself. "So, let's snort some." So he says, but he's the brains of the operation. The sensible brakes. He tests it first with a little color-changing solution to make sure it's safe. He looks both ways for a witness before bumping the vial. "Mmm, that burns like Hell, but I promise the come-up is quick."

Behind a granite mausoleum and a giant tree with fruit-punch-color flowers, we take turns lighting up our nostrils. From his phone, I put on a lo-fi fairy to whisper over glitchy, soft grunge guitars. Massage the boney shoulders under the split yoke of his cotton shirt.

We get grinny as our squints go grainy. The late-August scorch feels more like a spring breeze on the drug, goose-bumping our forearms and faces. I sink into the song, hallucinate a scantily clad angel to float-dance before me. Her skin's as white as the salt we sniff, the slave grave headstones she twirls between.

We make it through a couple dreamy EPs before I remember my body. From behind, Olive Eyes wraps me in an embrace and juts his chin like, Up, up. Time to go.

I stagger, glass-eyed like a doll on ball-joints. He lets me lean against him like a zombie into town. We pass the state-commissioned graffiti of neon eagles, buildings that look like mini–White Houses. A strip club sticks out from between them like the city planner's a comedy fan. Olive Eyes ain't into disco ball dance halls or the BBWs plastered on the promo photos outside, but I want him to do better than get shit-faced with me tonight.

I scratch-pet his lapel. "Is this the worst birthday ever?"

"Not even close."

"What do you normally do?"

"Study. Work. Don't think about it."

"Even on milestones like 16, 18, or 21?"

He nervously laughs, lowers his voice for fear of passersby. "Ehm, well, at 13, my father...procured? a hooker for me. He just sprung it on me after a mysterious car ride, then shuffled me into a motel room that reeked of Winston Lights."

I gasp, drum his arm. "What? That man was barely in your life but made a point to get his baby laid before he left? No wonder you're so wei— Well, I mean, how'd you do?"

He rolls his eyes, half-smiling. "I was too young to know what to do. Literally scared stiff."

"Was she pretty?"

"If she was a third as cute as you, I'd have ejaculated at the doorway instead of half a second after she left."

I press for details, declaring this type of ketamine the best. A truth serum, after all.

"Ehm, she was a dishwater blonde in a latex bikini, probably with a kid of her own, judging by the loose skin and scars on her stomach... Said her name was Honey after the Bond girl. Perhaps she looked like such a decade before. I don't know, I could hardly form sentences then... Out of pity, she played cards with me. Blackjack, specifically. When I won the third time, she leaned over the table and ruffled my hair with her breasts in my face. That was the most eventful part. Most eventful birthday."

"Until now," I say.

"Until now," he echoes, squeezing my hand.

"No, you don't understand. I'm making you a promise."

***

Olive Eyes comes out from our shoddy motel bathroom, smelling like tangerine dreams and the thickest ivory soap. In just low-slung, slim sweatpants and shadows, he looks exactly like the husband I always hoped for. But now that I've got us on the run, that delicious mouth on a perpetual pout, I owe him at least a bachelor party. This could be his redemption for half a life ago. Mine.

In just a lace-up bra and itty panties, I push him on the bed. Climb atop, offering a bullet with a wonky buzz. The drug is as lush as the "designer" label implies. A real mood and muscle lubricant. I grind against my lover to the slow string-beats of our latest Spotify obsession, excited for what's in store. A flesh gem to fly down to us like I saw in my last keta-lucination.

Know I'm a good snake-charmer but it's still surprising, sigh-inducing, to break away when there's a beast in his briefs, a knock on the door, and I'm dripping so much want through my panties.

Olive Eyes cocks his head up, tucks his other deeper down his pants, glancing around for his steel on the side table.

"Settle down. It's for you. No danger."

His expression doesn't change much, but he trusts me enough to stumble to the peephole.

"Got something to cheer you up. Spice things up!"

I let the gift glide through the door and she's as gorgeous as she looks on live. Even in a wraparound dress, you can tell her curves are killer. Her makeup is natural-looking, hair starlet-silk. Fake tits but real charm in that pre-giggle smile.

"Two blondes are better than one. That's what they say," I introduce her to Olive Eyes.

He sits up in bed, a brow perplexed. He stays silent so he won't wake from this dream.

She hugs and tongue-kisses my neck, a cop-checking trick I remember from my outcall outlaw days. I lower my head to meet her lips and discreetly slip some bills from my bra into her hand. She tastes like pink bubblegum and the cash disappears in seconds: good signs.

When she starts singing "Happy Birthday" like Marilyn Monroe and cat-padding her way atop him, he's no less confused but his vision sure isn't on the gun anymore.

I drape a robe over it before she notices, pull a condom from the drawer. "Do you remember her from my SodaCam streams? PeachiePie69, she'd come on a solo feed before me?"

He shakes his head, stuttering a no.

"I remember you," she probably lies, using what I told her on video chat while he was in the shower. "305Vices. You said you like feet and a sweet girl with some sort of accent. Now, I know you're not sick of your fiancée's Pennsylvania one, but how do you like my drawl? Southern belle sound good to you?"

He turns as red as I worried I'd paint the bed. Luckily, I got a stand-in so I can stay plugged up. "It's okay, Olive Eyes. Unwrap your present. Enjoy."

He looks at me, lips sliding without the traction of words.

"Not a trick," I giggle. "Well, sorta one, but go on, touch her. She's real."

She smiles Julia Roberts wide, arms at either side of his, caging him between the pillows.

Slowly, he leans back, cups her arms and slides up like he's checking for wires, disintegration, my jealous dissatisfaction or something.

I light some decorative candles I stole from the lobby, top the other night table with a tray of pre-cut lines. "Don't worry, Olive Eyes. She's like you were on your thirteenth birthday. A virgin. So no real expectations."

His namesake inflates. He jolts up, nearly knocking his face into hers.

She laughs and says, "Guess I'mma late-bloomer. Camming's been my whole life since I turned 18. No time for college or boys 'til your girl made me an offer I can't refuse." Her shrug makes her dress slink down, revealing the top of a blush-color nipple. She sets her pink-bowed box where mine was a minute ago.

I sit on the sliver of bed left for me, one leg hanging off. "Told her I got the perfect guy. Mint chip sweet. Said, 'He'll probably be as awkward as you, an even match—at first.'" My hand worms between where their two bodies meet, wriggling so they both get the tingles.

One of her dainty fingers tug-slashes down the middle of her dress, so the fabric separates, and we can see her flat, tan tummy and girly white panties.

"Yep. All I've known is the plastic and silicone you've seen me with before you got ready for Cherry's shows. She tells me you're her favorite toy these days. Said we could share. You wanna play with me, don't you, tiger?"

An animalistic grunt crawls out of his throat, and I smile.

***

Panting, I take a step back so I'm off the bed that's become damp with our sweat and saliva and excitement. My head spins as I still clutch the whore's hips from behind, driving her up and down, jiggling her tits and peach meat over my man. I kiss the small of her back as a temporary adieu as she pulses for him a third time. I watch her steamy little raindrops slip down to the reddening base of the condom.

Maybe the girl's just good at timing the beginning of her period or maybe there's a 5% chance she wasn't lying about a hymen. That's really more of housekeeping's problem. Hey, I tried to protect the bedding, but in for a penny, in for a pound. As in, with how good he was pounding her the last round, I couldn't be bothered to be self-conscious about a period penny smell or Rorschach sheets.

I shimmy to remove the tiny vibrator from between my lips, let it fall to my furled palm and go wash it in the sink, unseen. Feeling as light as the one I flick on, I pretend not to see a baby cockroach burrow behind the mirror. Won't taint my K high or the endorphin rush from my good "naughty" deed.

I feel the goofy grin overtake my face, hoping this will cement my status as the coolest girlfriend ever. That this will be his best day—not just birthday— of them all. Besides our wedding one, of course. (Guess I'll have to top that with a couple "bridesmaids" and bowl of ever-rare MXE or British molly, but whatever.) I clean everything including myself up, and amble back out.

Olive Eyes, silk-robed like a Japanese groom and stoned, sits with his legs frogged under the coffee table. The girl and her bling-clipped hair slouch against the wall on the other side. Between them is the tray I prepared.

"Like a chemical charcuterie board," she chuckles, kneading the slinky dress balled up in her lap. She's probably getting off for a fourth time, feeling the wad of cash I gave her.

"Are you a virgin in that way too?" I ask, dropping and scooting into Olive Eyes' lap.

He holds me, nooking my head under his chin, whispering a laughy-unsure, "Ehm, thank you very much for this."

"Have I taken drugs before? Oh, yeah. I mean, here and there at high school parties or movie premiers. Xan, coke, Percs."

"Don't feel pressured into it, but if you wanna sample, we're good for it. Man's a bit of a kingpin further south." I feel him pinch my knuckle to stay mum but ignore it. "We fenty test everything." I point out the lines: classic yayo, acidy 4-HO-MET to swig down with the last of our vodka, the pussy-pink stripe of Roxicodone to relax.

She takes a schnoz-sip of devil's dandruff, and Olive Eyes and I halve the opioid as some sort of ironic comedown. As we drift from the moon back to the slightly soggy motel carpet, she speeds up, fingers fidgeting with the clothes she's not wearing. We don't mind, her tits still hypnotizing us in two different directions. Olive Eyes teases us about how we come quieter on cam, and we him for tickling our piggies with his tongue or asking if we wanted water during. It's a good time but not too long 'til we're nodding out.

A few blinks and my memory razors like how they used to cut-edit old movie strips. Me hiccupping awake when I bump against Olive Eyes' slow-mo mouth. The girl redressing, her pocket looking pregnant. Me at the door, waving goodbye like she's somebody cousin-close. Olive Eyes telling me not to lean so far out the threshold. Now, my vision's blotted out by a glorious pillow I hug. I muffledly hear him knock around the room. There're question marks in his words, a rising aggression funneled through a happy pill haze.

He rips the shield from my eyes. Says as levelly as he can, "What did you do with the baggie of coke? And ketamine? And blue bottle of pellets?"

Takes me a second or four to process. "Nothing." I replace the pillow to count sheep easier.

He snatches it, throws it at the safe I tapped into for our guest. "Then. Where. Are. They?"

I slump over, groan, pull the nightstand drawer. "Right..."

"Right," he says between teeth.

This is when my heart should drop past my belly button. Understand why he parks the Ruger in his waistband and throws on a shirt. But I just feel a flutter in my tummy, my brain lagging a few inches behind my body. I find it funny my feet carry me out the door and into our car. I can't even grasp why we're in here, why he throws a water bottle and jacket at me.

Then he says, "You're practically naked."

"Oh," I say just because I like the way the word curves on my lips. "Oh. Ohhhhh."

"Sober up," he says shortly, knowing I don't really get it. "Drink if you're coming."

Feels like my lips are melting down my face. Or maybe I'm just drooling. I swipe my chin, but it just feels like there're buzzy bees in my fingertips and my skin is made up of the feathery stuff in flower circles. I laugh, realizing he's force-feeding me cold water, that the Buick's side mirrors got pretty patterns in them like glow worms. Their wiggle and the sky light that cycles from bright to dark on repeat like a touch-dimmer lulls me back to black.

I've got a Heavenly heat beneath my skin. Euphoria slurs. Makes me wanna sleep all C-shape and cocooned like a caterpillar. The car rumble and rhythmic cursing are unexpectedly comforting. "Thought she was uncut, pure," I think I mumble but maybe it's just to my mind.

If you know somebody for a year, even through a screen, it should count for something... Olive Eyes knew me that way...but still hasn't learned that I have to be watched. His good-time bunny can make for the slummiest trouble. I feel more water stream down my cheeks, but it feels so nice, I smile even as I start to put up a whiney defense.

"Don't start," he warns me, clenching the wheel with one rage-white hand. "We'll find her. Let me focus." He takes my phone, pops some sort of upper, and I blackout on his behalf.

***

My own humming seems to wake me. I've made a bed out of the backseat, his suit jacket a blanket over me. My mouth tastes like metal and rotten fruit. I gag, crack the car door to spit up. Stare transfixed at the puddle of booze I made on the parking line. A skinny pantleg appears in the corner of my frame of reference.

"I took care of it," Olive Eyes says in a way that makes me imagine his esophagus is steaming with oil.

"Goood," I say with many more fun Os as he twists up the contraband into his suit jacket and stuffs it under the front seat. As he shoves, his sleeve rides up and I notice the red streak on the side of his wrist. A curly, scarlet-tip hair hanging from it too long to be mine. I pretend it's from the fun times we had in bed. As loopy as I am, trying to remember what the coat lumps he hides are supposed to mean, I know better than to ask what happened. "Daddy, can I ride up front with you?"

"You still got that bullet of K?"

It's a fair trade. I fish the snuff tube out of my bra and hand it over.

He plugs his nostril and sniffs hard 'til it sounds empty, jitters like he took a hit of the grossest cough syrup. "At least you got us stocked on dissos..."

I'm too faded to feel the prickle of blame or wonder why he wants to dissociate so bad. As he slams our doors closed, I hobble over the console to ride shotgun. When the car starts, I smirk.

"What?"

I drink in the clock, saying, "'S well after midnight. Technically, I only screwed up the day after your—"

He shoots me a glare like could come from the metal in his pants.

"Promised the most eventful birthday... Think you got it," I mumble, untangling my leg from the seatbelt.

"Every day's a fucking event with you."

I frown.

He sighs, puts us back on the road, as his nose starts to bleed. It instills more confidence that maybe that's all that occurred with his hand.

I sink horizontal, cuddle up for forgiveness, clasping his right leg in a lazy hug. Yawn, "I'll make it up to you tomorrow."

He stares down at my head in his lap. "You can make it up to me now." He scrunchies my hair in his bloody fist as the other dials for a radio station to scream away any thoughts.

I give the smallest shrug. Getting him off is getting off easy, another excuse to close my eyes and see stars.

***

Swallowing penance, I pop up some time down the highway, the synergy of uppers and downers still squeezing and tuckering my nerves. "Still mad at me?"

"It's the thot that counts," he quotes me, rolling his eyes behind his head in sarcasm or Shangri-La.

"That's right," I play along and kiss his cheek now that we're at a stoplight. "Did you make a wish before midnight?"

He glances toward the backseat drugs then lingers on me. "Already came true." He holds my hand, index nail scratching my engagement ring. "Everything's been made whole, so I guess I can't complain. I've been made whole."

# ANTHROPODERMIC

## BY P. N. HARRISON

Anthropodermic Bibliopegy – the binding of books in human skin. Dr. Gerald Morgan had thought it was a myth until a few months ago. Sure, he had seen the movies – *Hocus Pocus* when he was a kid and *The Evil Dead* on movie night when he was an undergraduate. He had even read some Lovecraft in his *Introduction to American Literature* class. But those were stories and this thing – this book – sitting in a clamshell box on his desk was anything but fiction.

Henry Frank had reached out to Laerde University's special collections library four months prior. Frank was a well-known figure among museum curators and librarians in the southeastern United States. An antiquarian and a self-professed "adventurer," Frank was in possession of a private collection that was the envy of every university collection in the region; it even contained several notable items that eclipsed Laerde's holdings in interest and value. So, when Frank began to get rid of his collection in his old age, the university

jumped at the chance to acquire some of the rarer items.

Except Gerald and Henry hadn't exactly seen eye-to-eye. "Sensationalist"

and "more interested in attention than antiquity" were just some of the things

Dr. Morgan had said to describe Henry Frank in an interview with the school's

paper – *The Azure*. Despite the sizable fortune he had inherited, Frank charged

the public to view the wing of his estate that housed his collection. And what a

collection he had. Shrunken heads, a Ugandan shaman's staff, unique medieval

manuscripts on the occult and alchemy – these were just some of the items he

had compiled during his lifetime. All of these items needed, *deserved*, to be in a

museum or a university library. They were wasted in the hands of a private

collector, especially one who was more interested in making a buck than learning

about the materials in his care and educating the public.

But the "skin-book" had never been on display. This struck Gerald as

strange. In all logic, the item should have been the crown jewel of Henry Frank's

collection. People would surely have plopped down their hard-earned money to

feed their morbid curiosities. Yet, this book had been kept out of the public eye.

No, that is not quite true. When Frank had acquired the book in Paris, forty

years prior, he had made a big deal about it. *The Dallas Morning News* even ran

an article about it. Then, silence. After making such a damned spectacle about

getting the book, it seems as if Frank didn't mention the thing again for four

decades. Not until Gerald's phone rang.

It was February when Gerald got the call. Frank was to the point about it. He wished to offload the whole of his collection, and he wanted Laerde's library to have his rare books – for free. The only stipulation, he said, was that a certain one-of-a-kind item needed to be a part of the transaction. A seventeenth-century French book entitled *L'hérésie des Pauvres – The Heresy of the Poor.* The book's cover, he said, was human skin. As long as the school took the book in and kept it *preserved* – he emphasized that word – then the whole of his collection belonged to Laerde University. The decision was easy.

***

Now, four months later, the skin-bound *L'hérésie des Pauvres* lay on his desk. Gerald knew next to nothing about the book and its provenance. Of course Henry Frank hadn't supplied this information; he certainly didn't care about history any further than it could profit him. No, Gerald would need to find out everything for himself. He lifted the clamshell's lid and saw, for the first time, the book's cover. It looked like pretty much every leather-bound book he had ever seen. He closed his eyes and breathed in. The next part was something he had dreaded. Hesitantly, he ran his fingertips across the binding. He exhaled. It felt just like it looked – if he didn't know better, this could be the leather cover of a family Bible or an antique copy of *Paradise Lost.*

Except he *did* know better. As one of the stipulations for the sale, the library had required Frank to get the book scientifically verified. He had sent a small fragment of the cover to the Biology Department at the University of California, Berkeley. "There is no doubt," the letter that Berkeley sent back stated, "That the sample in question is human skin."

Skin, yes. But no one had told him *whose*. It was Gerald's job to find out as much about the book as possible, and that started with examining the cover and the book. Aside from the binding material, the cover wasn't terribly remarkable – blank on both the back and the front with only the book's title etched into the spine in black ink. After measuring and photographing both sides of the book and its spine, Gerald opened the tome.

The inscription on the book's flyleaf was faint, almost entirely faded. Still, an inscription is a jackpot for a librarian, especially on book this unique. He photographed the writing, loaded the image onto his laptop, and zoomed in. French. That was a small roadblock, but it was not one he wasn't prepared for. He could send the image to the Department of Modern Languages, and a translation would arrive soon enough. Surely one of their faculty would be eager to make a name for themselves researching the book. After all, once the word got out that the library had acquired a book like *this*, there would be publicity – news articles and interviews, at the very least. Maybe even a feature on a Netflix series about "dark tourism." He attached the image and sent off the email.

Honestly, there wasn't anything else of interest about the book's interior. No additional notes in the margins. No ending dedication. But the inscription on the flyleaf was promising enough. He could certainly get an article, maybe even two, out of it once the translation came in. Gerald placed the book back in its case and grabbed his jacket to go home.

***

Gerald dreamt that night. A woman's body, nude, lay face down on a metal table. A man, dressed in fine black clothing, stood above it. He glanced over the body, then reached over to a nearby tray. He grasped a scalpel and returned his gaze to the corpse. Then, with practiced precision, he began to cut. Starting below the left trapezius muscle, the blade ripped through the flesh on the cadaver's back. Viscous blood trickled from the incision; the man mopped it up with a towel from the tray. The scalpel's journey continued across the body's lumbar, then up the opposite side of its back. Finally, as the instrument completed its rectangular path, the hand reached over and began to peel back the flap of skin. The last thing Gerald saw before he woke was the sight of the man's smile.

***

It took another ten days for the translation of the inscription to arrive from the Department of Modern Languages. Gerald saw the email on his phone and rushed to his laptop to open the message:

*"A book about the poor deserves a cover taken from a pauper. This book was created for his own collection by Docteur Bouland from the corpse of Marie, a widow dead of consumption at the age of 30 at La Salpêtrière. – 1897"*

Gerald didn't recognize the name "*La Salpêtrière*," but a simple Google search showed that it was a women's hospital, the largest in Paris during the nineteenth century. "*Docteur Bouland*" was less of an enigma. Dr. Ludovic Bouland was a major figure in the history of skin-bound books, a fact that Gerald had come to know since he began researching the topic. Bouland had made a number of these books, and it was not uncommon for him to comment on his creations in the book's flyleaf. In the front of one book, he had compared the merits of different methods of tanning skin. Bouland had sold a small number of these books, often to others in the medical profession. Examples of his work resided at Brown, the Philadelphia College of Physicians, and (until recently) Harvard.

Bouland may have been an open book, but Marie was a mystery. Still, *La Salpêtrière* gave Gerald something to go on. The conditions of the sanitarium were notoriously poor – more like a prison than a house of healing. After a bit of digging, Gerald found that Bouland practiced there as a physician and a surgeon. The implication settled in his stomach like a bowl of rotten curry. Marie had, almost certainly, been one of his patients while she lay dying, eaten up from the inside by tuberculosis. He shut his laptop and rubbed his eyes for a moment.

As the darkness faded from the edges of his vision, Gerald thought that he saw the figure of a woman standing amongst the library's shelves.

***

Gerald was right; it didn't take long for word about the skin-bound book to get out. *The Fort-Worth Star Telegram* reached out to him for a short interview over the phone less than a week after the translation arrived. Jessica Chaloff, the special interest reporter, called him the next day.

"How did you get the book?" Jessica asked. Probably the most obvious question. Gerald told her about Henry Frank and his collection. The next few, in fact, were questions that he had anticipated. "How much did the collection cost?" "Who made the book?" He told Jessica about Frank's donation and Dr. Bouland.

*"Do we know whose skin the book is made out of?"*

Gerald had expected this one, but his stomach still turned. It made him think about how little he truly knew about Marie. Everything he could tell Jessica about her – that she was poor, that she was a patient at *La Salpêtrière* – he had learned from Bouland's inscription.

"As you know, Harvard recently destroyed their skin-bound book. Do you have any plans to do the same?"

Gerald hadn't seen this question coming. Jessica was right; Harvard had destroyed the binding of their anthropodermic book. They cited "the ethically fraught nature of the book's origins and subsequent history." Still, Gerald hadn't even considered the option. Not that he could destroy the binding, even if he wanted to. He hadn't mentioned to Jessica the condition to Henry Frank's gift, but removing the book's cover would certainly be a violation of their agreement.

"I certainly recognize the difficult moral questions that anthropodermic books represent, but we have no plans to remove the binding at present. We'll be treating the book as human remains, and we intend to respect the dignity of the deceased as best we can."

"And how do you intend to respect Marie's dignity?"

"Library visitors will need to prove a legitimate scholarly interest in the book to be able to view it. We don't want any gawkers."

Jessica thanked him for his time and hung up. It was for the best. The call had left Gerald uneasy, and he still had significant work left to do. He had started writing an article on Laerde's *L'hérésie des Pauvres*, and he wanted to make some progress before he left the office for the weekend.

***

He had the dream again that night. Once again, the corpse lay on the metal table. Again, the scalpel traced its precise design across its back. Except, this time, there was a distinct difference. With every slice of the scalpel, the body twitched and squirmed. It was still distinctly a cadaver; the pallor of the lips and skin, the lack of breath, all indicated its lifelessness. Still, it writhed underneath the blade, its eyes squeezing tight as the razor's edge did its work. Then, as the surgeon's hand began to pry back the rectangle of flesh, the vacant eyes bulged open.

Again, the physician smiled.

***

Gerald swore under his breath as he tapped the keyboard. The due date approached, and he still didn't even have a first draft. It wasn't that he didn't have enough to talk about –*L'hérésie des Pauvres* was a scholarly gold mine –, but he was just so damned *tired.* He hadn't slept well in weeks. It wasn't always nightmares, no, but it was like he couldn't find it in himself to rest.

Coffee. Another cup would help. Gerald made his way to the library's break room and began to spoon the black powder into the ancient Mr. Coffee. The coffeemaker burbled to life, and Gerald began to pace. The special collections were empty except for him, as they usually were after 5:00pm. He enjoyed walking through the stacks; they reminded him of why he became a university librarian in the first place. He had processed many of the collections himself, after all.

He had wandered fairly far into the stacks when he heard the coffee pot beep. He turned on his heels to walk back down the aisle. There, at the end of the row of shelves, was the silhouette of a woman, her back to Gerald. Odd, yes, but not unexpected. Sometimes the student workers from the main circulation desk came down to borrow a Styrofoam cup or some creamer. He called out to her and walked forward.

As he stepped forward, he noticed that the woman was naked. She stood, almost cruciform, with her arms splayed out outwards, hands pressed against the wall of books on both sides of the aisle. Gerald watched as two thin, deep lacerations began to form on her back. Blood oozed down her legs and began to pool at her feet as the two incisions met, forming a perfect rectangle on her skin. Then, slowly, she reached behind her back. Her fingers dug into the edges of the wounds. She began to peel back the flesh.

Gerald didn't move. He didn't scream. He simply stood as the flayed figure did her work. Then, as the last bit of skin separated from muscle and bone, Gerald squeaked out.

*"Marie?"*

Then, she was gone. No blood remained on the floor. The smell of gore no longer permeated the air. Just an empty space between two bookshelves.

Gerald didn't bother getting his coffee.

***

Gerald didn't come into work the next few days. As haggard as he had looked for the past few weeks, nobody really questioned it. But the article's deadline still loomed. He had managed to produce about half of its anticipated content – the book's provenance, the manner of its acquisition, its measurements. That brought him to the known history of the book's cover. He danced around the topic for a few sentences: "the book was obviously rebound during the nineteenth century"; "there is no way of knowing any information about the book's original binding." But the fact remained.

He would have to talk about Marie.

He would, he decided, lean on his historiographic training. After half an hour of work, he produced a short snippet, everything he knew about the binding's "donor":

*"There are few biographical facts about Marie. Researchers know that she was an impoverished widow, age 30, who was a patient at La Salpêtrière hospital in Paris at the time of her death from tuberculosis."*

Twenty-eight words. The entire testament to Marie's life. But he *did* know more about Marie. He knew that she had short, brown hair. He knew that she had a mole at the nape of her neck. And he suspected that she was a patient of Ludovic Bouland during the final days of her life. But he couldn't include any of this information. That would lead to questions about *how* he knew these things, and dreams and nighttime apparitions aren't exactly reputable sources for academic publications.

***

He dreamed a different dream that night. The woman was still there. Except, this time, she was alive. She sat upright on a cot in a small, white room. She was pale, dark rings around her eyes, sweat on her forehead. She coughed a rasping, thick cough into a crimson-stained towel. The door opened. A man – the surgeon – stepped in. They exchanged words; the language was one Gerald did not understand. The woman's voice came through between ragged breaths. Tears mingled with the sweat beneath her eyes. She became agitated, visibly distressed. Then, clearly, he heard the man's exasperated voice.

*Madame Allard.*

***

It took nearly two weeks for the information to come in from *La Salpêtrière*'s records. Gerald was, quite frankly, shocked they found anything at all. It had been more than a century since the patient's death, after all. It had taken another two days for the Department of Modern Languages to translate the hospital's note. And now, on the screen in front of him, was the information he was looking for.

*Marie Allard. Admitted 17 September 1887. Died 30 September 1887. Attending physician: Dr. Ludovic Bouland. Cause of Death: Complications from Consumption. Next of kin: Sophia Allard (daughter).*

Gerald stared at the screen for a long time. It was too late to include this information in his article; it had already been submitted more than a week ago. Anyway, there was no way for him to prove that this was the same "Marie" whose remains sat in the room with him, bound tight around *L'hérésie des Pauvres.*

But he knew.

***

It went against every bit of Gerald's graduate training. Still, the book lay on his desk, a pencil beside it. He opened the cover and, in his uneven script, began to write underneath Bouland's message.

*This book is the earthly testament to the life of Marie Allard, mother of Sophia Allard. Her skin was taken without her consent by Ludovic Bouland to make this book's binding.*

As Gerald looked up, he saw again the silhouette of a woman. For the instant she was in view, he saw her for what she was.

Whole.

Smiling.

# BRUTAL LOVE WEARS JACKIE O DIMESTORE SUNGLASSES
## BY FRANK REARDON

*Summer of Love*

A hippie wearing bell bottoms and a 'Jesus Christ Superstar' T-shirt vomited on the hood of Ray Conlon's black GTO after he parked. The hippie, plastered in silver glitter and explosive cheer, didn't offer an apology.

Ray looked at the red house and the people standing on the deck built off the side. Long haired men and women danced, laughed, and drank beer to the sounds of The Moody Blues. Ray dusted off the nothing from a dark blue work shirt that had his name stitched in cursive on the left side of his chest. The clueless hippies pretended not to notice him. It didn't bother him; he figured they were too busy being *groovy* to care about a jobholder. He reached into his front pocket, popped a Camel from the soft pack and lit it.

Natalie opened the front door and welcomed him with a hug, 'I'm Just a Singer in A Rocking Roll Band,' blasted out the door along with the scents of blueberry candles and patchouli.

"Come here, asshole," Natalie said, kissing him.

"A dancing hippie puked on my car."

Her arms wrapped around his thick neck. Blue eye shadow and Cleopatra eye liner, stared adoringly at a man who stuck out like a sore thumb in the middle of her love-in party. She looked outside the door and watched the puke culprit dance in the middle of the street.

"Oh, him," she said laughing, "That's just Micah. He dropped a ton of acid, doesn't know where he is right now."

"Want me to drag him back in the house before he hurts himself?"

She massaged Ray's biceps and shoulders and leaned back to get a better look at his face, his bright blue eyes and the scar that started on the forehead, traveled across his face, jumped the eye, and continued to the cheek.

"Finally, my knight has arrived," she said.

The hippies looked from around the corner, but when they noticed Ray, they lost interest immediately. They thought 'Narc' and 'Square,' then returned to their partying and talking about the state of the country and communes they wanted to build, but never would.

"You don't need to worry about Micah. He'll find his way back," she said. "Now get your ass in here and let's get you a cold beer."

Ray reached into his blue Dickies and pulled out an envelope and handed it to Natalie.

"Here you go."

She thumbed through the envelope stuffed with twenty-dollar bills.

"Well, well," she said, biting her bottom lip, "looks like someone's getting laid tonight." She tapped him on the shoulder with the envelope and side eyed him. "Follow me, Mister."


Natalie's hips swayed up the aqua-carpeted stairs. A long red velvet skirt moved to the sound of the music. Trinkets wrapped around her pale ankles banged back and forth. Shoulder length auburn hair moved molten with the sounds of the music. Random hippies greeted her with every step like an award was being presented. She smiled at every one of them, but unbeknownst to them each smile she threw out was a favor she'd one day collect on.

A tie-dye tapestry divided the living room and the kitchen, Ray moved it to the side and entered the kitchen full of appliances partially hidden by hippies passing joints and pulling tabs off beer cans. Men with headbands and rock band T-shirts talked to women in filthy jeans or long flowing skirts. Ray's stomach churned when a woman lifted her arm, and he could smell a body that hadn't bathed in months.

"I know, baby," Natalie said, handing him a beer. "I'm about to throw her in the shower myself."

"I wasn't…"

"You don't have to," she interrupted. "But if you think she's bad wait until I introduce you to her lover, Amos. He's a pig farmer."

"I didn't think it could get any worse."

Natalie reached up and touched his chin and lightly pulled him in for another kiss. He obliged. When their lips met, he tasted the candy flavor of her lip gloss, he thought, 'Man, am I lucky.' He had short hair, a two-day unshaven face instead of a beard. He worked for a living. Years before he was an up-and-coming boxer until he shattered his hand. He was a foul-mouthed Irish kid from South Boston built and hard as nails. He preferred spending his days drinking beer, betting on sports, and listening to Roy Orbison. He didn't fit in with the hippie world of Huntsville, Alabama. He pretended to like the music, understand the lingo, and trained himself to nod in agreement when they talked about saving the whales, building strawberry fields in the middle of a poor neighborhood, or when they talked about chaining themselves to a fence that surrounded a construction site.

One time he made the mistake of telling the hippies that the construction sites provided jobs. A woman in a puffy pirate shirt got in his face and yelled, "but the starving kids in Viet-fucking-Nam!" He didn't understand what it had to do with people building a museum, but he learned quickly about the power of an agreeable nod to save himself from the rants of the self-righteous.

Natalie towed Ray by the hand around the party, proudly introducing him to everyone. Most of them were not impressed with his face, worked hands, clothes, and short hair. But they all wanted something from her, whether it was her energy, or her physically doing something, so they humored him.

"Aquarius/Let the Sunshine In' played on the stereo system. Micah returned from his acid-fueled journey and was shirtless and dancing in the middle of the living room. His head pointed up towards the ceiling, long pale arms waved around above his head. Ray looked on in disbelief, then looked up at the ceiling. He wondered if Micah was drilling the air with the glitter of his arm movement.

"Come with me," Natalie said.

"Gladly," Ray replied.

She walked them into her bedroom, shut the door behind him and tossed the envelope of cash on the bed.

"You're not afraid one of those fuckers is going to take that?"

"Baby, ain't nobody taking from me. Besides, those assholes claim to hate money. Like it's evil."

Natalie pressed her curvy body against his. The beer landed on the dresser without spilling and he began to grope her hair, hips and back. She unbuckled his pants and let them slide onto the floor. Not letting their mouths break apart she pulled his boxer shorts down and let them fall on top of blue work pants. Her well-manicured fingers forced him onto a chair, underneath a giant statue of a Buddha. She climbed on him and started to move around on his cock.

"You like it baby?" She said, her head titled back as she moved up and down.

He showed her how much he liked it by digging in and slapping her ass. She moaned and told him to do it again. After she came, she kept going.

"Before you cum, I have a question for you, baby."

Ray ignored her and kept with the rhythm of her body. He clenched his teeth, eyes, and worked harder. A feeling of exploding swept across his brain like a wave of godly confusion.

"Baby," she insisted, "Before you cum I have a question."

"Yes?"

"Want to rob the Copper Top?"

When she asked her question Ray came inside of her. He felt at one with her body as she continued to grind on top of his delightful sensitivity.

"What? When?"

"In two nights."

"Wait, are you serious?"

"As serious as your leftovers leaking down my leg right now." She kissed him again. "You're obviously staying over tonight, right?"

"I planned on it."

"Good." She said, grabbing him by the hand. "We'll talk about it when everyone leaves."

"Let's make it over coffee in the morning. I plan to do that again."

"I like the way you think, Mister."

Natalie poured fresh hot coffee into two mugs. One black for Ray, and she added a touch of cream into her mug, followed by a half of a fresh strawberry. He didn't understand why she always dropped a half of a strawberry into her mug, but he thought it original, and it only added to her personality. She set the mugs on the table then sat across from him.

"That Micah guy make it home alright?" Ray asked with a smile.

"He left with some guy named Calico."

"He's gay? And Calico?"

"As gay as the music he was dancing to. Calico because he dresses up as a kitten."

"Hmph."

"Does that bother you? It's not 1366 anymore. It's 19-fucking-69."

"Nah, I don't care, kid. I didn't know is all."

"How could you not?"

"I thought that's how all you hippies dance."

"Oh, we do love the dance parties, Mister." she replied with a sarcastic glace. She removed a long clove cigarette from her purse and lit it. "But you only have to chat with him for five minutes and you know."

"Well, I didn't get a chance to talk to him. He was busy dancing, if that's what you call it, and vomiting on my damn car."

"Fair enough."

Ray lit one of his camels, and the tobacco smoke blended with Natalie's clove. The house was littered with beer cans and packed ashtrays. Ray noticed a woman passed out on the sofa in the living room.

"Who's that on the couch?"

"That's Beth, she's an artist."

"What kind of art?" He said, gawking at the tightness of her bell bottom jeans snugged around her hips, and her tiny Tie-dye tank top.

"She's a painter. Big Beatles fan too."

"How you know her?"

"She hangs around the food pantry."

"Cool."

"You know that envelope you brought here last night?"

"Yeah, well, I meant..."

"That it was short?"

"He said he'd make it up to you in trade or something like that."

"Connie, man! What's he think, that I want a piece of that Nazi memorabilia in trade?"

"He's not a Nazi, just collects World War Two junk."

"Not the point," she said. "I do a service for a person; I expect to be paid in full."

"What did you do for him?"

"You two are pals, let him tell you."

Ray cracked his knuckles and pushed out from the table and poured another cup of coffee. He noticed the strawberry still in Natalie's mug and knew she didn't need a refill yet.

"When you seeing him again?" She asked.

"We are going to the Copper Top later today and play the ponies in the back room."

"Let him know he can help us."

"Help with what?"

It wasn't often Natalie blew her cool, but she did in front of Ray on occasion because she trusted him enough to show her true nature when she needed to. She could be angry and weak in front of him. He liked it because the hippies only got the party version of her. There was an instant bond between the two. They could not see one another for days, months even, and come together like kindred souls. The year before she went to Amsterdam for the summer, and when she returned, they connected like they hadn't missed a day. Neither of them wanted to admit they didn't know how to survive without each other.

"Help with the Copper Top, Ray. That action they see every day in that back poker room. The cash running through the poker and horseraces and sports books. That belongs to you and me, Baby."

"I expected as much." She pulled the strawberry from the cup and took a small bite, "Beth is going to help too, but don't wake her up. I can't handle her energy right now."

"Is it bad energy?" Ray asked.

"No. She's the goods, but she's always overly thrilled by every damn thing she sees and does, like a kid at the zoo. It's way too early for that kind of energy," she said, holding out her empty mug.

Ray snatched it from her hand and filled it up. "You want an aspirin for that hangover."

"No," she said lighting half a joint and placing it the end of it on a clip. "I'm going to smoke this joint, then you are going to fuck me six ways from Sunday, and we'll sleep a bit more. I'll be good after that."

Ray didn't smoke weed, and she liked that about him. He wasn't part of the happenings of the late sixties. He reminded her of when she was a teenager, and all the greasy workers in the neighborhood. Men committing crimes, gambling to make ends meet. Men with dirty hands and beer on their breath. Men with bad backs who didn't have opinions because they kept it locked up inside. Loyal men who'd get angry if another man touched his woman. She screamed feminism, and even though she believed it, hippies couldn't screw like a working man. And they certainly wouldn't kill on command. She loved freedom, gentle words, kindness, and compassion, but she also understood it was not only a way of living, but also a currency. One she exploited like an expert bricklayer building a cathedral brick by brick, dollar sign after dollar sign. There wasn't a groovy mother fucker in Huntsville who wanted to owe her, nor dare get in her way when she had her mind set on something. Ray didn't mind being the meat behind the operation. When the time came to knock a poor bastard on his ass, or break a leg, he didn't feel an ounce of sympathy.

Ray buttoned up his shirt and pulled up his pants.

"Don't forget to tell Connie pay up or have his ass over here tonight."

"Will do, what time we going to meet?"

"Couple hours, baby. I'm still tired."

Ray kissed her cheek and left the room. The early afternoon sun pushed through the living room window. He adjusted his eyes to the light and saw Beth sitting cross-legged and hitting a bong. She looked up at him, pot smoke floating around her dark rimmed glasses.

"Hello!" She shouted like she hadn't seen a person in years. "Want a hit?"

"No, I'm good."

"You're Raymond, right!?" she asked, holding out the bong. He understood what Natalie meant. The energy bounced off the walls and slammed into his body.

"No one's called me Raymond since my mom."

"Natalie calls you Raymond."

"She does?"

"Yep. That's how I know she loves you," she said, her bones rattling through her skin like a child on Christmas morning.

"Well, nice meeting you," he said.

"You're leaving already man! Well, if you got to go, then peace, brother," she said, throwing up a peace sign.

Ray fumbled his fingers around, "ahh fuck it," he said, unable to return the peace sign in time. In the driveway, he noticed Micah's vomit had turned into a crust on the hood of his car. "God damn, hippie," he said. He walked to the side of the house and dragged a green garden hose over to the car and sprayed off the vomit. "Fucking patchouli puke all over my...god damn!"

"Jesus," Conrad said, throwing down his tickets, "Another loser. I swear, Ray if it weren't for bad luck, I wouldn't have any luck at all."

"All losers for me too," Ray said.

"We should ask Blondie the bartender to hook us up for the next race."

"We need to have to talk, let's go outside for a smoke."

"I brought a fatty. You care to partake," Conrad asked.

Ray couldn't take his eyes off Conrad's once white button-down shirt that he had Tie-Dyed. The purples, reds and yellows hurt his eyes. The pink and yellow ascot around Conrad's neck offended him.

"Her name is Aprul."

"Come again?" Conrad asked.

"Blondie behind the bar with the tatts, her name is Aprul. It's pronounced April, but she spells it Aprul. I have no clue so don't ask."

Ray signaled to Aprul. She walked over with a cold beer and handed it to him.

"Sweetheart," he said. "Can you pour a little Jack Daniels into a plastic cup so I can take it outside for a minute?"

"Sure thing, sugar." She replied. Ray touched her neck tattoo of a skull wrapped in a bed of roses and explored for a minute.

"Looks grateful but feels like porcelain. What does it taste like?"

"Like sweat and whiskey, sweetheart." A tired but sweet smile fell down her face. He noticed the sawed-off shotgun underneath the bar. The image of her shooting a would-be robber and peppering the bandit with buck shot turned him on. Ray respected anyone who took matters into their own hands, murder or fucking. It didn't matter, combing the two, even better. Aprul pulled her elbows up from the bar and walked away. Her denim clad rear with two red patches sown on the seat of her jeans swayed away from him. She snatched the Jack and poured some of the brown liquid into the cup. Her chest pushed out the T and the H of her Triumph motorcycle T-shirt.

Conrad lit the spliff and leaned on Ray's GTO, letting the feeling of being a loser fade from tense shoulders. "Street Fighting Man," played on the outside speakers of the Copper Top's patio. Ray set the plastic cup of Jack on the top of his car, removed his top denture implants, and dropped them into the whiskey.

"I didn't know you had fake teeth, man," Conrad said.

"Got them knocked out by some Swede in a boxing match back in the day."

"Swedes box?"

"Apparently so. His name was Alarik Bagge. Imagine losing a fight to a guy named Alarik Bagge?"

"How do you even spell that?" Conrad asked.

"I couldn't say. It's embarrassing though. I had the fucker, too. Fight went into the ninth round. I had him on the score card, then the fucker landed an upper cut that knocked me into the front seat of a UFO. I can still feel it. Messed up my teeth something fierce."

"I could imagine, brother," Conrad replied.

"Listen, Connie," Ray said, removing his brass knuckles from his back pocket and putting them on the top of the car next to his teeth. "Nat, she wasn't happy with the envelope last night."

"I told you, Ray, I'd have the rest to her this week."

"I know man, I get it. I really do, but you know Nat, Connie. She doesn't like half-assing anything. And money, kid, that's even worse, so unless you can cough up the other hundred and fifty, then I need to work you over a bit."

"Is there any other way? I wasn't planning on being knocked around today."

"It's the money or taking some lumps and helping us out with something."

"Help with what?"

"I'll tell you after, if you go that route."

"So let me get this straight, give you the money and I can go home and be out of the shit with her, or get my ass kicked and help out with something I won't know about until you're done kicking my ass?"

"That's pretty much the gist of it."

"I don't have the money, Ray."


Ray let the knuckle duster slide onto his fingers, then he hit Conrad in the side so hard a rib cracked. Conrad's red scruff shot out like tiny poison darts. He collapsed on the ground breathless. A sunburned bald spot gazed up at Ray's face.

"Holy...shit, Ray, you cracked my rib."

"One more time," Ray said, picking him up by the collar of his shirt.

"Not the knuckles man. Please."

Ray let the knuckles slide off his fingers and he hit Conrad square in the nose with his fist.

Conrad pranced around the car, gripping his nose.

"Fuck, Ray, I think you broke my nose."

"I'm all done, buddy," Ray said, looking at the blood flow from Conrad's nostrils. "Shit's not broken, pussy. Toss some ice on it. You'll be good in no time."

"There are no mantras to help you, Ray."

"Let's go back inside and get you some tape and ice for that nose."

"Fuck, Ray, my eyes are going to be black and blue."

They walked back into the bar, "Aprul," Ray said.

"Yes, honey?"

"You have a steak back there?"

"I do."

"Bring me a cold raw steak, a bag of ice, tape, and double whiskey for Connie here. And buy yourself a shot on me."

"Sure thing, honey."

Ray could tell Aprul had a thing for him, and he flirted a bit, but he kept it innocent. If he acted on anything with her, he understood that Natalie would have her beaten, even worse, killed.

"It's not too bad, Connie. Look in the bar mirror."

Enormous purple and black pouches swelled underneath Conrad's brown eyes. The white tape held his nose in place, and the whiskey did little to take the pain away.

"I look like a damn carnie."

"You are a carnie, every day of the week, man. Especially in that ascot."

"It's style. You wouldn't know anything about style."

"Sorry, Pierre Cardin," Ray mocked. "Aprul, two more double whiskeys for the road."

"So, what's this thing y'all need help with?" Conrad said, softly touching his nose and leaning to the side away from his rib.

"We are going to roll the Copper Top's back room."

"Wait, what?"

"Yep."

"Natalie is into the stick-up business now?"

"Appears so, carnie boy."

"She already owns the weed trade in the city. Why does she need to rob our hangout?"

"She needs a new fence."

"Fuck me, really?"

"No, but she could use a new fence. You rank hippies ruin her property every time she has a party."

"It's all about the love, brother. You could use love, Ray."

"I have plenty of love for those who deserve it. I don't walk around like a cult member handing out flowers and dancing away the hate in the universe. The world has been shit since day one, Connie. Yoga and chanting mantras aren't going to change that."

"Maybe try spreading more of that selective love of yours around a bit more than you do, and you'll see it grow."

"Should I walk up to the father who lost his son NAM and say, 'love you, peace?' Do you think the single mother working two jobs, trying her best to provide for her children needs to hear mantras? How about the old fucker dying off ass cancer, a man who hasn't shit straight in who knows how long, and cannot afford his medications, think he needs a bouquet of flowers and a peace sign? I have zero idea why you people think any of it helps. Truth is, it helps you feel better about being a shit person in a shitty world. You have no deeper insights, no deeper wisdom because you took acid. The world isn't going to wake up one day and say, 'oh fuck, world leaders are committing genocide, let me rub magic rocks on the earth. Mother earth will inspire the world leaders to become painters and musicians. Mother earth will make the KGB have an orgy. She'll open her goddess arms and hug LBJ's inner child.' The world doesn't work like that. Love is fleeting, it comes and goes. It's not a fashion pick of the day like you fruity fuckers think. Friendships, relationships, marriages, all that takes work."

"You'll see, brother," Conrad said. "It's the summer of love, my man. You'll see. Nothing will take it away from us. This movement you want no part of, our flower power, our love, all of it is going to prevail."

"Finish your whiskey. We need to get to Natalie's."

Natalie tossed a couple of black ski masks on Conrad and Ray's laps, "So they don't know it's you two."

"You going with?" Conrad asked.

"I'll be driving Ray's car. I'm the wheel lady. I drive faster than the both of you put together."

"We're taking my car?" Ray asked. "What's Beth going to being doing?"

"She'll already be there, drinking and packing a little Saturday Night Special in her waist band. When you two take the back room. She'll keep the bar cool."

"We are forgetting something," Conrad said.

"What? What am I forgetting Connie?" Natalie said, her eyes blood shot, patience thin.

"You know the cash that funnels out of there goes straight to the Dixie Mafia," Conrad explained. "I don't know about you, but I'd like to keep away from Kevin Connely and his goon squad of rednecks in Biloxi. Last time those boys came up this way they crucified John Printz to a telephone pole in Five Points. I don't know exactly what he did, something about skimming from the used car dealership he ran for them, 'Printz's Prize Hole?' Yeah, John got a big prize all right. And robbing them of their biggest source of stable revenue south of Nashville, we really need to consider what we are doing here."

"It's happening tomorrow night, Connie, so unless you can pay me, your ginger ass is in." Natalie said.

Conrad lowered his head. Fear rushed through his body, and anxiety kicked up from his legs and settled in his chest. Conrad didn't like guns, the idea of murdering people for cash gave him the shits.

"We both need a piece, hon," Ray said. "I can't get anything this short of notice."

"I got you covered," Natalie said, unfolding a blanket on the kitchen counter, "think these will do?"

Ray snatched up one of the Savage Fox double barrel shotguns. He opened the dirty steel and looked inside the empty chambers, "It only holds two shells, Natalie. We are not going hunting like a couple of aristocrats, babe." Natalie reached into a duffel bag she had stashed underneath the table and tossed a .38 at him.

"Do I get pistol, too?" Conrad asked.

"Yes," she said, putting a .38 with a taped grip on the table.

"I hate guns," Connie said, picking up the gun with his fingertips and a limp wrist. "Those guys are always packing automatics, knives, who knows what else. I don't even know how to use a gun. They'll kill me before I even remove the thing from my pocket."

"Let's hope it doesn't come to that Connie."
Ray practiced loading and reloading the shotgun, "How much you think they'll be holding tomorrow?"

"My person on the inside said the city's high rollers play the ponies and the tables every Thursday night. A ton of money goes through there, after that it heads down to Biloxi Friday morning, so we need to roll tomorrow night."

"What are you getting out of this, Natalie?" Conrad asked.

"Cash and control," she explained. "Maybe I want to put a dent in the Dixie boys. Maybe shut the fuck up, Connie."

"It's not a good idea," Conrad replied, looking down at the floor. "Ray, you think it's a good idea?"

"Raymond wants what I want, don't you, sweetie?"

Ray kissed her, then turned his head towards Conrad, "exactly what she said." Conrad shook his head and couldn't believe what he was getting into. He wanted to quote the Buddha, but his nose hurt too much.

"Connie," Natalie said. "You got a couple of bitchin' shiners, don't you?"

"I think my rib is broken too."

"My man nailed you pretty good, didn't he?"

"I don't see why he had to be so violent about it."

"Because you are a degenerate gambler who never pays on time. You'll think twice next time you ask for loan to play the horses."

"If you say so," Conrad said.

"Come here, Dr. Zaius," Natalie joked. "I got something for the pain."

"Did you just call me Dr. Zaius?"

"Sure did, the orange ape from Planet of the Apes, you look like him," Natalie replied handing him a codeine pill. "Maybe I should start calling you Zaius."

"Let's not," Conrad replied.


They sat around the table drinking coffee, each one wondering what the next night would hold. They all ignored what might happen after they pulled it off. Riches and greed filled Ray and Natalie's mind. Conrad stewed in anxiety. Anxiety the other two refused to acknowledge.

"Ray, baby, take Dr. Zaius home. He's killing the vibes but come right back. I need to get laid tonight."

Ray set the double barrel back down and covered it. "I'm going to bring the .38 with me tomorrow instead, leave the long barrels in the car." Natalie agreed with a nod. "Let's go Connie." The two of them headed towards the door.

"Oh, and Connie?" She said lighting a clove. "If you even think of skipping out on us, well, let's just say what happens to you will be ten times worse than what the Dixie boys did to John Printz. All of Five Points will see what Dr. Zaius' prize hole has to offer."

Conrad didn't respond. It bothered him because he knew they were both blind. Ray opened the door for him and looked back to give Natalie a wink, but she was too busy rolling a silencer on the table to notice.

*The Robbery*

Motorcycles lined the curb in front of The Copper Top. Across from the bikes expensive Cadillacs and Cobras, filled up the parking lot. Ray stepped out of the front seat wearing a green army jacket and jeans. He lifted the seat for Conrad who stepped out looking like a disheveled businessman, ginger hair a mess, candy stripped collared shirt half tucked into brown polyester pants. Natalie rubbed the gear shift and showed Ray a little thigh and blew him a kiss from gooey, candy-coated lips. It traveled in plain sight, moving the way love, trust, and loyalty should travel, straight to the heart of the recipient. Ray reached out and snatched it with his hand and stuck it in his pocket.

Conrad walked behind Ray towards the door. The Buchanan Brothers hit, 'Son of a Lovin' Man,' traveled out the front doors, hit a light post, then went straight back into the bar and rubbed the shoulders of the patrons sitting at the bar. Bikers, constructions workers, plumbers, farmers, and junkie hippies crowded the inner workings of the bar. Aprul moved fast, filling cups, and serving drinks to shit talkers and wannabe magicians.

Ray reached back and touched the back of his pants to feel the handle of his .38. Conrad pointed out Beth at the end of the bar. Her messy brown hair fell over her glasses and the chestnut tips tickled the lettering of a Beatles T-shirt. Ray leaned into the bar next to her, a nervous Conrad stood inches behind them.

"You didn't come in with masks on," Beth said.

"Keep it down," Ray replied.

"I just thought it would be more like the movies is all."

"This isn't 'Point Blank,' Beth. And I'm not Lee Marvin," Ray said looking back. "And Connie certainly is no Angie Dickinson?"

"Angie Dickinson ain't all that," she said.

Ray smiled at Aprul with two fingers up. "What's wrong with Angie?"

"Nothing, I just don't get why all the boys drool over her."

"Rio Bravo, The Killers, Oceans 11...What's not to like about Angie? Did I mention Rio Bravo?" Ray replied, taking a beer from Aprul, and handing the second one to Conrad.

"I'm not a big fan either," Conrad interrupted. "I'm more of a Bettie Page person myself."

"Thank you, Connie." Beth said.

"What!? Page is not actress. She's a fetish model," Ray said. "And you would like her better, Connie. King Cuck over there with his ascots and sensitivity."

"Beth," Conrad said. "Ray don't get high fashion."

She took a sip of her beer, "He doesn't know shit about models and movies either."

"I don't know shit about film. I named three or four brilliant films with Angie Dickinson in them."

"They don't reflect society," she said. "All they do in those movies is kill people. And with Vietnam, and civil rights, movies like those don't speak to a collective consciousness. You got Lee Marvin going on a killing rampage to get his cash, then at night he goes to bed with the hot red head with a nice ass."

"She's right, Ray."

"Those movies are holding up a mirror to society. They don't need metaphor and thank God for that. So, what if they throw in a couple shoot outs and a nice 'rack' or two to make the boys whistle. And by the way," Ray exclaimed, "Angie is a good actress. Her chops were as impressive as Lee Marvin's. People don't need artsy-fartsy movies like 'Persona,' or 'Peeping-Tom,' to understand how the world works. All those long dragged-out metaphors wrapped in distorted colors where's the fun in any of that? There's no fun at all. You two knuckle heads are full of shit, in love with what's hot rather than what is, and 'Point Blank' is what is."

"All I was getting at," she said. "Was I thought you two would come in guns blazing. Then I get metaphor this and art that. You really are a long-winded mother, aren't you Raymond?"

"We came for the back room, you know this."

"How do you expect to get past the whole bar after you are done with the backroom. You two didn't think about that did you? Because this place is packed. I guarantee half the bikers and a few of these crackers in business shirts are balls deep in the Dixie Mafia."

"Guess you should've paid more attention to 'Point Blank," Ray said with a smile.


Ray ordered two more beers and handed one to Conrad, "Drink up, Connie, things are about to get desperado in here. "

"Be ready, Beth," Ray said. "If we need you as back up, be ready."

"Yeah, whatever" She replied, "Just hurry the fuck up. I got a painting at home to work on, then I'd like to hit up the Sisters Against the War meeting."

Chills ran up Ray's arms. Anxiety flooded his lungs. He felt trapped, neither Beth nor Conrad took the job with an ounce of seriousness. Ray bumped Conrad's arm, motioning him to follow.

They walked back to the bathroom that was adjacent to the poker and sports gambling room. Ray called it the 'hole' because he spent days, weeks, owning money before he got lucky and paid up. They both entered the bathroom. Ray reached into his jacket pocket and pulled out his ski mask.

"You really going to wear that?" Conrad asked.

"Yes," Ray replied, "and so are you."

"What's the point? The entire bar saw our face."

"I don't care about the drunk idiots in the bar. Whoever is behind the door, that's who I care about."

Conrad begrudgingly followed Ray and removed the ski mask from his pocket. The two of them put the masks over their heads and collected their breath. Ray reached under his coat and pulled out the .38, Conrad stood there.

"You got your piece?"

"I don't," Conrad replied.

"What the fuck, Connie? I mean what the shit?!"

"I don't believe in killing, Ray. I figure one gun is as good as two, isn't it?"

"So, your plan was to stand there like an idiot while I do all the work? What happens if one of these assholes takes a shot at me, hits me even. What's your plan then? Sit down with them and have group meditation until all the bad feelings leave the room?"

"That's the smartest idea you've had since we got here," Conrad replied. Ray couldn't believe his friend left him in the lurch to manage the entire robbery. He looked at Connie's eyes staring at him through the eye holes of the ski mask. The stupid tie-dye ascot tied at the bottom of the mask. Ray moved towards the door without saying another word to his friend.

A dozen men sat around a poker table. Some of them were in overalls, others wore suits. Car dealership owners, gentleman farmers, doctors, lawyers. They all smoked cigars and cigarettes. In the corner, behind the table, sat two television sets piped into the horse track in Nashville. Men of means stood around the sets yelling and screaming for their horse to win. The back of the room a bored woman in an open window took money and served drinks.

"Everyone shut the fuck up now!" Ray shouted, holding up the .38. Ray walked over to the table and snatched up a giant canvas bag holding chips and decks of cards and dumped it on the floor. "Put the table money in here," he said throwing the bag on the table. "Then pass it over to the window and put the money in the bag. And while you are at it, what's ever in your pockets and wallets. In fact, just drop the damn wallet in, the wrist watches too."

"Son," an old man with slicked white hair said. "You haven't thought this through, have you?"

A fat man in a brown suit stood up from the table, "Boy," he shouted through double chins. "Do you know who you are robbing here?"

"I don't give a fuck," Ray said. "Put the money in the bag."

The men around the table dropped their wallets, watches in the bag one after the other. The dealer opened a box and dumped stacks of cash. The bag made its way to the television sets and the men betting on the ponies dropped their cash in the bag. Ray walked over, snatched the bag, "Connie, watch my back," he said, knowing very well Conrad didn't have a gun and he'd stand there pretending none of it was happening. That he'd try to transport himself to a place he loved, like a Zen beach.

"Lady, put the money in the bag."

She dumped a cigar box full of cash into the bag.

"Lady," Ray said with calm urgency, "The money in the safe. The real damn money that'll be sent to Biloxi tomorrow morning."

The woman with blue eye shadow and honey blonde hair up in a beehive removed the key from a chain from around her neck and opened a small safe at her feet. She pulled out banded stacks of cash and dropped them into the canvas bag. Ray flung the canvas sack over his shoulder and backed away. "Everyone on the floor," Ray said. The men all climbed on the floor and put their noses into the carpet.

The fat man in the brown suit looked up. The overhead colorful lights shined down on the masked bandits like LSD and a Grateful Dead concert in Las Vegas. He could feel the small revolver strapped to his ankle.

"Everyone count to five hundred after I shut the door," Ray said. Ray heard "Daddy Sang Bass, "playing from behind the door. He looked at Conrad and motioned him to the door. Ray turned around and faced the door to open it. A pop from behind went off. The blood painted the door and Ray's shoulder. Plasma and bone traveled from Conrad's skull and landed on the ground next to Conrad's feet. Muffled silence mixed with fear gripped Ray's heart when he watched a look of disbelief take over Conrad's face. Unable to understand why he had to die at that moment, in the back room of a shitty bar. His chunky body fell to floor in pool of his own insides.

Ray walked over to the fat man holding the smoking pistol, stood over him and pulled trigger. The fat man's head split like a melon killing him instantly. The woman at the money window screamed. Ray shot her from across the room, a bullet ripped through her chest. Men reached into their coats and pants, and removed pistols and pointed their weapons at Ray from the floor. Ray opened the door and ran out. He grabbed a nearby chair and slammed it underneath the knob. He pulled off his ski mask and put it in his coat and dropped the sack down by his side. When he turned the corner, he saw April on the telephone. Johnny Cash switched to The Mamas and the Papas, "California Dreaming."

She dropped the phone and reached underneath the bar and snatched up her sawed-off horse cock and pointed it at him. The entire bar looked at Ray then took cover underneath the tables and on the floor.

"Drop the sack, Ray," April demanded. "I really dig you, sweetheart, but I value my neck a lot more."

"I'd put that down right now," Beth shouted, pointing her pistol at April's chest.

A biker moved on the floor by Beth's feet, she turned around on the barstool and shot the man in the head. Skull blood splattered her bell bottom jeans and her cheek. She pointed the gun just as quick back at April, "Do you think I'm fucking around?" She said. Ray slowly moved back to the door. In the distance Natalie had the headlights on. Smoke from the tailpipe rumbled in the dark, traveling in synch with the air and lights. The two women held their guns on one another. Ray heard people weeping, others trying to hold their breath. Beth pulled the trigger. A bullet passed through Aprul's chest and hit the liquor bottles, shattering the glass shelving. Bottles gathered from each end of the shelf and collided above the breaking glass before hitting the floor. The horse cock fell from Aprul's hand, her body followed the gun to the ground.

"Connie?" Beth asked.

"Didn't make it." The men trying to break down the heavy door had given up. "We better get going, I know those fuckers in there are on the phone to Connelly and Dixie.

They left the Copper Top and walked up the parking lot towards Ray's GTO.

"How much did you get?" Beth asked.

"I don't know how much," He replied. "A lot."

"Yeah, but how much is a lot," she asked. "If you had to guess."

"I don't know, the sack is full to the grip, so a lot. I didn't count it."

"You mean to tell me neither you nor Connie counted it?" Beth asked.

"There's no time to count when I was the only one packing."

"Connie wasn't packing?"

"No. He developed a conscience."

"You are an idiot, Raymond Conlon."

"How am I an idiot? The way I see it is this bag of cash cost me the lives of two of my friends, and some fat bastard I didn't know. No one had to die tonight."

"You mean that trailer trash bartender was your friend?"

"She was good people."

"She had a gun on me, what was I supposed to do?"

"Put one in her leg? Let her go? I don't know, take a pick."

"She was trailer trash, Ray. Trailer trash that would've killed you."

"For a fun-loving hippie always going to anti-war rallies and art gatherings, you sure do like carnage, death, and talking down to those who have less than you."

"What's that supposed to mean?" She said planting her foot into the asphalt.

Beth didn't notice the double barrels of the Savage Fox resting on the open passenger window. The blast from the barrels lifted Beth off her feet and threw her corpse back five yards into a maroon Cadillac. Her head bounced off the steel and knocked her glasses somewhere into the darkness.

"Get in," Natalie said, lighting a clove.

He tossed the sack into the back seat, and she dropped the car into gear, screeching the tires against the asphalt.

"The fuck, Nat?"

"She wasn't getting in on this. It was always about me and you, baby. I was going to cut her out. I didn't plan to kill her, but she wouldn't shut up," Natalie shouted. "Blah, Blah, Blah. I swear Ray, I told you about her energy and how it digs into your bones. The girl never knew when to shut up."

Ray lit a Camel and leaned back into the seat. Natalie drove them onto the ramp and headed south.

"We not going to your place first?"

"Can't take the chance, baby. Miami is on their way."

"Miami who, what?"

"My supplier. I owe them."

"How much?"

"A-fucking-lot," she said laughing. "I've been spending more than I can sell."

"Jesus Christ, Natalie. You owe Cubans? You know they are backed by the Italians in New York. They'll never stop hunting us, never. We could get away for twenty years and think we are fine. It could be 1987 and we are sitting by a pool somewhere in Denmark, and they'll find us. It's not about the money at that point to them, it's about the principle. Fuck. I came here to escape that life. Boston Irish killed my parents over two thousand dollars. I had to fight in fixed boxing matches for a long time to pay back what they owed plus interest."

"This money is ours, baby. We are going to get us a Podunk motel in a shitty Podunk town for the night, then we are on a plane to wherever you want to go. Tahiti, China, France...Shit, baby, you want to go live in Antarctica, we can go there."

"Why did we even bother hitting the Dixie Mafia. We could've just taken whatever money we had and left. Now we have two groups of lunatics after us."

"You worry too much, honey," she said, gripping his chin.

He pulled his face away from her touch, something he'd never done before. He could see in her eyes and hear in her voice that the entire mess they were in, the money, the deaths, excited her. Killing is a dirty business that a person cannot escape from. If the law doesn't catch you, regret does. It made him nervous she laughed at the gravity of the situation. At any moment, a bunch of chainsaw wielding Cubans could find them and give them neck ties. Maybe the Dixie Mafia was following them, and they'd dump them in tubs of acid, or feed them to blood thirsty dogs.

*Poland*

They crawled around in the sheets together, naked, sweating and fucking on the king-sized bed of Starlite Motel outside of Birmingham. A red and green door motel owned by a tobacco-chewing porn aficionado named Brian Townsley. They both kissed and moaned, looking at one another in love. Ray came inside of her, and she didn't seem to mind. She loved him and in secret she dreamed of having a family with him. Ray rolled over and lit a clove for Natalie and a Camel for himself. They both stared up at the ceiling, smoking, and letting the fluids and the day drip from their bodies.

"Poland," Ray said.

"What baby?" Natalie asked.

"We should go to Poland."

"Why Poland, are you Polish?"

"No, but they'd expect us to go somewhere exotic, or to a place like France or Italy. No one runs away to Poland. Ever see a movie where the gang runs away to Poland?"

Natalie let a dozen movies run through her head, "I can't say I have, Ray."

"We hide out in Poland for a few years, then we go to a nice place like The Philippines."

"You are suggesting two places ravaged by war twenty years ago. I don't think we have a chance in either place. Pick somewhere else."

"You said anywhere."

"That was in the moment, baby. I was jacked up, and with Beth and Connie, I didn't know what I was talking about...Man, but that Savage Fox knocked her a fucking mile though, didn't it?" She said with a laugh.

Ray lit a second cigarette, and tried to forget her reckless words, "How about Portugal?"

"Now you're talking sweetie," she said, climbing on top of his body, "ready for round two?"

"Always."

Fear woke Ray at dawn. The faces of the dead from the night before haunted his dreams. He got out of bed and walked over to the window. Through the curtains he saw the sun come up over a field. A cough rang out and he looked at the office. Townsley spit a hunk of chew on the ground, and he unlocked the door of the office and went inside. He looked at the beautiful woman in the bed. Her naked body wrapped up in yellow sheets and her auburn hair a mess on the pillows. He reached the nightstand and picked up his teeth and put them back in his mouth. He mouthed the words "I love you," to the light sounds of her snores.

The shower loosened his muscles, and he began to believe in her plan. If they moved every so often and were smart about money, they'd have a chance. He started to believe in the lies he told himself, they were the only things he owned. He left behind all his books, photos, records, in his apartment in Huntsville. The long piss he took was even better than the shower. The sun shined through the bathroom window, the yellow tiles and yellow porcelain sink glowed. Hope rested in his lungs. He used a plastic comb and slicked back his hair, and put on his clothes from the night before, leaving his short sleeve button up shirt open. "There's something to this love business, "he thought.

"Hey baby," Natalie said sitting up in the bed.

Elation filled his being, love did away with his scars and anger. He walked towards the bed; he'd never seen a woman look so beautiful as Natalie did in the bed. Naked, thick pale and freckled legs wrapped in the sheets. Pale blue eye shadow hugging green eyes.

"Love you," he said.

When she didn't return the sentiment, he noticed the silencer pointed at him, partly hidden in between two pillows. He didn't even bother arguing or pleading with her. He completely surrendered; she'd made up her mind days ago. She dropped her head to the side to get a better look at her love. "You were my favorite, Raymond. You need to know that. Ten years from now, shit, thirty years from now, no one will ever take your place." She popped the trigger hitting him in the chest three times. She immediately swallowed the tears when his body collapsed on the blue carpet underneath a railing holding swinging wire hangers

Paulette Lindberg's blonde hair and grin hung over the large headlight of a Rolls Royce when Natalie entered the front office. Townsley didn't bother closing or putting down the May issue of Playboy.

"Good morning," he said from behind the magazine.

"Good morning, sir." Natalie replied.

"Your husband with you?"

"That's what I came here to talk to you about."

Curiosity took hold of Townsley. He put down the magazine and gazed over his blonde goatee. The canvas bag rested next to knee high black boots and a knee length wool plaid skirt. Her blue blouse royal in color didn't take away from her over-sized Jackie O sunglasses. She had all but abandoned her summer of love hippie wear, and to Townsley she resembled a woman who attended polo matches, the lover of a detective in the movies, a woman who seduced men at high stakes card games in the Riveria. Her lips curled, then smiled underneath the large sunglasses. She pulled out a stack of cash from the canvas bag and placed it on the desk of the motel office.

He'd never seen that much money in his life. He looked back up at her and she was biting her bottom lip, the Jackie O sunglasses now in her hand.

"That's for you," she said. "Might be a bit messy up there. You might need to hide something, but that's five thousand reasons staring you right in the face to look the other way. You can have the car too," she said, tossing a set of keys on the desk next to the money.

Townsley picked up the Playboy magazine and returned to gawking at centerfolds, "You have a nice day, ma'am."


The cab picked her up at the motel twenty minutes after she called from the parking lot pay phone. "All fancy," the old cabbie said.

"Going on a trip," she said.

"Airport in Birmingham?"

"Yes sir."

The cab moved at posted speed past cotton fields and old barns. The view turned into working class neighborhoods, where kids played, and adults argued. The neighborhoods turned into city scenes with businessmen and women walking in and out of buildings in a hurry.

"Birmingham-Shuttlesworth," the cab driver said.

"Thank you," she said, handing him a twenty.

"Ma'am the ride's five dollars."

"Tip."

"Thank you, and ma'am."

"Thank you, sir," she said to the old man, nervously touching the black frames of her glasses.

She entered the busy airport with a small suitcase that contained a change of clothes and the canvas bag full of money. She arrived at the TWA counter and put her suitcase down.

"You have a reservation ma'am?" A woman in a red TWA uniform asked.

"I don't." She said, "I want to take a journey."

The ticket counter woman tilted her head like a robot, "anywhere in mind."

"How about Poland?"

The lady flipped through papers, and took note of a monitor, "Well, you'll have a long layover, but I can get you to Atlanta, then New York City, on to Paris, arriving in Warsaw tomorrow."

"Sounds peachy," Natalie said.

The woman wrote down notes on a ticket and handed it to her. "They are serving cocktails in the lounge. Your flight leaves in two hours."

Natalie grabbed the ticket and picked up her suitcase.

"Can I just say that I love that blouse with that skirt and those sunglasses of yours. You look to die for."

Natalie replied with a smile.

"Have a nice time in Poland."

She sat down in the lounge and a waiter brought her a scotch on the rocks. She thought of Ray and missed him. The only man she ever loved, his facial expression of complete surrender right before she shot him in the chest. He didn't try to talk his way out of it because he loved her. It hit her at that moment that she had been living in a world of fashion that she and her friends created. Love was not something you wrote on posters and put on a T-shirt. It wasn't screamed by people holding fistfuls of flowers at a demonstration, but something to feel and share with others through actions and complete surrender. In the motel Ray had surrendered his life completely to her.

Meditation, love-ins, drugs, music, beads, it was all bullshit, and he knew it. They were fashionable things to do, things to hide behind to manage a world of hurt. Ray accepted who she was, the astrology, the mantras, the peace signs, all of it. He loved her unconditionally even if he wasn't like her. Contentment settled in her chest, knowing that she showed him love, but she knew she could never surrender to any human, not the way he did in the last seconds of his life. It hit her that he was comfortable enough in his own skin to love something completely different than himself, to give up his life so her life could continue.

She took a long sip of her scotch and felt tears starting to take ahold of her bones. She covered her eyes with the Jackie O sunglasses to keep others from seeing her weak. A plane pulled up to the gate from Miami. The waiter bought another drink without her asking for it and noticed the water behind her sunglasses. She wiped away the tears and put up her hand to let the waiter know not to bother asking. After he left, she downed half the glass, a cold and slithering void wrapped around her soul, 'who grifted who?' she wondered.

# THE RETURN OF THE GRIEVOUS ANGEL

## BY DAVID SCOTT HAY

I.

On the twenty-seventh day, long past when the trio should have turned back, the hard earth yielded her treasure under an evening redness.

Scorching days and freezing nights had revolved around the fortune seekers until their coffee grounds surrendered nothing more than grit. Thunder raged in their heads, the weak brew no match. Their bellies grumbled and growled, unsatiated animals rearing their heads. They watched through half-lidded eyes as the last of the beans boiled over unattended, their bodies stubborn and lethargic after a fruitless day.

But now, their leader, Elijah Bettis stood shoulder deep in one of the several dead-end holes. Pus ran from an open blister under the gold ring he refused to take off. "Like attracts like." He took another swing of his pick axe, pus and sweat mingling on its hickory handle, creating little mud balls where they fell like rain, the likes of which the deep earth had not seen in a century.

The Good Book clutched to his chest, his partner William solemnly gathered up their equipment and broke camp, folding tents and bedrolls with the stomp of his dusty boots as Elijah stayed hell-bent while William's daughter, Lucinda, tended to the wagon for departure. The japes regarding the book burning the hands of a fornicator had petered out along with their rations.

Despite the lack of sustenance during the last week (hunting game had cost them water and calories with no luck), Lucinda lounged in the back of the wagon organizing wares, forgetting with all the rations they'd gone through, maximizing space was no longer a priority. Her head throbbed, a thumping in her skull behind her left eye. She would gladly trade her cherry for a cup of coffee to quell it.

A strong cup, mind you.

The girl did have standards.

Her idle hands found a new task, fingers massaging her dungarees at the crotch, as she watched Elijah slowly disappear deeper into the hole, his thinning hair barely visible at ground level, the pickaxe raising up and coming down, raising up and coming down. It reminded her of a train piston, a machine fed not with coal or steam, but with hope and fortitude. Traits she admired. (If they struck gold, her father would certainly betroth her to Elijah, strengthening their brotherly bond.) With their predicament a week's ride from help, she noted that she felt no desperation, but a euphoria.

Freedom?

And wondered if sunstroke brought on horniness.

Elijah yelped, "The unholy fuck is this?"

**2.**

The treasure map looked as if it had been drawn by a child. Cartoonish mountains, funky shaped waterways, an inked circle passed across itself so many times it damn near wore through. These big landmarks occupied one side and a more detailed map filled the flip side. As though a teacher had guided the hand of a child, giant dashes lead to an X marking a spot, drawn as rudimentary skull and crossbones.

The smell of gunpowder tickled Elijah's nose as he perused the map. He liked that smell, as much as he did a tight cigar or a freshy washed pussy, both of which thumbed a nose at the memory of his father, a self-taught preacher of the weepy variety. Obscuring a few of the details of the map was blood, not his, but from the one-armed German dandy who lay not ten paces away, his bucket kicked.

Lucinda had bamboozled the German man in a game of three card monte called Chase the Lady. Though Lucinda had cheated (being a practiced grifter and an amateur magician), the German did short-change her, so judge her as you will. When she politely called the German on his miscounting, he indicated his half-arm neatly cloaked in a tailored jacket of exotic material, as though it had impeded his calculations. Regardless, Elijah found enough justification to draw, though William did point out the German's wobbliness indicated an excess of Kentucky creek water and perhaps the miscounting of this country's new currency had been an honest error.

Elijah holstered his Colt.

"Maybe."

Elijah was a man of action.

Judge him as you will.


The German had refused to pay up, cussin' (so assumed) them in that phlegm-gargling language muffled with a lacy scarf pulled up just over his nose. Perhaps, he chose this instead of a trail bandana to dissuade folks from thinking he had ill intent. Elijah noticed him earlier boasting in a grandiose (Lucinda's word) way about a treasure map to an inebriated group of prospectors. With a round or two of firewater, Elijah coaxed a retelling of the eavesdropped, half-remembered translation from the piano player (he, too, of German descent) manning a beat-up Steinway. The prospectors dismissed the German when he stopped buying rounds.

"Loco comes in many disguises," the piano player said.

Some loco is easily dismissed. Some not. Some loco hid a dark center. And occasionally a pearl, Elijah thought, palming a tip from the top of the piano.

And when the sobering dandy engaged in a three-card monte dance with Lucinda, Elijah decided this foreign oyster worth a shuck.

So, they robbed him.

The killing just a by-product.

A doctor might say it was death by violence.

A philosopher might say it was death by greed.

A native might say it was death by trespassing.

Elijah Bettis might say he should have been quicker on the draw.

And, in fact, he did.

"Shoulda been quicker."


**3.**

Lucinda, only fourteen and still looking like a boy from twenty paces, toed the German's body over while her father, William, held the reigns of Cactus and Tumbleweed even though Lucinda was the true whisperer, having broken a few broncos, bones, and hearts in her short tenure on the earth. She frisked the body expertly looking for hidden pockets, seams, and wallets. She found a gold watch and left it fastened to its chain. Maybe an honest soul would come along and trade its worth to bury him, she thought.  Optimism had yet to scar Lucinda, and kept her curious. Curious enough that she had to see the German's face.

Nothing surprised Lucinda.

She tugged the lacy scarf down and jumped back, startled.

The exception to the rule, however, knocked her on her ass.

The dead German had no skin below the nose. Missing like his right arm. "This poor dandy's also missing a slab of face."

"Huh. Take his scalp, too," Elijah said. He was not one to dwell. "Throw them dutifully sworn officers of the law off the scent."

"Should we draw straws?" William said. He wore his drawers backwards, but his companions said nothing, still irked they had to roust him midthrust at the town brothel.

"No sir," Elijah said. "I'll leave that up to you."

"Don't mind if I do." William drew his knife and spoke to the dead man, "No sore feelings." William slipped his knife under the suspenders so Lucinda could pull down the dungarees. Her small hands spidered around the dead man's clothes as William scalped the poor bastard.

"Huh," Lucinda said. "He ain't got no pecker, either."

"Missing an arm, face, and his pecker," William said, fidgeting with his crotch, even as he picked up the German's Bible. "You reckon he was going to follow that map, get rich, and buy replacements?"

They all laughed an uneasy laugh that died quickly. William, in an attempt to keep the merriment going, declared to the wind that he'd rather die than live without his pecker.

As any true cocksmith would.


4.

Opposite their rope ladder at the corner of the hole, now widened to qualify as a pit, a blackness oozed like a tree tapped for sap in the short days up north.

Lucinda asked, "Is that oil?"

"I don't know what it is," Elijah said, staring at the pearlescent liquid, viscous and flecked with who knows what.

William shaded his eyes with the Bible and peered into the hole.

"Whatever it is, it ain't gold," Elijah said, and swung the pick axe at the vertical side of the pit above the ooze, as Lucinda and William lay on their bellies peering into the hole.

"I can't go back," Elijah said like a mantra. "I can't, I can't, I can't."

William scooted back a bit, maneuvering the Bible in front of him as if to ward off the unknown. Oblivious, Elijah swung the pickax again striking the hardened earth. The blade sparked off stone, damn near breaking Elijah's wrist. "Fucking rock."

"Wait!" Lucinda barked.

No, not a rock.

Elijah scraped carefully, exposing a thin vein of gold.

"That's the spot," William said, lowering the Bible.

The trio hooted and hollered loud enough to wake the dead. Spurred by his discovery, Elijah started swinging, widening his area, uncovering another three vertical veins of gold. He slowed only when the blade met a curious resistance between two veins as if a skin of thin leather stretched between them.

The pearlescent ooze continued to pool at his feet laying atop the dirt like cold syrup on a stale pancake.

Elijah knew that they'd have to mine whatever they could this day and leave. They'd eaten one of their two horses ("Cactus." Against Lucinda's protestations, who ultimately did the deed), their attempts to preserve it halfhearted at best lest the smoke draw unwanted attention, so they ate well for two days, their bellies extended. Eating and vomiting and gorging again, like a Roman bacchanal. And no matter how they camouflaged the hole, a claim jumper might be eyeballing them with a spy glass and sitting on a 30lb bag of rice and beans. On occasion, the scruff of Elijah's neck bristled and the air felt electric. Did sunstroke bring on paranoia?

As the jubilation ebbed, Elijah scraped the membrane from the stick-thick veins, as if clearing glass from a broken pane. Behind the membrane a negative space existed.

No earth.

No rock.

Just emptiness.

Lucinda almost flipped over into the hole, leaning and squinting as far as she could to get a glimpse of something in the darkness. William clutched the Good Book to his chest.

"I see something peculiar," Elijah said. The earth has its own mind regarding what it took in and what it gave up, he thought. Elijah motioned to Lucinda to join him. And as much as she was curious, satisfaction did not motivate this kitten. Elijah nodded to William, and William unceremoniously pushed Lucinda over the edge.

She splashed in the black ooze, a pig in shit. She said nothing, for what would one say? Elijah, without taking his eyes off the dark hole, motioned her forward. Slowly, each step added a kerplish in the pearlescence ooze which the earth had not yet absorbed, if it would. He pointed into the darkness, past the veins of gold.

Lucinda saw a glint of something.

"Two eyes," she whispered, and then the creature spoke, which was not as shocking as the fact it spoke German.


**5.**

Lucinda worked a fingernail under the edge of one of the black goo stains on her body. It peeled off like a glue, taking a smattering of fine hairs with it. She did it as William kept repeating the same questions.

"What did it say? What did it look like?"

To which Elijah would say, "It looked like a little troll, maybe waist high, black and wrinkly. And it talked German before it skittered back into the dark. It had to be German. But none I knew."

"Maybe it's a monkey," Lucinda said, however her comment gained no traction.

William nodded thoughtfully. "That is peculiar, Elijah."

Lucinda said, "Pa, eating horse out here in the middle of godforsaken land is pretty damn peculiar. Killing a dandy with no arm, cock, or face and taking his treasure map is pretty damn peculiar, too. I'd say we left normal once we stepped off the train at Cottonwoods."

William couldn't help but laugh as he opened the Good Book.

Elijah disapproved. "There ain't no answers in there."

But William flipped through the book and showed Elijah a picture of the gold gate sketched in the Good Book. A rudimentary but reasonable facsimile of the one in the hole. "There's some other scribbling here and there, like the dandy found all this information and wrote it down quickly and the only thing he had near him was this Bible. It might have his name in the front." William started to flip through the pages when Elijah swatted him.

"I don't give a fuck what that dead dandy's name is, what I give a fuck about is why is there a creature in an earthly jail down there on a fucking treasure map? Is the gate the treasure? Is the creature the treasure? Is it like some kind of genie? We're going to rub its little cock and it's going to squirt out three wishes?"

"Elijah, oh Elijah." The thought tickled William. "I reckon if we treat with it, Lucinda should do it. She's got the magical whisper. Things flow off her tongue and her lips. Calm a horse, maybe a calm a Kobold."

Elijah asked, "A what?"

As if obvious, William tapped the book. "There's a word scrawled in here. Kobold. K-O-B-O-L-D. I think maybe that's what it is."

"Hmm."

"And it's behind a golden gate."

"All right," Elijah said. Nothing he'd heard so far dissuaded him from the fact that there was gold in the hole. "We need to come up with a plan because we only got a day or so of horse meat, I don't want to rebury that thing."

"Maybe we should," Lucinda said. "What if them veins ain't a gate but a cage?"

Elijah waited for her to say more and when she didn't, he reloaded his Colt replacing the two spent shells that put down her horse. "I want that gold."

William shrugged in a fair-game gesture. "Kobold rhymes with gold."

## 6.

Things went missing.

Now any doctor worth his salt might suggest that a lack of decent meals and sunstroke would contribute to carelessness. But these were items that fell outside the bounds of carelessness.

Elijah's ring, William's Good Book, and Lucinda's— well, nothing went missing. They accused her of taking things.

"Now what the fuck would I do with a Bible out here in the middle of nowhere? Pa, you think I'd interrupt your praying for all of us so I could do a special prayer for myself? You're an idiot," Lucinda said. "And you, that ring would fall off my finger the second I put it on. Am I going to wear it on a necklace like your sweetheart? Am I going to bury it with the Bible and hope a fucking Adam and Eve apple tree sprouts up...?"

They said nothing, though Elijah's face blossomed with an extra shade of red.

"...with gold rings just ripe for the picking?" Lucinda said. "You have lost your mind, Elijah Bettis."

"If I don't find my ring—"

William coughed lightly.

"—and William don't find his book, come sun-up..."

"What?" said Lucinda, "You going to eat my horse? Again?"

Neither William or Elijah had a rejoinder.

"Great," Lucinda said. "I can put plain foolishness on the list of dysentery, starvation, dehydration, and greed. Congratulations, Elijah. We're rich with disaster."

The Kobold in the pit snickered.

They all turned around and looked towards the hole.

Lucinda stomped off to tend to their only horse, Tumbleweed.

William and Elijah traded looks.

"She's trying to fuck us over," Elijah said.

William said, "I don't know what my daughter gains by stealing your ring and my Bible. Maybe we ought to let those things go for right now and, focus on—" he nodded his chin towards the hole. "That thing, find out what it's guarding. Maybe we can a strike a bargain or trick it. I've been feeling awful faint, Elijah."

"Hmm."

"We ain't got food."

"Maybe we do," Elijah said, eyeing their last horse.

"That horse is the only thing that can pull our wagon out of here, whether we get gold or no."

Elijah nodded. Sound observation.

"Maybe we just bury it, come back out here better stocked," William said. "We'll know where to look."

"Hmm."

"We know the map works," William said.

"I can't go back empty-handed." Elijah's stare burned through William's eyes and out the back of his partner's head, and William thought better than to speak. Elijah rubbed his finger where the ring used to be. "You know that."


**7.**

They each took turns down in the hole "conversing' with the Kobold, scrambling up and down the rope ladder when frustration would peak. Its German accent was thick and it got frustrated when they asked it to repeat itself repeatedly. Pantomiming and charades only made them feel foolish. More often than not, the Kobold would throw dirt clods at them, squealing in frustration.

Other times it just laughed as if they were the slow, unsure ones. They danced with caution, neither party close enough to grab through the bars.

Despite their desperation, when the sun was at its zenith the whole gate glowed so bright you could hardly look at it for too long without it burning into your retinas. These ghost images haunted Elijah when he slept. They couldn't leave it. None of them got much rest, though. Exhaustion, though making one weak, did not allow for a restful sleep. There was nothing edible left of the butchered horse and you couldn't drink Lucinda's occasional tears. When the wind shifted just so and the aroma of the horse carcass blanketed you, death felt close.

It was Lucinda, though, at the encouragement of William, who was the most patient at communing with the ugly, twisted thing and soon got a clear enough picture of their circumstances: "We shoulda gone back weeks ago," Lucinda said. "We're fucked."

## 8.

This gate of gold can be taken, Elijah proclaimed as if a steady voice would increase their odds of success.

Lucinda warned without a trade or an exchange with the Kobold, they would, in her estimation, be cursed. This was not news to William. They were already cursed. A treasure beyond their dreams, if they could dig it out without the Kobold doing Kobold things, with no way of hauling it to a bank, no way to protect it. If something out of the ordinary didn't happen, they were all going to

die of starvation and dehydration. Hunting had been eerily scarce near the hole.
And the only potable water sat in the wagon's water barrel, a skin of dark algae
spreading on its surface.

"Hell, we already done dug our grave," William said to Elijah, nodding
to the hole. He shuddered at the thought of being buried in the hole with that
ugly twisted thing with a gold gate as an underground marker. He thought them
a gang of racoons refusing to let go of the bait to save its own life.

Mine. Mine. Mine.

Of course, with any gate, you had to wonder was the purpose to keep
something in or something out? William's attention wandered and Elijah had to
snap his fingers. William nodded with his chin over Elijah's shoulder. In the
distance, a lone rider streaked across the horizon. Saddled bags stuffed and full,
the rider urging the horse on, as if racing the devil hisself.

"It's a Pony Express," Elijah muttered.

"'Orphans preferred,'" William said, quoting their recruiting posters.

"They're trying to reach California before war breaks out between the
North and South."

"Huh."

"This is our last chance to stake a claim before all hell breaks loose."

"Maybe we could hike up there, that trail, and catch the next rider
coming through."

"He ain't going to be carrying enough water and food for us," Elijah said. "Hell, he might not have enough for one. We'd probably get two of us on that horse, split the rations."

"That horse and Tumbleweed would be enough to pull the wagon."

"One of us would have to stay here."

"William, I just ain't got it in me, I ain't got it in me to return with nothin'."

"You think the best move is gonna be dealing with whatever's down there?"

"I do."

Lucinda's head popped up from the hole. "I think," she said, "it's made an offer."


**9.**

The Kobold reached into the folds of its tattered clothing and produced Elijah's ring. It produced William's book and a brooch unknown to the men. Lucinda gasped and patted her chest.

Elijah became indignant, as it was one of his weapons. "You got all this gold probably sitting on a mother load and you're taking a ring from a fella what got that from his grandpa? You takin' a Good Book, the Lord's book, for a man turnin' over a new leaf? And I don't know where the hell you got that brooch."

Elijah was not as smart or as quick to connect dots in some matters.

"That's Lucinda's," William said quietly.

Lucinda said nothing, perhaps nodding her head imperceptibly, as if to convince herself.

"None of that stuff you stole," Elijah's said, "is worth near anything next to this gold."

The Kobold grumbled and spat a loogie of tar.

"What are we gonna give you, now that you got our treasures?" Elijah asked. "And unless you got a chuckwagon back in that hole, there's nothing goin' keep our belts tight. So, I think your little game of purse snatchin' might have backfired ifin' you're planning on using us for playthings."

The Kobold cocked his head, pointed at its own mouth, and then pointed at them.

Elijah wasn't quite sure what to make of it as William shrugged; parlor games not their bailiwick.

Lucinda said, "I think it wants to give us something to eat in exchange for the things it stole."

"Oh. Ain't the way I normally do business," Elijah said. (Which is to say a lot of murder and mayhem.) "But yeah, I could eat."


Elijah shifted, not uncomfortably, as the hole was cooler than it was above on the ground. "Well, what have you got for us?"

The Kobold swung from bar to bar on the gold fence, like a primate in a zoo. In fact, it made similar noises to it.

"That thing's crazy," William said.

"No," Lucinda said. "I don't think it is."

Elijah commented. "That's what he thinks of us. Monkeys. Just trying to grab something shiny."

"I tell ya, Elijah, we should just fill this hole and take our chances with—" He nodded in direction of the Pony Express, not mentioning it, not wanting to tip his hand but Lucinda narrowed her eyes. Her ears were just as good as her tongue.

The twisted thing dropped to all fours. Showed its behind and like a mother insect laying eggs, an oval shape emerged slowly and splashed into the pearlescent ooze.

"Is it shittin'?"

The oblong pearlescent coal-like nugget was the size of Lucinda's fist. It shat out more. William counted, like a school kid watching a magic act.

"One...

"Two...

"Three..."

Three little pearlescent egg-like objects.

"Be fruitful and multiply," William said to no one.

The Kobold toed the objects to the edge of the fence one, two, and three in front of Lucinda, Elijah, and William. Then it reached down and shuffled them just as Lucinda had shuffled the cards in three-card monte. There was no Lady to follow in this game, however. The Kobold gestured for them to each pick an egg, pick their fate, pick their treasure.

None could be certain of the creature's folly.

Elijah coaxed an egg forward with the back of his hand as if it was too hot to touch with his palm. William used his leg, pulling it towards himself with the instep of his boot like a hook removing a vaudeville performer.

Lucinda leaned forward, different than the boys, and picked one up gingerly as if it were, in fact, an egg. She held it in her cupped hands, like a small bird might emerge.

"Feels like a potato."

She brought it to her face, as she inhaled deeply.

"Smells earthy," she said.

The tip of her pink tongue protruded and she touched it gently. William gasped a little, and Elijah stared with intense curiosity as Lucinda took a little nibble of the pearlescent egg. Then she took a bigger bite, chewed and swallowed. Like a striking rattlesnake, William took a quick bite of hers before she pulled it back from him, swatting him. He raised his hand as if to backhand her, but her glare didn't go away. Elijah counted to thirty, waiting to see if her eyes rolled back in the head, as if to watch her brain stop working while her body seized with poison.

But it didn't.

She took another bite, and chewed enthusiastically.

"Never thought I'd be eating a shit potato," he muttered to himself, and took a bite. William commented that it needed salt, which they all agreed.

The Kobold, giggled and jiggled, rolling around on the ground, happy with their consumption.

Once they had finished, they realized how dark it had gotten in the hole, and that it was probably time to climb out. That's when William said the obvious, that they all could see, but probably needed to hear to verify. "The ladder's gone."


**10.**

"Someone pulled it up," Elijah said.

"Boost me," Lucinda said.

Elijah interlocked his fingers and she stepped into the stirrup and he boosted her strongly enough that her foot left his hands. Lucinda hooked her arms over the edge with legs akimbo, scrambled out of the hole.

Or she would have, save for the boot to her face.

She yelped in pain like a puppy, fearful and startled. Luckily, William and Elijah broke her fall while keeping their bones intact. Her knees and elbows did them no favors, however.

"The hell?"

Elijah spit a mouth full of blood and half chewed shit potato.

Two shots rang out, and the thump of what could only be the weight of a dead horse hitting the earth was felt.

"Tumbleweed..."

Moments later, a face appeared over the edge of the hole. A man with a lacy kerchief around his face.

"No..."

"I'll be damned."

He tugged the scarf down enough to reveal the missing lower half of a face. It was the one-armed German man.

The Kobold squealed, in fear or delight was a matter of perspective beyond the trio's.

"Guten tag, sweethearts," the dandy said with a skinless smile.

**II.**

"I stand before you a man of deep remorse, true, but also a man of redemption." He spoke German to the Kobold as if translating. To them: "My brother slew my father who brought this creature from the Fatherland to sniff out gold. And as Cain slew Able, I slew my brother over that map. Was it revenge or greed?" He shrugged.

The man's face mesmerized, muscle and sinew exposed like a skinned rabbit. Lucinda thought he'd be wet from blood, but it resembled a tanned buffalo hide, dry and weathered. Like a burn that had healed. When he talked, his mouth pulled to one side as if the skin had tightened too much.

"Regardless, I opted to chase the lady and lost." He indicated his missing arm. "As for my sins, I repent. I can now only hope to break even, as they say."

"Shoot him," Lucinda whispered.

Elijah quick drew and fanned three shots, before the German could react. But all the shots resulted in muted clicks. Elijah flipped open the cylinder. Unloaded. "The fuck...?"

William cleared his throat. "I fed them to the Kobold."

"What the hell you do that for?"

"Dunno." William shrugged like a child. "We were bargaining."

Elijah slugged William, his ring opening a cut below his eye. William cowered, apologetic mutterings dribbling from his mouth.

"Soon this young country will devolve into war where brother slays brother," the dandy said. "And I will be back in the Fatherland." The earth pulled the sun lower and the trio now stood in shadow as the dandy adjusted his hat to shade his eyes. He consulted his gold watch. "And now the Game."

**12.**

The German spoke to the Kobold and it chittered in glee, and shat three more black eggs.

"In one, maybe two, of them is a bullet," the German said. "If you think you chose a bulletless egg, you can hold. If you don't then you have the chance to play a game of three card monte. If your egg has a bullet, I shoot you, like you shot me. If it doesn't, you get the gold. If you play three card monte and find the Lady, you win; the gold is yours. If you lose, I get my choice of your personal possessions."

"What gold?" Elijah said. "The gate?"

The German barked a word they did not recognize in a language seldom heard even by foreign winds.

Again, the Kobold drops its pants and shat out three more eggs.

Gold eggs.

They plopped into the ooze and sank halfway, like a lead weight in mud.

Like raccoons, Elijah and William reached for the eggs. But the Kobold hissed at them until they backed away, while Lucinda asked the dandy: "How come you ain't dead?"

"Curses come wrapped in many colors," the German said. "Some with a bow."

"I don't cotton to your double-talk," Elijah said.

"And if we don't play?"

"I bury you alive and let the geschöpf show you all its tricks." The German grinned a lipless smile. "Select your egg, fräulein."

"How can we trust you ain't a cheat?"

"I've left my thespian skills back in Berlin and can promise you," the German spat into the hole, his loogie resting atop the pearlescent ooze. "I'm just as fair as y'all."

A cry of dread escaped William's mouth.

"Pick one," the dandy said.

William took an eternity forever to pick his egg. He clutched it tight to his chest where his hammering heart threatened to crack it. Lucinda picked one and tossed it to Elijah and selected the last one. Elijah took a long hard looky-loo at Lucinda's as though he might demand a trade.

The Kobold chittered with excitement.

"I'll keep mine," William said.

"Hold it tight," the dandy said.

Lucinda tossed hers in the air and caught it as if weighing it. She nodded towards Elijah's. "These two have the bullet, I think. They felt the same weight. I'll Chase the Lady."

Smart girl. "Same," Elijah said. Lucinda had initially confused him with the trade, and William seemed divinely sure whereas Elijah wondered if he wasn't already laying outside the hole with the sun frying his brains with a sizzling nightmare.

The German bit into Lucinda's potato egg and didn't crack a tooth. No bullet.

She should have held. By process of elimination, his and William's eggs had a bullet.

"Please, please, please." William sank to his knees in prayer, splashing the ooze.

"No sore feelings, Willie," the German said as the Kobold grabbed William by the neck and choked him tight against the gold cage and groped at his crotch before letting William fall despondent into the ooze.

"Time to Chase the Lady," the dandy said.

But Lucinda opined an obvious question: "How you going to shuffle with one arm?"

**13.**

The Kobold shuffled the three cards, leapfrogging them two handed, one-handed at times with a deftness that surprised Lucinda. Their pattern is different. Palming anything would be harder. Should be harder. She'd never seen that. The German had tossed it a crisp pack, a gesture of fairness. Though the creature probably tipped those scales, if we're shootin' straight. Gone were the Kobold's hysterics as if the dandy and the Kobold had a connection.

Could such a creature be trained...?

Nervousness distracted Lucinda. Her eyes flickered off the cards to the dandy and she lost track of the Lady.

Shoot, she thought.

No idea.

She picked a card at random. No Lady. That was my mistake, she thought. Don't look at the dandy. "Do you mind pulling your bandana back up? I find your face distracting."

With a lopsided grin and a tip of his hat, he honored her request.

She nodded. Ready.

She kept her eye on the Lady. The Kobold's shriveled hand passed over it. Did he pick up? Did he drop? She couldn't miss this. The dandy's shadow flickered over the cards.

Don't blink.

She blinked.

The Kobold stopped, looked to her expectantly. Lucinda looked to Elijah, then William as though they might have a clue. Elijah shrugged, while William sat like a pig in shit, making peace with the origin of ham and bacon.

She picked her card.

The Kobold turned it over.

It was the Lady.

One for two. This next one would determine her fate.

Elijah spoke up. "Let us see all three cards."

In turn, the Kobold held up one. Then the other. Then the other. There was indeed one Lady and two Aces.

Square and fair.

The dandy cleared his throat. Nodded to Lucinda. Ready? She nodded. Ready. This time the geschöpf shuffled much faster, as if he had lulled her into—well, shit, she thought. She couldn't keep up. As soon a sit stopped moving the cards, she picked one at random. It turned the card over. It was not the Lady.

Loser.

The Kobold chittered and somersaulted before throwing a dirt clod, hitting William's bald spot.

"No sore feelings," the dandy said.

She stepped aside, head down. Lucinda assumed she knew what he wanted. From a young age, she knew what men wanted. She unbuttoned the top button and the next on her shirt. Maybe she'd get that cup of coffee.

"Nein, nein," the German said. "I have another game to finish before I collect from you."

**14.**

It was Elijah's turn.

He fared no better.

He glanced at Lucinda, hoping for some indication that she too had been following the Lady, but she looked away, staring at William, whose tears rolled down his face, disappeared into his beard, leaving clean tracks. After the first shuffle, Elijah picked and missed. The Kobold slowed down its second shuffle, but it mattered not.

Elijah picked again and missed.

Now all three treasure hunters had lost.

A foreign feeling bloomed in Elijah's gut. Perhaps regret; perhaps remorse.

"No sore feelings," the German said. "Now the games are complete and it's time to collect." He reached into a satchel at his feet, unseen to them from their vantage point and pulled out a rusty bone saw. "Elijah, from you, I want your right arm below the elbow." The dandy wiped the blade with his sleeve. "Cut off his right arm, fräulein."

"And if I don't oblige?"

"I'll execute all three of you now. However, complete the task and I swear on the soul of my father, I'll let you live and perhaps even gift you a bit of gold to take back to Cottonwoods or Mexico."

The Kobold squealed in defiance.

"Stille, geschöpf."

It quieted down.

"See, I'm more generous than you were."

Elijah looked up defiantly at the German. "I'm going to need a tourniquet."

"Not if she's quick enough," the German said. "That black goo will staunch the bleeding. Simply smear it over your stump. Will even help with the pain. More so than any whiskey."

"Alright then," Elijah said. This was all a dream, a bad dream. Hallucinations from sunstroke, sun heat. He wasn't in a hole. He was laying out on the ground, baking in the heat. His mind going all whirly in these last minutes.

**15.**

The German tossed Lucinda the bone saw. She too thought it might be a dream, and aimed to be quick and efficient, but the bone saw had not kept a keen edge and Elijah cried through gritted teeth. True to the German's word, the black ooze stopped the stump from spraying and numbed the pain, but did nothing for Elijah's sanity.

"Now your turn, fräulein."

She undid another button on her shirt. She thought of her future wedding night. Would she still be accepted? And if she was betrothed to Elijah, could she accept him with one arm. Doubts plagued her.

Another button.

"Nein."

The German took out a Bowie knife, tested its edge with his thumb. "Upon reflection," he said, "I probably should have done you first. Now Elijah's got to cut off your face with his left hand."

He tossed the knife to Elijah.

Elijah caught it lefty.

Lucinda closed her eyes as tears streaked down. She preferred the dandy let her keep going with the buttons. Elijah might not take her to a marriage bed now.

"You have a luscious mouth," the dandy said. "I do hope it fits."

The Kobold laughed and did cartwheels, like a circus monkey.

I should have asked for a cup of coffee, she thought as Elijah scalped the lower half of her face.

With two cupped hands, she splashed the black ooze on the lower half of her face. Blood trickled out from underneath it here and there, until Elijah dabbed a bit or two of the black ooze. She might have tried to say something, but nobody could hear anything over William's cries.

"William, the last piece to restore myself..." the German said, through Lucinda's lips, "... will be claimed by teeth."

Like a child on a beach, William tried to bury himself in the ooze as his bottom lip quivered and snot glazed his beard.

The dandy asked, "Any volunteers?"

The Kobold chittered.

William screamed.

### 16.

"My suggestion for you fine leute is this: Find a fool to play this game and maybe you'll win your flesh back." The German made vowels sounds and moved his jaw as though chowing on a turkey leg. The new skin stretched tight and his speech was crisper.

"Or maybe you'll live with what you got, and go deeper into that mine. The geschöpf can be quite generous, if not fickle. There's a motherlode waiting for those willing to barter."

The dandy's new arm had a limited range of motion, but enough to thumb down his dungarees. With a quick piss, the new cock proved not only ready and able, but a significant upgrade. This pleased the German dandy.

"As for me, having experienced both sides..." He let out a low whistle, and doffed his hat, exposing the dull skull underneath. "I prefer being intact."

**17.**

In the distance between the hole and the horizon, a dust cloud from an appaloosa broke the stillness. A young rider barely Lucinda's age cantered his horse up to the camp. Staples littered the ground near a wagon as though it had regurgitated its cargo under the unforgiving sun. A waxed canvass tent fluttered in the gusts of the plains, its flaps ragged like forgotten flags.

From a square hole near camp, the young rider heard the most curious laughter. Like a child's, high-pitched and trembling with glee. He spurred his horse closer, leaned over. Heard prayers more pointed that cactus nettles.

"Hello...?"

A small voice answered, "Guten tag."

**18.**

A prospector might say a mine is only worth the gold you can carry.

A misanthropist might say no saintly deed goes unpunished.

A recruiter might say orphans preferred.

And with good reason.

# DOMESTICATED
## BY
## RON CLYBURN

You ever hear a sound when you're half asleep, and you can't figure out if it's real or part of a dream? And then, when you figure out it's real, you roll over and decide to ignore it and go back to sleep, only to discover the burrito you were eating last night before you passed out was next to your head on the pillow the whole night, and all you can think about while that noise grows louder and louder, is... *Why did I get guacamole? I must have been hammered.*

No? I guess it's just me then. I'm different that way. In fact, I'm different than everyone. More on that later.

I sat straight up to get away from the funky burrito smell. The sunlight beaming through my curtainless window meant it was morning, or maybe afternoon. I had no idea. But I found out quick that the noise I heard was someone knocking on my door.

I rolled out of bed and hit the floor. I mean, literally hit the floor on my hands and knees. My bed was basically a mattress in the middle of my apartment's living room. I jumped up and rushed toward the door, kicking a frying pan across the linoleum into a pile of dirty clothes. That hurt. I limped the rest of the way and looked out the peep hole.

It was a woman. Maybe in her forties, dressed nice with lots of jewelry. Probably not a bill collector, but I couldn't be sure unless I opened the door. I thought I'd paid all the late bills with the cash I made from my last case, but I'd been on a three-day bender, so anything was possible.

I unlocked the deadbolt and looked down to kick an empty pizza box out of the way and noticed something was missing.

*Pants. That would be nice. Not a good first impression.*

I hurried to the bathroom, my big toe still throbbing from the frying pan, and found my Cincinnati Reds robe hanging on the shower curtain rod. Thank God it wasn't on the floor. Anything that ends up on the floor of my bathroom should be incinerated.

I rushed back to the door and the lady was still knocking. She really wanted to talk to me. That was either good or bad. Probably bad. I didn't get a lot of visitors. Mainly because, I didn't have many friends. Unless you count the one guy on the Dayton Police department, but that's only because I made him look good on a couple cases. And, I think he feels sorry for me.

I gripped the door knob and glanced back at my apartment. It looked like a frat house had exploded. I can't be the only 33-year-old who lives like this. Oh well. Maybe the cluttered chaos would scare her away.

I jerked the door open and stuck my head out. The woman drew back and inhaled sharply. And she hadn't even seen the apartment yet. This would not go well.

"Mr. Joe Cooper?" she asked.

"I made the payment already," I said, avoiding eye contact. "Sorry I was late. Last week... not a good week for me."

"I'm not here to collect anything, Mr. Cooper. I'm Mrs. Sandra Collins, and I want to hire your services. You're the private investigator, correct?"

I looked up. She was prettier than the distorted image I saw through the peep hole, but I sensed an air of elitism. Her shoulder length blonde locks were styled with perfection. Not a single hair out of place. She wore a green, very dressy pants suit and held a purse just like the knock-offs they sold at the flea markets. I had a feeling the one she clutched was real. The combined value of her earrings, necklace, and rock on her finger was more than my salary back when I was a police officer. One thing was certain, this woman came from money. With her green suit, she even looked like money. Or, the queen of the leprechauns.

Oh, and I used to be a cop. But that's another story.

"I'm sorry for dropping in unannounced," she said. "But when I called the cell phone number I had for you, it said the line was disconnected."

*Dammit! That's the bill I forgot to pay.*

"My bad," I said. "Come on in."

I stepped back, kicking a couple beer cans out of her way, and tried to open the door farther, but the pizza box wedged under it like a door stopper. She gingerly squeezed all the way through. Her eyes widened as she scanned her surroundings.

"What happened here?" she asked.

"Oh, uh..." My brain searched for a plausible excuse. "My maid quit."

"Really," she said, still looking around at the mess that was my life. I could tell by the look of disgust on her face, she didn't buy it.

"Mr. Cooper, you were very highly recommended as the best investigator in Dayton." Her tone made it sound more like a question than a statement.

"Yeah, by who?"

"My attorney, Michelle Green."

The name sounded familiar. "Oh, yeah. Michelle. Nice legs. We went out on a few dates."

Mrs. Collins' jaw fell open. "You? And Michelle?"

"She didn't mention that to you?"

"Definitely not."

"Oh. Well, they weren't exactly dates, per se."

She scoffed at me. I was almost offended, but if she didn't believe me about the maid, she had no reason to believe that I'd actually seen her attorney's tramp stamp.

"Where are my manners?" I said. "Would you like something to drink?" I stepped over the piles of debris to the kitchen and opened the refrigerator. "I've got... beer?"

"It's nine in the morning."

"Right." I grabbed a can and popped the top. "In high school, we called it... riding the school buzz." I took a drink and noticed she was looking at the window in my living/bedroom. Two squirrels were sitting on the window sill, looking inside. When they both saw me, their tails twitched excitedly and they pawed at the glass. I rolled my eyes.

*Not now, fellas.*

They quickly jumped out of sight.

"Rodents. You feed them once and they won't leave you alone." I looked at Mrs. Collins. I couldn't tell if she was confused or just uncomfortable. She was definitely out of her element, and I'd bet my miniscule bank account she'd never met anyone like me.

"I need to make a phone call," she said, pulling her cell phone from her purse. "Do you have somewhere private I can go?"

I belched and looked at her feet. "I wouldn't recommend the bathroom, but you've got high heels on, so you should be good. Unless you're squeamish."

"I think I'll just step outside."

***

Sandra stood on the landing just outside the apartment, looking at the top of her Mercedes in the parking lot and watching the cars roll up and down Far Hills Avenue. She drummed her meticulously manicured fingernails on the white plastic railing and pressed her cell phone's speed dial number for her attorney. The line connected. "Michelle Green."

"Who the hell did you send me to?" Sandra said, her tone harsh and direct.

"Sandra? What are you talking about?"

"Joe Cooper, the private detective. You said he was a 'hot mess.' At the time, I thought it could mean anything. But this man is a total disaster."

"Sandra, calm down. I know he looks rough, but—"

"Rough? He needs a life coach with a PHD in lost causes."

"I'm telling you, he's the best. He solves cases the police can't figure out. I don't know how he does it. If anybody can find your brother, it's Joe Cooper. I'd bet my professional reputation on it."

*Reputation. How ironic. I have to ask.* "Did you sleep with him?"

"Did I what?"

"You heard me."

"What did he say?"

"He said you had a few... dates, per se."

"Um... That's... a personal question."

"Oh my God, you did!"

"I... Well... Look, I met him at a bar. We had a few drinks..."

"I don't want to hear about it. I just need to know if he can find Paul."

"Yes, Sandra. Trust me."

***

When Mrs. Collins squeezed back through the door, I was in the bathroom combing my hair and holding my breath. I'd found my flip-flops under last week's underwear and summoned up the courage to relieve myself and attempt some personal hygiene, but my bar of soap was on the floor behind the toilet, so I opted out.

I walked out into the hallway, where cleaner, safer air was in ample supply, and found Mrs. Collins standing very still, holding on to her purse with both hands, and looking around like she expected some kind of creature to crawl out from the under my mattress and bite her ankles.

"Everything okay?" I asked.

"Yes. I wanted to confer with my attorney, Michelle. She assures me you're the man for the job."

"And by job, you mean... investigative work?"

She scoffed again. "Yes, of course."

"Good. I was scared there for a minute. The only problem is, ma'am, I'm kind of on a self-imposed sabbatical." That was the best way I knew to describe excessive day-drinking that carried on into the night and early mornings.

She took out a pen and checkbook from her purse. "I'll give you twenty thousand dollars."

"Ma'am, I'm really... Wait. What? How much?"

"Twenty thousand."

"Okay. I'll do it."

"Good. When can you start?"

"When can you give me twenty thousand dollars?"

"I'll pay you half now, and half when you find Paul."

"Okay. Who's Paul?"

"My brother... the one who's missing."

"Oh, yeah. I should have asked that earlier. Would have been helpful."

Mrs. Collins sighed and rolled her eyes as she made out the check. "If Michelle is wrong about you, I'm going to find myself another lawyer." She tore the check out with a quick snap and handed it to me. I read the embossed names: Dr. Robert Collins and Mrs. Sandra Collins.

*A rich old man. At least I don't have to worry about the check bouncing.*

I took my beer out of my robe pocket and chugged the rest of it down. "Mrs. Collins," I said, trying not to belch in the face of my new client. "I'll find your brother. Just do me a favor."

"Yes?"

"Next time you talk to Michelle, ask her to look for my Ren and Stimpy boxer shorts. I can't find them here anywhere."

Damned if she didn't scoff at me again.


***


The first thing I did after depositing my $10,000 check was pay my cell phone bill. And my Internet provider. And my car insurance. Responsibility is so overrated.

I did a little Googling on Mrs. Collins, and found out her missing brother, Paul Gibson, was a former Marine who did two tours in Afghanistan. He also had multiple arrests for OVI, drunk and disorderly, and possession of a controlled substance. My guess is he suffered from PTSD. Right away, I felt for the guy and my new case became a little more personal.

I rolled into Ghost Light Coffee on the southern edge of Dayton and ordered a salted caramel, peanut butter, mocha latte, with a triple-shot of expresso and cayenne pepper. I was one of their regulars and Nichole, the barista, who I "dated" a few times, created that concoction just for me. She called it "Joe's Hangover." I felt honored.

I sat down with my Hangover and Detective Tony Ortiz from the Dayton Police Department walked in. He's the cop I mentioned before, who I helped out on a murder case and basically made his career. He agreed to meet with me, but said he couldn't do me any favors. I'd have to convince him otherwise.

"Is that you parked in the handicapped spot?" Ortiz asked, pulling out a chair and sitting down at my table.

"Well, I have gone to therapy," I said.

"I'm betting that's psychological and not physical, and doesn't guarantee you a spot next to the front door. And what's with all the beer cans in your floorboard? Do I need to call a unit in here to give you a breathalyzer?"

"Uh, those aren't from today. How do you know that's my car, anyway?"

"I can still run plates. Besides, you're the only guy in town who drives a Pontiac Fiero."

"It's a classic. Look, I need a favor."

"I told you I couldn't do you any favors."

"C'mon, man. You owe me. If it wasn't for me, you would've never found where that guy hid the murder weapon."

Ortiz let out a sigh and turned his eyes away. He knew I was right.

"You know, I still don't know how you found that knife," he said.

"It didn't matter at the time though, did it?"

He sighed again. "Okay. But on one condition."

"What's that?"

"Get your shit together, man."

"What exactly does that mean?"

"You know what it means." Ortiz leaned forward in his chair, making direct eye contact. "I read about you when you were a cop in Cincinnati. You were the man. Distinguished service award, K9 officer of the year... You've been through some shit... I get it, but you're maybe a step away from living on the streets... or worse. The man I read about is in there somewhere. You just have to try to find him."

"Since when did you become a counselor?" I said, my comfort level with the conversation wearing thin.

"I know a few. And, I know the lady who runs a PTSD support group for cops. I can get you in."

I took a long drink of my Hangover coffee. "Is she hot?"

"I'm serious here, Coop. If you want my help, you have to put some effort into getting your life on track."

I resisted the urge to look away. That would have tipped him off that I was just telling him what he wanted to hear.

"I'll work on it."

"Give me your word," Ortiz said, reaching his hand over the table to seal the deal with a shake.

I paused, looking at his hand. It felt like the moment before you sign a high-interest loan contract. I extended my arm and tried to match his firm grip.

"Word."

"Cool. So, what do you need from me?"

***

I parked my classic 1984 Fiero two blocks away from the Rebuilding Futures half-way house in the Oregon District. If "classic" meant backfiring whenever I killed the ignition, or one of the hide-away headlights forever stuck in the up position like a one-eyed road pirate, my Pontiac fit the bill.

The Oregon, one of Dayton's oldest neighborhoods, with gentrified houses and small mom-and-pop businesses, was THE place for young professionals to celebrate their progressive lifestyles. Fifth Street in the Oregon was home to numerous restaurants, bars, and a couple adult-oriented stores, that I may or may not have visited on occasion. Every Halloween, they have a massive block party called Hauntfest, attended by thousands, all dressed in crazy costumes. I brought a girl from Cincinnati down here a few years ago, and saw a guy dressed up like a vagina. Last week, I saw that same guy wearing that same costume in broad daylight, and nobody batted an eye.

Ortiz knew all about the missing person's case on Paul Gibson, who had apparently disappeared without a trace three weeks ago. After Ortiz and his buddies turned up zilch on their initial investigation, Paul's name, date of birth, and description was entered into a missing person's database that all U.S. law enforcement agencies had access to. That effort turned up zilch as well. The man was just gone, and with his past drug history, Ortiz expected to hear a report of Paul's bloated, decaying body washed up somewhere along the banks of the Great Miami.

Rebuilding Futures was the last place Paul had been seen, according to their lead counselor, Mark Jefferies, who Ortiz interviewed personally. Ortiz told me that Paul left really pissed off one day, and they hadn't seen him since. When I asked why Paul was upset, Ortiz said, "They didn't know. Apparently, he was prone to erratic behavior and violent outbursts. Common behavior for drug addicts."

Funny. I knew plenty of people prone to that kind of behavior, and none of them were addicts.

For some reason, I smelled a rat. Actually, standing on the sidewalk, looking at the old, two-story brick house where Rebuilding Futures ran their non-profit counseling center, I could hear rats talking to each other somewhere in the basement.

*"There's no food down here."*

*"I never said there was food down here."*

*"You said, 'There's meat in the basement.'"*

*"No, I said, 'Let's meet in the basement.' You've got ticks in your ears."*

That's how I'm different from everyone else. And also, how I maintain a 99% close rate on all my cases. In reality, it's more like 100%, but no one would believe that. Just like no one would believe that I can talk to animals. I'm like the real-life Doctor Doolittle, but without the English accent and the big pink sea snail.

From what I was told by my mother, it's a gene that's passed down in my family every few generations. When I discovered my ability, Mom sat me down and told me stories about my great-great grandmother, Myrtle Ann Davis, who, as a young girl in the hills of West Virginia, would go off into the woods to play and talk with the animals until sundown. Some of the backwards-ass hillbillies spied on her, and accused young Myrtle of being possessed by the devil. The local pastor got involved and threatened to burn her at the stake, until he figured out they could use her to coax the animals into town, so all his God-fearing brethren could shoot them like fish in a barrel, then butcher them up for supper.

Myrtle Ann couldn't stand for that, so she ran away and ended up in the Ohio Valley where she married a poor dirt farmer.

So yeah, I'm the lucky one in my family with the gift. Or the curse, depending on how you look at it. Sure, I can convince a vicious dog to back down, and talk a runaway horse into trotting back to the barn, but there are lots of things I can't do. Like go to zoos. Or aquariums. Or any wildlife natural habitat. The first time I took a nature hike, I looked like Noah leading the animals into the Ark. Animals can sense me, and are naturally curious, so if I'm near, they seek me out. It's annoying. Sometimes I can mask it, like if I focus on baseball or my last incredibly painful STD experience.

To sum it all up, I can hear their thoughts and they can hear mine. They also think I'm a big deal, because... well, I'm the only human who can communicate with them on a level they truly understand. And what most people don't know about animals is they can see and remember almost everything. So, do I exploit them? No. Do I use my ability for profit? You bet your ass.

To get a better picture of what happened to Paul, I needed to talk to the counselor, Mark Jefferies, or anyone else who'd seen him on the day he disappeared. To get an even bigger picture, I walked down an alley that ran next to the half-way house and found a dumpster filled with overflowing bags of trash from the neighboring restaurants. Behind that dumpster, looking for lunch, was a tom cat. He was predominantly black, with white patches on his belly and feet. He stepped out into the alley and I introduced myself.

*"Hi,"* I said, projecting my thought into his mind.

*"You're him, aren't you?"* he asked. Word travels fast in the animal community.

*"Yes. I'm him. You can call me Joe. Do you have a name?"*

He held up one of his fuzzy paws. *"A little girl, who used to give me food, called me Socks because of my white feet."*

*"Okay, Socks. Nice to meet you. Do you live here?"*

*"I live lots of places, but I get food here all the time."*

I looked over at the foul-smelling dumpster and wondered how long he'd been living on the streets. *"Socks, I need some help."* I took out my cell phone and pulled up Paul's mug shot that Ortiz sent me earlier. *"Have you seen this man before?"*

He looked at the picture. *"What's in it for me?"* Most cats can be a bit self-centered.

*"I can guarantee you a nice meal."*

*"I can get a meal right here."*

*"Yeah, but the food I have doesn't smell like Bigfoot's butthole."*

*"You know Bigfoot?"*

*"Not personally."*

He looked disappointed, then studied the image a little closer. *"I've seen him. He's been to that house a few times, along with his friend."*

*"Friend?"*

*"Yes. Another man. Smaller and skinnier. They always came to the house together."*

*"Did they?"* No one had mentioned anything about Paul having a friend. Not Ortiz, not Mrs. Collins, nobody. I needed to find out who this friend was and find him.

*"Socks, how would you like a really good meal?"*


***


When I opened the door to Rebuilding Futures, an electronic tone announced my entry. I stepped in to what was once a living room in the house built over one hundred and fifty years ago, renovated into a comfortable greeting area with cushy chairs and a wooden desk for a receptionist. The walls were painted a blue-grey color and adorned with signs imprinted with positive affirmations, like "Hope," and "Believe." The matching blue-grey carpet was plush and clean, and the air had a hint of lavender. The décor was very calming, and seemed perfect. Almost too perfect.

A door behind the desk opened and a woman walked out. She was also perfect. Mid-twenties with long, flowing red hair and a body like she'd stepped out from one of the magazines I kept under my mattress. She wore skin-tight, leopard-print pants and a low-cut blouse that I'm sure was on clearance at Strippers-R-Us. Her eyes grew wide, and she looked me up and down like I was the main course at a sausage party. I smiled, puffed out my chest, and wished I didn't have to lie to her about who I was.

"Hi, welcome to Rebuilding Futures," she said with a smile, showing her perfect teeth. "I'm Jennifer. How can I help you?"

"Hi, there," I said. "My name's Joe Mannix, and I'm looking for a friend who I served with in the Marine Corp. I heard he was going through some hard times and I wanted to see if I could help. His name is Paul Gibson."

"Oh, yes. I remember Paul. But he stopped coming here a few weeks ago."

"I see. How well did you know him?"

"I remember Paul was a kind man, but very troubled. You said you served with him?"

"Yes, that's right."

"Rebuilding Futures specializes in helping veterans. I could schedule you a session with one of our counselors?" Jennifer sat down at the desk and placed her hands on the keyboard. She looked up at me with inviting green eyes and bountiful cleavage, waiting for an answer. I continued my charade.

"No, I'm good. But the last time I talked to Paul, he said he was working with someone here named... Jeff?"

"Jeffries. Dr. Mark Jeffries? He's our founder."

*So, Jeffries is more than just a counselor.* "That sounds about right. Is he here? Maybe he has some information on Paul that could help me find him."

"No, I'm sorry. He's out of town at a conference."

*How convenient. I need to step this up.* "I have to say, Dr. Jefferies is a lucky man to have someone as gorgeous as you working for him."

She blushed and acted like she'd never heard that compliment before. "Oh, my goodness. Thank you. You're so sweet."

"Just stating the obvious. Oh, one more thing. Did Paul have any friends? Maybe someone else in your program that he hung out with?"

"No, Paul was pretty much a loner," Jennifer said, her green eyes darting quickly to her computer screen as she answered.

I sighed and tried to look disappointed. "Oh well. I won't take up any more of your time. But... If I do decide to talk to a counselor here, why don't you give me your number and I'll call you."

Jennifer smiled and wrote her number down on a Post-It Note. She looked up and handed me the paper, her eyes filled with the kind of curiosity you only see in barrooms and back seats. "Call anytime," she said.

"I'll do that." I stuck her number in my pocket and turned toward the door. I paused for a second, then looked back at Jennifer. "I really like what you've done with the interior here. It's very soothing. But... I think it's missing something."

"Really? We've tried so hard to create a very peaceful environment. What are we missing?"

I opened the door and when the tone sounded, Socks ran in and jumped up on Jennifer's desk. "How about a house cat?"

"A kitty!" Just like that, Jennifer turned from a smoke show to a giddy school girl.

*"Okay, buddy. Turn on the charm."*

Socks literally jumped into Jennifer's arms, purring and nuzzling, just like I'd told him to do in the alley.

"I love him," Jennifer said. "He's adorable. He looks like he's got little socks on his feet. Where did you find him?"

"Oh, just out here on the street looking for his forever home. I think he likes you."

Jennifer laughed and giggled while Socks purred and rubbed his head against her neck. He stopped long enough to look right at me and wink. That was my cue.

"Okay, bye. I'll call you." I stepped out the door, listening to Jennifer cooing baby-talk to Socks. I was certain he'd get tired of that real quick.

I walked down the sidewalk towards my car, feeling the sun on my face. I smiled and took a deep breath, filling my lungs with the early fall air while admiring the turning leaves on the trees growing along the street in the Oregon. Yes, I'd set Jennifer up for disappointment with Socks, but she clearly lied to me about knowing Paul's friend, and deserved as much. It was times like these that I really enjoyed my job and almost forgot that I hated myself.

I walked for about three minutes, then turned around when I heard the scratching of multiple squirrel feet on the sidewalk behind me. I dropped a few peanuts that I kept in my pocket and told them to beat it. When you're a guy who draws a crowd of animals wherever he goes, it helps to be prepared.

I quickly stepped back inside the half-way house and left the door open. Socks was on the desk, still putting on a show for Jennifer, until he jumped off, darted out the door, and ran like a shot down the sidewalk.

"Sorry to barge in, but I think I left my sunglasses here."

"Oh no! Mister Pickles!" Jennifer said, clearly distressed.

"Uh... who?"

"My cat. Mister Pickles. He ran out the door!"

"Oh, gosh! I'll go get him. You stay here." I closed the door behind me and ran in the direction of my car. When I got there, Socks was sitting on the hood, licking his paw and rubbing the back of his ear. I opened the driver's side door to let him in and he took the passenger seat. I slid in behind the steering wheel and started laughing.

*"What's so funny?"* Socks asked.

*"You tell me, Mister Pickles."*

*"Ugh. I've eaten mice smarter than her."*

*"Maybe, but she's fun to look at. Did she make a phone call like I said?"*

*"Where's my meal?"* he said, licking his chops. I opened the center console and sorted through the peanuts, dog biscuits, and bird seed until I found a bag of cat treats. I placed a few nuggets in my hand and held them out. Socks devoured them in ten seconds.

*"Will that do?"*

*"For now,"* he said. *"Yes, she did talk to someone in that little box you humans carry around. It was a man and she said this to him: 'You asked me to call if anyone showed up asking about Paul. A guy showed up here today and said he served with him in the Marines, but he didn't look the type. Said his name was Joe Mannix. No, he's kind of hot. Yeah, I'll send you a picture. Will I see you tonight? Okay, bye.' That was all she said besides the ridiculous babbling."*

*"A picture?"* I said. *"There must have been a security camera hidden in there somewhere that I couldn't see. Now somebody knows what I look like and that I'm looking for Paul. You didn't happen to remember the phone number she dialed, did you?"*

*"I don't know what that means."*

*"Forget it."* I leaned back in my Fiero's bucket seat and thought about my next move. What I was about to do was totally outside the law and could put my PI license at risk.

*"Joe,"* Socks said.

*"Yeah."*

*"Here she comes."*

I looked out my windshield and saw hot Jennifer walking towards us on the sidewalk, calling out, "Mister Pickles!" over and over again. I laughed, even though it was not the weirdest thing I'd seen someone do in the Oregon. I started my car and did a U-turn out of my parking spot.

*"Where are we going?"* Socks asked.

*"Cyber space."*

*"Oh. Is there food there?"*

***

It was beginning to look like someone had a hand in Paul's disappearance. If that was the case, the police needed to know. Or did they? I needed to find out who Jennifer called and tipped off about me, which would involve a warrant signed by a judge, and taken to the phone company, requesting the call records of the number I had in my pocket. That process, followed to the letter by local law enforcement, would take a week, maybe two. Farah could get that information for me in a half hour.

Farah Petrovic's parents were Bosnian refugees who fled to the US in the 90s to escape the war in the Balkans. They ended up in Dayton, which ironically, was where the leaders of Bosnia, Croatia, and Serbia all met to discuss a peace deal that would end the war.

Two years ago, Farah's older sister was murdered during a robbery at their family's bakery in North Dayton. The police had a suspect, but no murder weapon. That's when Ortiz called me and asked if I'd help out. On the down-low, of course. After some candid conversations with a rabbit, two chipmunks and a duck, the murder weapon was found with the suspect's fingerprints all over it. Case closed, and Ortiz got a big fat promotion.

The first time I saw Farah was at the murder trial. I stopped by the day of the sentencing to see if the dirtbag would get life in prison or not. Farah was twenty-two and pretty, but had a lot of hardware in her face and dressed all in black like she'd listened to too much Emo. When Farah and her parents walked past me on the courthouse steps, she ran over and hugged me, whispering, "Thank you," in my ear.

How she knew I helped on her sister's case was beyond me. How she managed to steal my cell phone right out of my pocket without me knowing was another mystery.

I'm not a big fan of technology, but I needed my phone back. So, like a cave man, I looked in an old phone book and found her address in East Dayton. When I pulled up, she was sitting on the front steps taking selfies and playing Subway Surfers on my phone.

"You really should lock your phone down better," she said, right before tossing it to me. I tried talking to her, but I could tell she was socially awkward and prying words out of her was like pulling teeth. Once she warmed up to me, I found out she was incredibly smart and spent a lot of time on her computer, claiming to be a "hacker in training." I asked her if the curriculum included cell phone thievery, and she said, "I saw the look on your face and it reminded me of me. So, I thought we could be friends. I don't have any."

"A simple, 'Hello, I'm Farah,' would do," I said. That concept was too much for her, and she jumped up to go back inside, but before she did, she turned to me and said, "If you want to be friends, it's okay. I'll let you."

At first, I thought she was trying to come on to me, which was bad. I mean, historically, after a few rounds of bedroom rodeo, all my relationships with women end up trampled like the bull rider. And Farah wasn't really my type. She was a little young, and I definitely didn't have enough black clothes to meet her standards. Besides, my life was screwed up enough. I didn't want my epic failures to bring her down too. Or, maybe I just didn't want this kid to see how big of a loser I was.

She started texting me on a secure chat app she installed on my phone, and I figured out what she really wanted was a big brother type. After her sister was murdered, her parents sold their bakery and fell into a deep depression. They rarely spoke and it was like she didn't exist. Farah said the feeling of being alone, and the isolation didn't bother her. It was the feeling that her life didn't matter that really hurt. So, I text with her a few times a month to check in and make sure she's okay. In my mind, I'm the last person someone should look up to, but I'm all she has.

I hadn't seen her in person since that day on her front steps, so showing up at her house out of the blue and asking her to hack a major wireless communications provider, might threaten our pseudo-sibling relationship.

When I knocked on the door, her parents showed me in and led me to her room. They didn't seem to remember me from the trial and didn't seem to mind that I carried a cat. I knocked on Farah's bedroom door and waited.

*"Is this cyber space?"* Socks asked.

I chuckled. *"Not even close. But we may be at the threshold."*

Just then, the door opened and we saw Farah in all her Gothic glory. Short, jet-black hair with multiple piercings, a black tee-shirt for a band I'd never heard of and black jeans with more holes than a golf course. She didn't say a word. She just looked at me and Socks with a blank expression on her face, then abruptly turned and walked to her computer chair where she sat down and began typing.

I looked down at Socks. *"She's not much for conversation."*

*"She's not much for color either,"* he said.

I walked into Farah's room and sat on her bed, positioning Socks on my lap. The room was small and dimly lit by the four computer monitors Farah seemed to be working on simultaneously.

"Why do you have a cat?" she asked, still typing away.

"It's a present," I said.

"For who?"

"For you."

Farah stopped typing. She watched a group of white text characters scroll from the top of her screen to the bottom, then swiveled around in her chair and looked at Socks.

"Why?" she asked.

"Well, he needs a home and you need... something."

Socks looked up at me. *"I don't know about this,"* he said.

*"You'll be fine. Go say hi."*

He jumped down on the floor and walked over to Farah's chair. He sniffed her jeans and she surprisingly reached down to pet his head. Socks sniffed her fingers.

*"She had tuna for lunch."* He arched his back and rubbed up against her legs, starting his purr engine. For a fleeting moment, the corners of Farah's mouth curled up into a smile.

"I will not love him," she said. "But he will be loved, I promise."

"Hey, whatever works for you. And him."

Farah stood up and reached down, picking up Socks and holding him to her chest. She walked to her bedroom doorway and stepped into the hall. "Mom... I'm getting a cat," she said, loud enough to reach her mother at the other end of the house. Her mother replied with something in Croatian, but it didn't sound like an approval. Farah rolled her eyes and sighed, then walked back and sat down in her computer chair with Socks.

"She said no, but I don't care. I'm moving out soon. I have enough money to buy a house."

"Really? Where?"

"Oakwood's nice."

Oakwood was a ritzy suburb south of Dayton. In today's market, you can't even walk inside a starter home in that neighborhood for less than 400K. The only people I knew who lived in Oakwood, rented apartments from the rich people who lived in Oakwood.

"So... how much money do you have, Farah?"

"If I told you, you'd be an accessory."

"Can you give me a hint?"

"It's mostly crypto."

"Superman's dog?"

"No. Crypto currency. How old are you?"

"Look, you know I'm lost like the Donner party when it comes to this technology stuff. From the sound of things, it's better that I don't know. But since we're on this subject, I have a favor to ask."

"I knew it! There's always a catch with you men."

"What?"

"Every guy I talk to online just wants to see pictures of me naked. They have no idea how a real relationship is supposed to work."

"Farah, a real relationship involves being physically present with a real person."

She pulled Socks a little closer to her chest. "I'm not ready for that yet."

"Fair enough," I said. "I've always been straight with you, right?"

"Yes."

"So, are you going to help me, or what?"

She sighed and gave me a look like I'd just asked her to clean her room and take out the garbage. "Alright. What do you need?"

I took hot Jennifer's number from my pocket and handed it over. "I need to know who that phone number called today about 1:30."

"That's it?"

"Let's start with that."

She spun around in her chair and reached over Socks to her workstation. Windows popped open across the four screens, her fingers attacking the keyboard like a gamer on cocaine. Before I knew it, she was in the cell company's phone records and accessed Jennifer's call log. She found the number that was called at 1:33 pm, then copied that number into a webpage and hit enter. It only took about thirty seconds.

"The number is registered to a company," Farah said. "Legacy Pharmaceuticals."

"A pharmaceutical company? Can you find—" She had the company website open already.

"It's been in business about ten years... CEO is a guy named Mark Jefferies, PHD."

"You're kidding me?"

"Can you not see the man's picture on my screen?" Farah turned her chair around to face me. Socks was in peaceful slumber on her lap. "What's this all about?"

"It's a case I'm working on. Missing person, last seen at a half-way house founded by Jefferies, who was also the missing guy's counselor. What's his bio say?"

"Nothing about being a counselor," Farah said, turning back to her screens. "Spent most of his career in research. Got his PHD in Biochemistry at the University of Michigan."

My suspicion meter was pegged into the red. I'd been through enough counseling over the last few years to know that a PHD in bio-chem was the wrong credential to practice Psychotherapy. Not even as a hobby. I'm an easy-going guy, but I could feel my blood start to boil.

"Where does this asshole live?" I said, my voice gruff.

Farah changed screens and after a few clicks pulled up a few addresses.

"Jefferies' home address is on Wayne Avenue downtown, but... his company has an office in Ann Arbor... and owns a farm in Jamestown, Ohio."

"A farm?"

"That's what I said." She brought up the Google Earth image on her screen. "Here it is."

The farm looked to be around one hundred acres and very isolated on the eastern side of Greene County, about thirty miles from downtown Dayton. There was an obvious house in the middle of the property and one very large building that could possibly hold equipment or keep livestock. Maybe Jefferies was recruiting guys out of the half-way house to work cheap labor, picking pumpkins and herding heifers. That was actually the best scenario in this entire case. I locked the farm's address in my phone and stood up.

"I have to go," I said.

"Where are you going?"

"Looks like I'm going down on the farm. Thanks for your help. And, for taking in my little buddy here," I said, motioning to Socks, who was still napping.

"You don't have to bring me presents whenever you need help. A simple, 'Hey, I need help,' would do."

I shook my head in amusement. "I'll try to remember that. Oh, his name is Socks, by the way."

Farah gently scratched her new friend behind his ears. "It fits."

Socks opened his eyes. *"I think I'll keep her."*

***

I pulled into my apartment complex and one of my squirrel buddies, who I called Spaz, was hanging off the side of a tree at the edge of the parking lot. As soon as he saw my red Fiero, he leaped on the ground and ran into the middle of the road in front of me.

"What the…" I slammed on the brakes, screeching to a stop. Spaz immediately jumped on the hood of my car.

*"Joe! Don't go in your nest,"* he said, very agitated.

*"Why? What's going on?"*

*"Men in your nest, Joe. Scary men. They scared me."*

My "nest" was on the second floor of an eight-unit complex. I leaned forward and looked out my windshield and sure enough, my door was wide open.

*"How many men, Spaz?"* I opened my glovebox and took out my Glock 9mm.

*"Two. Two men. Very scary."*

*"Okay, get back in the tree. I'll be fine. Thanks for the warning."*

Spaz leaped off my hood and scurried up the trunk and into the branches, out of sight. I pulled back the slide to do a press-check on my Glock to make sure I had a round in the chamber, then found a parking space in the lot. I got out and ran to the stairway, keeping watch on my open apartment door as I moved. I carefully crept up the stairs to the second-floor landing. With my cop instincts in full gear, I extended my Glock out in front of me in a low-ready position. I had a feeling Dr. Jefferies had sent some goons to scare me off Paul's trail. Either that, or some local boneheads decided to rob the messiest apartment in Dayton.

I stepped quietly down to my door and stopped to listen. I heard no footfalls or movement. I peeked quickly around the doorframe and saw nothing but my mess. I took a deep breath, raised my gun up to eye level, and rushed in. I cleared the room from left to right. The kitchen was empty, so I entered the living room, and that's when I saw him. A man standing by my mattress. He wasn't armed, just dressed in a pair of jeans and a red flannel shirt that looked strangely familiar. He faced away from me and stared down at the floor. My heart was pounding and adrenalin pumped through my veins, but I sensed something weird about how the man just stood there. Like he was in trance.

"Turn around slow, and show me your hands," I commanded. He didn't move. "I said, show me your hand, mother f—"

Another man stepped out of my back bedroom into the hallway. He had on a blue suit and looked just like the guy in the picture Farah pulled up on the Legacy Pharmaceuticals website.

"Doctor Jefferies," I said, swinging my weapon in his direction. He walked towards me with the kind of smirk on his face that only douchebags wore. When he reached the living room, he placed his right hand inside his jacket pocket.

"Don't do it!" I yelled, lining my sights up on his chest. Jefferies slowly pulled something out of his pocket. It looked like a pen, but then he removed a long plastic end cap. It was a hypodermic needle.

"Paul, would you kindly subdue Mr. Cooper?" he said, calmly.

The man standing by my mattress slowly turned and looked up, and I almost loaded my pants. It was Paul Gibson. The flannel shirt was the same one from his mug shot. His eyes were glazed over and the right corner of his mouth curled up into a snarl.

"Paul?" I said, keeping my gun trained on Jefferies. "Hey, there's a lot of people looking for you, buddy. Why don't you tell me what's going on?"

"Now," Jefferies said.

Paul was on me in less than a second. He moved so fast, the trash on my floor flew up into the air from his wake. He grabbed the barrel of my Glock and rotated it against my thumb, breaking my grip and disarming me. He tossed my weapon into the kitchen and I drew back my right arm and punched him in the jaw. His head snapped sharply to the left. Then he slowly turned back and glared at me, with a look like he wanted to eat my face.

Let's get one thing straight. I can handle myself. I was a cop on the streets of Cincinnati for eight years. I've thrown hands with plenty of guys, some bigger than me. But Paul was strong. Freakishly strong. He grabbed the back of my shirt and slammed me down on the floor hard. That move knocked the air out of my lungs. As I gasped for breath, Paul pushed my head down on the floor. I felt a beer bottle cap and a piece of old pizza crust dig into my cheek, then felt something sharp stick in the side of my neck. I tried to turn my head to see what was happening, but I saw stars and little Tweety Birds flying all around my apartment. One flew up my nose and then everything went black—

***

You ever hear a bunch of sounds when you're half asleep, and you can't figure out if they're real or part of a dream?

I woke up with the worst hangover I've ever had. And I've had plenty. The sounds in my head were cries for help from animals.

*"Are you awake?"*

*"Can you hear me?"*

*"Help us!"*

*"Get us out of here!"*

I opened my eyes and tried to focus. I was on my back looking at rafters high above me and rows of florescent lights hanging from wooden cross beams. I tried to get up, but couldn't move my arms or legs. My wrists and ankles were bound by leather straps to a gurney. My mouth was as dry as cotton and there was a chemical odor in the air like in a hospital, but more pungent. I looked around and guessed I was in the building that looked like a barn in the Google Earth image Farah showed me. But it was no ordinary barn. From what I could see, the interior was enclosed by finished drywall and the floor was smooth, clean concrete. The room was sectioned off by thick sheets of clear vinyl dividers, like the kind used in meat packing plants.

I looked to my right and saw a row of about twenty animal cages lined up against the wall. Most held dogs of various breeds, but in two of them I saw monkeys. I guessed they were rhesus monkeys, the kind most used in scientific testing.

This was a lab. Doctor Mark Jefferies-Frankenstein and his Paul-monster had taken me out to the farm on the edge of Jamestown, where Legacy Pharmaceuticals was undoubtably testing some diabolical concoction on these poor animals.

I looked to my left and laying on another gurney a few feet away from me was Paul. He looked unconscious and his arms and legs were bound just like mine. A chrome hook held an IV drip that fed into his arm. How did he fit into all this? Did he discover what Jefferies was doing? Was Jefferies experimenting on him too?

"Paul," I said, hoping he'd come out of it and I'd get some answers. He stirred just a little. I had to try harder. "Paul!"

He moaned and turned his head in my direction, his eyes barely open.

"Who are you?"

"You don't remember kicking my ass?"

"I never remember anything when he injects me." Paul turned his head back and closed his eyes.

"Hey, man... don't fall asleep," I said. "Is Jefferies using you for testing?"

"Yeah. And my friend Nathan."

"Nathan? Is that your buddy from the half-way house? Is he here?"

"No. He's dead. Jefferies killed him."

"What?"

"He'll kill me too when he's done with me."

"What is he testing on you?"

"It's a serum," Paul said, turning his head toward me, fighting against the drugs to speak and keep his eyes open. "He's trying to... create super-soldiers. It makes you strong... obedient... mean. He'll sell it on the black market."

"So, he moved on from animals to humans," I said.

"There were more animals here. Jefferies injected them... made them fight each other... to the death."

It was all making sense to me now. Jefferies was a genuine mad-scientist, kidnapping down-and-out veterans for experimentation. A feeling of dread came over me, and I knew if I didn't get the hell out of there, he'd turn me into one of his psycho Winter Soldiers.

On the other side of Paul, I saw a row of shelves holding a glass terrarium. I didn't think much about it at first, but when I looked again, I saw rats. Maybe ten white lab rats, to be exact, and they were all pressed up against the glass looking at me. I had an idea.

*"Hey guys. I bet you're tired of being locked up all day."*

They all said, *"Yes,"* in unison.

*"If one or two of you can get out of that cage and chew through these straps, I'll make sure you all go free."*

Rats are pretty smart. It doesn't take them long to figure things out. At the mere mention of the word "free," they all began jumping up to knock the screen off the top of their rat prison. But the aquarium sides were too high, so they climbed on top each other and made a rat pyramid, allowing one rat to reach the top and push out under the lid. Four rats eventually made it out of the cage, and as soon as they hit the floor, they ran off in different directions. I shook my head in disgust. You just can't trust a rat.

*"We had a deal!"* I said, knowing damn well they heard me. All the caged dogs threatened to eat them and the two monkeys threw turds and screeched obscenities like a pair of sailors. Two of the rats finally came back and made it up on the gurney.

*"Sorry,"* one of them said. *"We're really scared. Bad things happen here."*

*"I get it. Now, start chewing."*

Both rats gnawed furiously on the strap that held my left wrist until there was only a small piece of leather left. I flexed my bicep and broke free. As soon as I unbuckled the strap on my right arm, all the animals went silent. I looked over at them. The monkeys cowered in fear and the dogs whined and sulked to the rear of their cages. They could hear something I couldn't. Finally, I heard footsteps. It had to be Jefferies.

*"The bad man is back,"* one of the monkeys said. The rats were gone in an instant. I looked over at Paul. He was out cold. My heart started pounding and I quickly secured the buckle on my right wrist and put my left wrist back in the strap the rats chewed, hoping Jefferies wouldn't notice I'd broken free. Then I did what anyone would do while they waited to be turned into a brain-dead zombie. I whistled.

I was on the second verse of Guns N' Roses' "Patience" when I saw two figures on the other side of the vinyl dividers. A pair of hands split the panels and in walked Jefferies, still in his blue suit, and followed by hot Jennifer. When she saw me, she rushed up and grabbed a sidebar on the gurney and gave it a shake.

"Where's Mister Pickles?" she shouted.

"Beats me. I guess cats have a thing about living with lying whores!" I said.

She drew her arm up to smack me, but Jefferies grabbed her by the shoulders and pulled her back.

"Now, now, my darling," Jefferies said. "We don't want to injure Mr. Cooper before he has a chance to participate in our program. Be a dear, and ready a vial of serum, will you?"

Jennifer glared at Jefferies, then turned in a huff and stomped off through the divider panels. I tried not to watch her backside as she walked away, but I couldn't help myself.

"I have to hand it to you, Jeffries," I said. "You know how to pick 'em. She'll be popular in prison. So will you, for that matter."

Jefferies roared with maniacal laughter. "We'll be in the Caribbean once I sell my serum to the highest bidder. I only have a few more tests to run, and my project will be complete." He took a rubber strap from the tray connected to my gurney and began tying if off around my right bicep. "Make a fist, please. Jennifer will be back soon."

"How about I punch you in the face with it?" I said. He laughed again. I didn't think it was that funny, and the spot I was in wasn't funny at all. I needed some help, and my only option was the rats. I focused and reached out to them.

*"Hey guys, I could really use some help right about now."*

"Rats!" Jeffries said.

"Huh?" I answered. How did he know what I was doing?

"My rats," he said, looking straight at the aquarium on the shelf. "Four of them are missing."

"Uh... I don't know what you're talking about."

"I had ten rats in that cage. Now there are only six."

"Really? What do they look like?" Suddenly, I sensed all four rats underneath the gurney.

Jefferies shook his fists and his eyes were wild with rage. "Like... like rats, you idiot!" He was clearly insane, not to mention incredibly anal about his rats. Just then, Jennifer walked back in holding the vial and an injection needle. I reached out with my mind to every animal.

*"Do something now!"*

All the dogs began barking. The monkeys did somersaults, screeched, and threw more turds. That drew Jennifer's and the doctor's attention away from me. I pulled my left hand loose and unbuckled the strap on my right arm. I looked down on the concrete and saw the wayward rats, sniffing the air and scurrying around like rats do. One of them stopped and looked up at me.

*"What do you want us to do?"* he asked.

*"I don't know... pretend they're food."*

Two rats jumped on Jennifer's foot and she let out a scream that pierced my eardrums. She kicked them away and ran back through the vinyl flaps, dropping both the needle and the vial. When the vial hit the floor, it busted, spilling Jefferies' demon semen onto the concrete.

"No!" he shouted. "That's the last... AHHH!"

I freed my legs and slid off the table to see the other two rats climb inside Jefferies' pant legs. He yelled and kicked and smacked at them, but they kept burrowing under the polyester like gophers until they reached his crotch, then went to work on his jewels and Johnson like they did on that leather strap. He fell and writhed on the floor, screaming in falsetto. I looked on and cringed thinking they must have really been hungry.

I ran over to the monkeys and opened their cages. "Let all the dogs loose," I said. They both took off and I hurried over to Paul and unbuckled his straps.

"Hey man, we have to get out of here." He was barely coherent. I pulled the IV out of his arm and helped him off the table. We walked past Jefferies, who was passed out due to massive blood loss and not having a penis anymore. Bloody little footprints trailed away from his pant legs across the concrete.

"What happened to him?" Paul asked.

"He's not the man he used to be," I said.

\#

I commandeered a Dodge Sprinter van that still had the keys in the ignition and helped Paul in the passenger seat. Thankfully, there was a large sliding door on the side so that twenty dogs, ten rats, two monkeys, and a guinea pig one of the monkeys found, could all fit in. The farm set way back off the road at the end of a long gravel driveway. The tires spun and kicked up a cloud of dust as I hit the gas, speeding past the old, desolate looking farm house. Hot Jennifer, who was now bitch Jennifer, was nowhere to be seen, but that didn't matter. Ortiz wouldn't have any problem finding her after I gave him all the details. The detective, after coping with the initial shock of Jefferies' genitalia mutilation, would probably want to know why I didn't call an ambulance or give medical aid. Maybe he didn't need to know all the details.

I knew we had a long drive ahead, so I covered some ground rules with the animals. No barking, biting, fighting or humping. They didn't cause any problems, but there was an excessive amount of licking and butt sniffing. I was surprised at how much profanity the monkeys knew, and used with proficiency and vigor. They would have both made good cops. Overall, the menagerie was just happy to be out of that torture chamber and I was happy to liberate them. "You sure have a way with animals," Paul said. "Who are you, anyway?" He was coming out of his drug induced stupor, holding and petting a small poodle-mix that jumped in his lap.

"I'm a private investigator, but I, uh... used to be a K9 cop." I didn't talk about my past much, but that was the only possible explanation as to how I could keep a van packed full of animals from going bonkers.

"Really? Why'd you quit?"

I didn't answer him right away. I just drove down the bumpy gravel drive, staring out the windshield until we got to the road. When I turned right to head into Jamestown, we hit a large pothole and the van rocked from side to side, stirring up the dogs a bit. I looked in the rearview and noticed, for the first time, that one of them was a German shepherd.

"My partner was killed and it was my fault. After that, I just couldn't do the job anymore."

"I hear you," Paul said. "Survivor's remorse. I deal with that every day. Half my squad was killed in Afghanistan because I made a bad decision. Should have been me. That's why I got mixed up in this. Nathan said Jefferies could help me, but he bought into the lies and paid the price for it. When Nathan went missing, I went to Jefferies to beat the hell out of him and make him tell me where my friend was. But he got me with the needle. I can't tell you how many times I've wanted to off myself. But after going through all this... I just want to get better, you know?"

I took this job because I needed the money. Then I became personally vested after learning about Paul's past. It wasn't until now that I realized just how similar we were, and that I could have easily fallen into the same trap he did, or even worse, ended up like his friend Nathan. I shook my head and wondered how long it had been since I'd feared the possibility of death.

We'd made it through Jamestown and turned on to State Route 35, heading west toward Dayton, when I felt a tug on my shirt. I looked down to see one of the monkeys holding the Guinea pig.

*"Can I keep him?"* he asked.

*"Please, God. No!"* said the Guinea pig.

I had to hold back my laughter. *"I don't know where you guys will end up, but I'll make sure each one of you are taken care of. Okay?"*

*"Thank you. Here, I found this. What is it?"* He held up a cell phone that looked a lot like mine. Jefferies must have left it in the van when he and Paul took me from my apartment.

*"That's something humans use to talk to each other over distances and spend countless hours wasting valuable time on. I'll take that."*

I opened the phone with my thumbprint and saw several missed calls from Sandra Collins. I looked over at Paul, who seemed to be enjoying his new friend licking his cheeks. He looked at me with a smile and I handed him my phone.

"Now might be a good time for you to call your sister."

***

I'd just made my eighth trip to the dumpster and started another load of laundry when Michelle, the lawyer, knocked on my door. She was wearing her usual business attire, and a skirt that showed off her long, incredible legs. I let her in and she walked into my new and improved living room without having to traverse any obstacles.

"Looks like you're busy," she said.

"Yeah, just doing some rearranging, and cleaning. Domestic stuff."

Michelle laughed. "Joe Cooper... domesticated. Doesn't really suit you. I just wanted to stop by and congratulate you on finding my client's brother, and give you the other half of your fee." She smiled and handed me a ten thousand dollar check, signed by Mrs. Collins.

"Oh, great. Thanks." I took the check and walked into my kitchen that was freshly sanitized for my own protection.

"So, how long will all this take?" Michelle asked, gesturing around my apartment with her hand.

"Um... I don't know. It's a work in progress. Why?"

"Well, I just had a new hot tub installed at my place and I'm dying to trying it out with someone. You interested?"

I took the check and placed it under a magnet on my refrigerator, right next to the picture of me and my old K9 partner, Tex, that I'd found under a pile of mail that was at least three years old. I let out a sigh, glanced one more time at Michelle's legs, and couldn't believe what I was about to say.

"Maybe some other time, Michelle."

She raised her eyebrows up in surprise. "Are you turning me down?"

"Yeah, I am. I mean, who knows what will happen in a few weeks, or even months, but today…" I opened the door to my fridge and pulled out a bottle of water. "It's a work in progress."

# THE FISHERMAN

## BY GABRIEL HART

For a finite body of water in the middle of the desert, the Salton Sea appeared a vast ocean with no visible shore besides the one Jacob and Colby stood upon, especially when the fog refused to dissipate.

Or rather, what the two boys called fog was the evaporating miasma suspended in the desert's thick unrelenting heat; a stench you could *see*. Since the boys had moved in with their grandparents one long month ago, they had acclimated to its putrid effluvium, their recall of fresh air forgotten. They had yet to learn that the Sea's coarse, pebbly sand formed from intermingling with layers of decayed fish vertebrae.

"Whatcha thinking about?" said Colby.

"What do you *think* I'm thinking about?" said Jacob, annoyed. He threw a rock at one of the countless dead tilapia floating on the surface. "I'm thinking about dad."

"Well, he's not coming back. You should probably just think of something else."

Jacob took pause so he wouldn't blow up at his brother again, something he had recently promised his grandparents. He steadied his view on the non-horizon, the jaundiced mist hovering just high enough to seduce his gaze, yet low enough to feel trapped on Bombay Beach. He turned his head to his grandparent's half-sunken salt-eroded dock where their algae-infested 1970 Chrysler Cadet ski-boat was tied. It bobbed ever so slightly from the Sea's humble ripples, as if it was nodding right back to Jacob.

"Okay," he said. "I'm thinking about something else now. Follow me inside the house, I've got an idea..."

Jacob ran ahead, assuming his brother was following. But Colby stood transfixed on the water; an uncharacteristic four-foot wave cluster traveled *sideways* across the lake, incongruent with the typically meager ripples that lapped its rotting organic matter to shore.

Attention-deficit gears changed quickly as Colby ran to catch up with his brother.

***

"You boys need help with something?" Grandpa said. "You've been staring at that map for twenty-minutes now."

"Grandpa, do you mind if we take it off the wall? We'll be super careful."

"Well, I suppose... Just put it back up on the wall when you're through then."

Gently, the two lifted the framed map of southern California from its hinges, leaving a clean rectangle glaring from the accumulated grime where it hung for over fifty years. Each grabbed an end like two pallbearers as they walked it gently into their bedroom, laying it on Colby's bottom bunk.

Colby locked the door before joining Jacob, who was already tracing the outline of the Salton Sea on the map with one finger.

"Let's see... we are right—here," he said, pointing to the right-side bulge of the Sea where the ruins of their Bombay Beach now lied in decay. Holding their spot on the map, his other finger moved through the Sea's big blue blotch to its Southern end, stopping at a stringy trickle forming a pathway out of the country.

"And there's where we are gonna go," Jacob said. "The New River goes from the Salton Sea all the way to Mexico. We can finally go there and see everything that Mr. Vera always tells us about."

"Maybe since it's so narrow it won't be that dangerous?" Colby said.

"For sure. Then once we get to Mexico, we'll be free to do whatever. Mr. Vera makes it sound like there's no rules there."

"Should we talk to him first, let him know what we're doing?"

"No way. What if he tells grandma and grandpa? Do you think they know we talk to him?"

"How could they? All they do is watch TV all day. I don't think they've ever even said hi to Mr. Vera."

"Okay, well it's 5:30—he'll be home from work any minute. Let's go wait on his patio."

***

"Okay so let me get this straight – you boys are gonna do what?" Mr. Vera said, amused to chuckles as he brought out two glass-bottle Cokes for the boys, a Budweiser for himself. He sat down and fanned himself with his palm straw Stetson, preparing for a long story.

"We're gonna take grandpa's boat and sail the whole Salton Sea to the New River, then take that all the way to Mexico," said Jacob, no flinching.

Mr. Vera slapped his gut as his head flew back in laughter. "No, no, no...You boys are fucking psychos, man. You don't wanna go in the Sea and you *definitely* don't wanna go in the Rio Nilo, trust me."

"The Rio Nilo?"

"A lot of people call the New River *Rio Nilo.* You know, like The Nile River, because it's so long. But when we were growing up in Mexicali, we would call it *Ni Lo Huelas.*"

"What does that mean?"

"That basically means 'You don't even want to *smell* that river.' It's all raw sewage coming out of Mexicali, then it gets mixed up with all the pollution from the maquilladoras along the border like where I work. To be honest, I'm ashamed to admit how much chemical we dump into that river. But the worst part—guess where it all goes? I'll give you one clue: the river actually flows North. Here."

The boys looked over their shoulders to the Sea where Happy Hour was just beginning for the seagulls. They swooped down on the noxious smorgasbord, consuming layers of freshly dead floating tilapia. Plucking out their eyes like appetizer olives, beaking larger chunks out of their water-bloated bodies, littering the shoreline with countless gristly brittle fish skeletons with just the heads and tails remaining. Piles of aquatic rot accumulated like seaweed until the fish bones decay into the beach's unique coarse sand. A circle of life eclipsed by a Venn diagram of death, neglect, and denial.

"Grandpa says it was just 'cause the Sea got too salty?" said Colby.

"That too," said Mr. Vera. "The disaster of the Sea is like a perfect storm. But since it barely rains here, the storm comes from below, not above. We can't even begin to imagine what's at the bottom. At my factory, where it overlooks the river, we've seen fish with three to four eyes. And that's just in the shallow parts where all the industrial foam collects on the edges. Think about what is happening in this big body of water after decades of toxic run-off, what it must do to the sea life?"

Colby turned his head to check his brother's reaction to all of this. He saw Jacob rolling his eyes.

"But if we're in a boat, who cares?" said Jacob as he raised his arms. "It's not like we're gonna be swimming in it..."

"It doesn't matter, boys. There's stuff out there you're not gonna want to see."

He paused too long, a contemplative thought.

"Your grandparents tell you about The Fisherman yet?"

"The Fisherman?"

"Maybe what's left of one, anyway. There's a little rowboat out there on the other side of the Sea, sometimes you can see it on a clear day. Someone or something is in there, kind of hunched over... but no one has ever seen him dock or leave the shore. Whatever it is, he's just floating out there, with God knows what else..." Mr. Vera shook his head and grabbed his crucifix necklace.

"Aw, come on Mr. Vera!" The boys were now convinced he was putting them on.

"Hey, I'm telling you nothing but the truth, so help me God," he said, continuing his hand's caressing the cross. "But the Fisherman isn't what really freaks me out, man. You boys spend enough time staring at the Sea—you ever seen those big-ass waves come sideways all of a sudden?"

Colby's stomach dropped. He remembered what he saw earlier but kept that wild card close.

"What about 'em?" he said.

"I wish I knew," Mr. Vera said, shaking his head. "Waves don't go sideways, that's all I know. Hey, and besides—how do you even know if that boat's motor runs? You try it out yet?" Mr. Vera was already walking over to the boat, possessed by his own curiosity and penchant for mechanics. "Damn," he whispered to himself as he saw the key was carelessly rusted into the ignition. He turned it, but no turnover. He double-checked that it was in neutral gear, then kicked the side.

"I hate to break it to you guys, but this thing's dead in the water," he said, relieved.

Jacob leaned over to his brother. *"Don't worry. I already knew the motor didn't run. I've got it figured out,"* he whispered. But Colby wasn't concerned the boat wouldn't run as much as he was worried what they might find out what laid beyond the haze. He slapped Jacob on the knee to signal Mr. Vera returning to the patio. He sat back down at the table, took a sip of his beer and looked at the boys, pondering.

"Can I ask why you boys wanna do this so bad?"

Jacob and Colby looked at each other, then looked at Mr. Vera. They were tongue-tied, lips squirming to form.

"Is it because your father died a Navy man?"

Both boys shrugged their shoulders, heads downcast until Jacob found the guts to nod his head in silence.

"Listen, I know it's tough to process. It's gotta be confusing that your father died at sea. That still makes him a hero, you know? High-ranking officer, man. But sometimes danger doesn't care if you're a professional who knows what you're doing..."

He paused until he made sure they were making eye contact.

"... but none of this matters, because you boys aren't going out on that boat, right?"

Silence.

"Right?"

"Yes, Mr. Vera..." they grumbled in unison.

"Good. Hey, one more thing—is there any way we can get your grandma to stop singing in the middle of the night?"

The boys rolled their eyes.

"Sorry about that, Mr. Vera," said Jacob. "You know that blue building between 4$^{th}$ and 5$^{th}$? Well, that's the old Bombay Beach Opera House, where she used to sing ages ago. Grandpa says she thinks she's still there sometimes, even though it's been closed for decades."

"Oh, I see..." he said, embarrassed for prying into her senility. "Well, forget I said anything then. About your grandma. Take everything else to heart, yes?" Mr. Vera sternly tapped his own heart to punctuate his point.

The boys nodded as Jacob slapped his brother on the thigh. "Let's go, it's getting dark. Follow me," he whispered. Jacob took the lead back home but only to grab a hammer from his grandpa's toolbox. He led them to a quick right on 5th, then a left on Avenue H.

"Where are we going?" said Colby.

"We're gonna make a quick stop at the old Yacht Club so we can make the boat run. But we gotta be real stealth so no one sees us."

"What? That place has been closed forever..."

"Duh, I know! We're not going in – we're going up."

While a few hundred residents still held on to their properties since its commercial abandonment, Bombay Beach was a lawless ghost town of shut ins. The demographic didn't waver—you were either a senior, a dipso-tweaker, or both—so it was a rare sight to see anyone out walking besides a trip to the only functioning business: the liquor store. No one would bat an eye at the sight of two kids climbing up the drain-gutter to the top of the old abandoned Yacht Club.

"Man, what the hell are we doing, Jacob?"

"Just shut up and keep watch," he whispered.

Colby stood in awe, watching his brother take a hammer to the shuttered business's sign. Two real paddles in an X-formation had cradled the words BOMBAY BEACH YACHT CLUB until he shoved the hammer's claw into the rusted nails, liberating the salt-eroded but otherwise unused oars whose true purpose was to take them into the unknown.

"You're a genius, Jacob."

"I know I am," he said, throwing his brother a paddle with a smile. "C'mon, let's get out of here."

***

Grandma cooked them their Tuesday night tuna-mac and the boys competitively doused their congealed cheese mounds with hot sauce to mask the taste of fish. Eating fast and hearty; the swifter they ate, the quicker her and grandpa would go to bed. After washing their plates, they went to the porch to pace and gaze, knowing they still had to contend with that hour of their grandparents slack-jawed in front of Fox News.

Eyes in the back of their heads, they felt the living room lights go off.

Their stomachs tightened.

"Okay, let's do this quick," Jacob whispered. With urge to beeline straight to the boat, they had to be smart, gather enough supplies; they had no idea how long this adventure would take.

Like two conspicuous stripped-shirt ninjas, the boys tip-toed into the kitchen. Colby took a fresh loaf of Wonder and laid every piece in two rows. Jacob grabbed the peanut butter and handed his brother the jelly. In five minutes, they had constructed ten sandwiches and Colby stacked them back in the bag, spinning a cinch for air-tight containment. Jacob grabbed one of the twelve-packs of Coke off the top of the ever-replenishing stack in the pantry. Luckily for the boys, their grandparents seemed more concerned with keeping stock of soda than their own health.

They inched down the hall and paused, just to make sure they were asleep. They heard their grandparent's snoring alternating peacefully through the particle-board door.

"Let's go," Jacob said, eyes wide.

"Should we leave a note?" Colby asked.

"No. A note would just make them panic. You want the cops ruining our trip? They might even put us in a foster home. Grandma and grandpa won't even know we're gone until supper tomorrow."    Jacob paused with one last detail. "But we should count our money real quick."

They overturned grandpa's old cigar box where they stashed their chore cash. Jacob smoothed out each bill, organizing it by denomination. "Forty-three dollars."

Colby exhaled. "Let's do this."


Into the night they scampered toward the boat, no looking back. The porch light now behind them, the pitch-black desert eve offered no illumination apart from the moon's long path mirroring on the water into the opaque vapor. They stepped in gingerly, placing their supplies of sugar and starch in the rear where the two paddles laid in wait. They each took a side of the bench, taking a paddle into both hands. Slowly, they ladled the murky water behind each blade in broad strokes until the boat propelled forward, replacing the anxious dread in their bellies with invincible juvenile adrenaline. They whipped their heads to one another, exchanging the same lip-biting smile.

The boys stabbed and flung into the fetid Sea like they were each digging a hole on their respective side. They reached a steady pace until Jacob suddenly paused, ruining their momentum which in turned the boat a half circle. They completed a 180, now facing backwards towards the horizon.

"What are you doing?!" said Colby.

"Shhh... listen. Is that grandma?"

In the distance towards the dock, which they could no longer see since they were now enveloped in the fog, they could hear grandma singing a sour aria; the dramatic shanty "Senta's Ballad" from The Flying Dutchman. Eerily, it bounced off the thickness of the mist as if she was right there in the boat with them.

*Johohoe! Johohoe!*

*Hohohoe! Johoe!*

*Have you met the ship at sea*

*with blood-red sails and black mast?*

*On the high deck, the pale man*

*The master of the ship keeps endless watch..*

Colby dropped his paddle, unable to recall ever being this scared of his grandma. The two of them sat looking off into the obscured shores from which they came, too unnerved to move an inch.

"Is she singing a song about dad? It sounds like she's saying the name Joe?" said Jacob.

"I don't know, but now I can hear why she's been weirding out Mr. Vera..." Colby whispered.          While terrified of the tune, they remained silent to make her words audible.

*Hui! How the wind howls – Yohohey!*

*In bitter gale and raging storm*

*he once tried to round a cape*

*he cursed, in mad fury, and swore:*

*"Never will I give up!"*

Jacob punched the air victoriously. "She must be singing about dad." he said, constructing a desperate narrative.

"Let's keep paddling. This is way too early for her to be up, and I don't want her to catch us out here," said Colby.

The boys resumed their vigorous rowing, determined to make as much distance between the shore and whatever the hell was out there. As they advanced, Grandma's voice began to fade.

*Hui! And Satan heard it! Yohohey!*

*Hui! Took him at his word! Yohohey!*

*Hui! And damned, he now roams*

*the sea without rest or peace..."*

***

Jacob and Colby rowed in silence, surveying the veiled landscape the best they could. It was past midnight, the moon now directly above them. The lunar rays cast a shadow from Jacob's side, darkening his view of the water. Colby's side was slightly moonlit, allowing him to witness the strange behavior of the fish below, an observance he immediately tried denying as a sleep deprived hallucination. But once the largest tilapia completed the morbid survival sequence, he couldn't help but say something.

"Uh, hey Jacob?"

"Yeah?"

"These fish are doing weird shit."

"Yeah? Well, they're fish. Fish are weird," said Jacob, whipping his head around with an exaggerated pucker of his lips, a de-fault wide-eyed "fish-face" meant to make his brother laugh. But Jacob wasn't laughing. He was still staring down at the water.

"No, this is like, really weird. I just saw a little fish get eaten by another fish, then another fish tear apart that fish, then the same kind of fish three times their size eat that one."

After various stuttering false-starts, the only insight Jacob could offer was half-hearted.

"Well, nature is weird, I guess..."

A fluid stretch of time passed. An hour, maybe two, but nothing in their obscured view could punctuate their journey as progress. Neither brother would admit it, but the excitement of their independence was slowly being overshadowed by a worry they might have no idea where they were going, no view of either shore to stabilize their navigation.

"Jacob, how do we know where we are headed? It's gonna be fucking dumb if we just end up at Salton City on the other side of the Sea."

"Oh, don't worry. I've got dad's compass right here," he said, handing it over to his brother. You can hold on to it for a while, just make sure the red arrow keeps pointing South."

Colby gripped it tight, thumbing the edges where the glass met the brass backing, thinking of dad. He began to whisper, a babbling yet focused prayer to their patriarch beyond the grave.

"What are you doing? Can you stop that?" said Jacob.

"Why? I'm just talking to dad?"

"Well, stop! You're freaking me out."

"Oh what, you can be all obsessed with dad and I can't have my moment with him?" Colby started to tear up, his pent-up emotion of the last month finally bursting from the dam.

"Give me that, you can't have it anymore if you're gonna be all weird about it."

Jacob threw the paddle down on the floor and tried yanking it from his brother. A struggle ensued, a sentimental tug of war that would only award them with disaster; both Colby's paddle and dad's compass plopped into the deep black water. Like a part of dad dying all over again, leaving them rudderless with despondence.

"Fuck!" Jacob screamed. "Now look what you did!"

"None of this would have happened if you just let me hold onto the compass, Jacob!" Now in full inconsolable sobs, Colby's layers of shame and rage felt useless to reconcile.

"Well, who's gonna row now, all by themselves, spinning us in a dumb circle in the middle of nowhere?" snapped Jacob. It was a sharp point in the dark physics of their predicament.

Colby grabbed his brother's paddle off the floor of the boat. In tearful hysterics, he straddled both sides of the boat, pathetically dipping the wood into the water back and forth as the boat rocked precariously. Only demonstrating it was impractical, he threw the paddle back down on the floor in  forlorn tantrum.

A wash of remorse fell across Jacob. No words spoken, he reached in the back, tore open the thin red cardboard and retrieved two cans of Coke. He flipped the tab and handed it to his brother, looking him in his moist eyes as his lips quivered.

"Sorry."

"Not as sorry as I am," Colby said.

"Oh fuck..."

"Jacob, you better stop cursing all the time, 'cause you're just..."

"No, shut up—look!"

Materializing in the distance, a silhouette unmistakable against the milky gloom.

The Fisherman.

Just like Mr. Vera described. A tiny boat with someone—or something—hunched over their fishing rod hanging over the side. The boys sat transfixed, barely breathing. Now that they had stopped rowing, a strange current dragged them towards The Fisherman and whatever lay beyond.

"What do we do?" Colby asked.

"I... don't know," Jacob replied, defeated. All his tough posturing began dropping, knowing this could be one of many reveals that Mr. Vera was telling the truth.

"Just, maybe don't look at it?" he suggested, but the flow of the Sea was already turning their boat ninety-degrees, now directly facing them towards the foreboding sight. With no idea who or what The Fisherman was, they could ascertain he must an insane man for being out there at this time of night.

Then, the far grimmer thought: what would that make them? Two boys who once had a choice not to go through with this insane idea.

A choice, since expired.

Suddenly, the Fisherman's arm outstretched like a whip-crack, pointing back toward their tread path.

*"Go back!"* said the cloaked man of bad posture. *"Go back or I will make you go back!"* A warning negated by threat from a wheezing voice drenched in pain.

The boys froze. Nothing else they could do but continue being carried by the current gaining strength by the second, terrifying them to further paralysis.

*"Do you want to die!"* The Fisherman screamed, not a question, but assured mortal intimidation. He stood up, drunkenly rocking his skiff as he hurled an object through the moonlit blackness. A shatter of glass on their boat's rear triggered two tandem bursts of squeal. Panicked and scrambling they leaned over each side. Jacob struck the water with the remaining paddle like a jackhammer, while Colby pathetically attempted to paddling water with his small hands. But the boat bobbed violently, rocked by an inexplicable swell of waves coming in from their ever-changing left-hand side. The Fisherman shrilled gratingly, rising in volume with the surge of the tide until the crashing water began to drown him out, his unholy hollering now just another indistinguishable texture in the aquatic cacophony. Both boys held onto their sides with death-grip determination, crying impressive obscenities as their boat surrendered to the circular flow, like the outermost orbit of a drain. Nowhere the boys could look back to, nothing past The Fisherman speeding toward them with a flailing lurch. Nowhere to look forward to beyond the massive whirlpool forming a quarter-mile radius, an inverted tornado plummeting into the water's foaming depths.

Then, jutting fangs: some half-formed while others so pointed they resembled ivory stalagmites. Hundreds of agonized eyes like scattered marbles, all displaced and misshapen over a scaly mound of tortured life. The shape of a whale or a small island emerged from the spiral, vomiting an unsightly geyser of stinking brine like festering pus from a scratched-open abscess, its healing forever interrupted. The heavy spray rained down, the sludge smearing solid on the boy's faces drenched from the turbulent waters as they both lay fetal on the floor of their vehicle. Jacob's head pressed into his hands, his brother demanding one more look at the monstrosity's thrashing mass creating its own cruel weather system the boys were now falling victim to. As it jumped in mid-air he saw its entirety: this bloated uncanny tilapia, magnitude of a blimp, hyper-evolved from its interspecies cannibalism yet glitched and stunted from toxicity. A writhing, gelatinous kink of creation beginning to howl, displacing water out its blubbery mouth in order to steal another un-fresh breath. Trapped between breeds and thirsts of survival, its shriek presented its very existence as sadistic torture, as if its own scales were double-sided barbs enforcing perpetual internal bleeding, yet nothing tangible to blame for its birth but the very waters it was entrapped in.

All bets off except the law of gravity, the aqua-behemoth crashed back into The Sea like an asteroid, the impact deafening as a cargo-train wreck. When it bobbed back up to the surface, Colby saw its countless demented eyes flash to their boat, its pupils blurred multitudes like black spots on albino ladybugs. It resumed its flapping rampage, trudging their direction, nearly serpentine in its motion. The incoming wave flipped the boat, capsizing the boys underneath until they felt what could only be tentacles wrapping around their arms struggling in vain to tread water...

***

Jacob opened his eyes to a nearly puncturing rhythmic pain on his chest – frantic CPR being administered by Mr. Vera. The boy gagged, turning his head to the side, expelling the atrocious fluid of the Salton Sea. He turned his head the other way to see him jumping over to Colby, repeating the process until his brother heaved Coca-Cola colored bile onto the pebbly sand of the shore. Disoriented, the boys looked up to see the sun just about to rise over the mountain range behind them. To their left, their grandparent's trailer. For the first time since their father passed, they were glad to be home.

"You boys okay?" he asked, wheezing as if he was in need of resuscitation as well.

The boys nodded, humbled by their aborted mission. They were grateful to be alive as much as they were mentally blasted by what just happened.

"Good. Now, let me make a deal with you. I won't tell your grandparents you stole and lost their boat as long as you don't tell them or anyone else that I'm the fucking Fisherman, okay?"

They nodded in solemn agreement, though it wasn't quite good enough for Colby.

"Okay, Mr. Vera, but truth—what are *you* doing out there?

Mr. Vera was almost back into his speedboat but paused mid-step, staring at the boys contemplatively. "Okay, but again you can't tell a soul... "

... I'm out there every night, fishing so I can feed El Basura Demonio. So far, I've been keeping him it out there in the deep end so it won't go terrorizing the rest of the Sea – I'm keeping him away from *here*," he said, pointing down.

"Yeah, but why you?" Jacob asked.

"Why not me? Because I know how this all happened... and I know that no one else at the factory will do anything about it. My co-workers know we've helped give birth to Basura Demonio, but no one has the cojones to talk about it," he said, reluctantly kicking a pile of fish rot back into the water. "Least I can do is make sure that whatever happens in the Sea, stays in the Sea." he said, stepping his other foot into the boat.

The boys sat on the beach mystified at Mr. Vera, their shoreline gargoyle. Not only did they owe him their life; they owed him their trust and never would they doubt him again.

"So, I gotta go back and finish – when I saw you boys were out there, I had just barely caught my first bite. But hey, at least you can tell people you made it all the way to the mouth of the Rio Nilo!" He smiled, amused with his accidental pun. "Ha—the mouth!"

Jacob and Colby cracked a smile, offering each other a look of relief.

"Oh, and hey, one more thing? Can we *please* get your grandma to stop singing one of these days? Last night she really, *really* had me spooked out there..."

He started the boat with an animated stab and turn of his key, saluting the boys with the other. Into dawn's creeping light he sped, getting smaller in the distance as he faded back into the mist.

# IT FELT LIKE A KISS

## BY COLIN BRIGHTWELL

Nikki wakes from nightmares filled with dead girl groups and beehive hairdos. Those songs from the oldies station always did have a little too much blood and heartbreak: bad-boy-with-a-heart-of-gold lovers crashing their motorcycles, teenage runaways learning that the real world is absolute madness. Not that Nikki is a sad teenage runaway. In her mid-thirties, she's understanding that running away can be a wonderful thing. Those old gals had it so wrong. But her nightmares, filled with Ronnie Spector and Lesley Gore, Mary Weiss and Patsy Cline, these women standing on stage with their beehives about to catch fire from under the hot lights, their heels about to snap, their voices strained and demonic from singing forever, make it seem like they have something to tell Nikki. She lies in enough sweat to fill a kiddie pool and her heart beats like the opening of "Be My Baby." She stares at the ceiling and tries to think of something like Metallica to push the girls away. Ronnie sticks around.

She reaches a clammy hand over to Johnny, grounds herself to the here and now. The ceiling flashes pale blue. Her phone. It can't be any later than seven and already someone is texting her. Johnny will be getting up soon to spend the day at the funeral parlor, comforting families whose own teenage runaways have ended up in the gutters of Kansas City, or crashed with their tragic lover. Those songs about blood and heartbreak, they ended like they usually do in real life. It's the perfect job for Johnny. Soft-spoken with kind eyes, like he was born to help families bury their dead. He wasn't the first-person Nikki met when she ran away to Kansas City, but he was the first not to judge what she ran away from. Not that Nikki told Johnny everything, just enough so she wouldn't be a stranger after living together for two years.

When she's sure that Ronnie Spector and Lesley Gore and the other singers are out of her head, she grabs her phone. Hard sleep crusts in her eyes. She rubs it away and sees the text from a New York City number. She goes blind for a second. This isn't real, she thinks. It can't be real. This is another layer of her beehive-filled nightmare. Soon enough, Mary Weiss will crawl out from under the bed, her mouth open and the vocals from "Leader of the Pack" sounding like they're being broadcasted from the end of the galaxy, and that goddamn motorcycle crash will stab her eardrums. She squeezes her eyes shut then opens them. The texts are still there. There are three messages: a link to the Orlons' song "Don't Hang Up," a picture of the bar she works at, and a simple little "; )."

She tosses the phone at her feet and sits up, careful not to wake up

Johnny. She looks at the phone as she gets out of bed and walks to the bathroom,

expecting it to start blowing up in an endless stream of messages from Rossi.

Instead, it's her head that blows up. How he got her number, how he found out

she moved to Kansas City, how he found out where she works. She thinks

maybe one of the other girls she chatted with online months ago, saying how

easy it was to get out, to buzz that beehive down.

She doesn't remember letting any personal details slip, just playing Big

Sister to the rest of the sad tragic imitation girls of the Supremes, the

Chordettes, the Shirelles. Rossi's favorites were the Shangri-Las and the

Ronettes and Nancy Sinatra. His clients preferred them, too. And Nikki was his

favorite little Shangri-La. All the high-rollers wanted to see her sing "Leader of

the Pack" with that blood-red curtain behind her.  Like they were part of the

Rat Pack. Rossi told her one night after his nightly private show, him always a

little too rough and lasting one Ronettes song, that it was all part of the fantasy.

You're selling them a dream, baby. These old guys live in the past. They wanna

think they're seeing some oldies girl group. And the chance to *really* see them,

that's where the money for Rossi was. Whether he really was in a five-foot hole

with some of the bigger city players and had to pay it off, Nikki and the others

didn't know. They only knew that he told them they were worth so much and

then took most of that away.

That blue light flashed again. Nikki grabbed her phone and wasn't surprised by the latest text. A link to another song, the Angels' "My Boyfriend's Back."

Making his own playlist. Letting the music do the talking, the way he usually did. Until he got angry. Nikki dug a trench in her memory bank, trying to pull out songs that he would send. She knew them all by heart, could sing them as good as any *American Idol* dope. But never as good as the originals, and Rossi made sure Nikki understood that. In his way. She closes her eyes and pictures the dance routines Rossi hammered into her and the other girls' heads, all that shoulder strutting and hip-shaking. It was all in the hips, Rossi told them. The hips made money.

Nikki burns those memories away and slowly gets off the bed. Johnny stirs and starts to wake. His work day starts soon. Nikki throws some faded jeans on, slips her phone in the back pocket, and tip-toes out of the bedroom and gets coffee ready. As the water hisses and the dark roast smell seeps in the kitchen, Nikki goes to the small closet by the front door and shuffles around through the layers of shoes and boots and heels. The trim on the back wall can be pulled away and she slips it off, reaches her hand in the darkness between the wall. Feels the culmination of years of dust bunnies and cobwebs, and maybe how the hand of Ronnie Spector or Rossi will grip her wrist in that darkness and drag her down, down, down. She closes her eyes and finally feels the envelope that's been sitting here since they moved in a year ago. It used to be fatter, as thick as a bible, when she first got into Kansas City in a 1999 Honda

CRV with a leaky transmission and shaky muffler. Funny how the years cost money.

It hadn't been much; this wasn't the lottery. Just what Nikki thought four years of her life were worth, when she itemized. All those nightly shows for Rossi, and the meaner of the clients – boys who didn't know how to share a ball in kindergarten and would kick you in the shin and smile that grew into men – convinced her that sixty-thousand was enough. The foot cramps from dancing in heels, all those beehives and bombshells, all those harmonies. All those sugary-sweet songs about how you can never go home again when you run away with the boy you loved. All the things Rossi liked to do alone.

She counts the money that's left – twelve-thousand – and feels her phone vibrate. The song this time is the Shangri-Las' "He Cried," followed with a ": (." It all comes back to her without having to hear it. It's like riding a bike. "Lose your shoes?" she hears Johnny behind her, speaking into a yawn. Nikki stuffs the envelope under her shirt and grabs a pair of sneakers that were white in another life.

"Cleaning the floors tonight," she says. "These guys won't mind getting a little dirty."

"They won't even notice," Johnny says.

They give each other a good morning kiss and he makes his coffee, says he's gotta rush; it's a long day of grieving families ahead. He takes his coffee to-go, jumps into a gray suit, and leaves. In the seconds between coffee and clothes, Nikki manages to tell him not to wait up for her tonight, that because it's

Thursday all those college kids from Rockhurst are going to gather at the Taproom to drink enough to last them the rest of their lives and it will take forever to finish up last call. In Nikki's hand her phone vibrates again and she knows it's not her boss. Johnny doesn't think twice about what she says, he understands she loves working late nights. Whatever brings in cash and makes her happy.

He leaves and Nikki feels self-preservation pump through all four of her heart valves. She looks at the phone to see another song from Rossi. This time it's the Crystals with "He's Sure the Boy I Love." That turns Nikki's mind into those stupid abacus toys she had as a kid: zigzagging and looping thoughts to figure out if Rossi has some hidden meaning with this song. Like, she thinks, does he mean *he's* the boy I love? Or, and this zigzagging turns her stomach over as well, does he mean *Johnny*? She shuts her eyes, pictures Rossi with a gun pointed at the back of Johnny's head. He already knows where she works, so she must think he knows about Johnny. And where he works. Unless she's overthinking. Her heart beats so fast she can't even feel it.

*where r u*, she texts back. She bites the inside of her cheek until she feels blood, mad she gave in so quickly.

Instead of answering her, another song pops up on the screen. Lesley Gore's "She's a Fool." Yeah, she thinks, tell me something I don't already fucking know. A fool for thinking she could rip-off sixty grand. A fool for thinking the world's creepiest music aficionado would let it slide eventually. A fool for thinking she could do what all the girls in those songs could never do and runaway into the crystal blue free and clear.

Rossi doesn't even wait for Nikki to reply when he sends the song that gets her into nuclear mode. Another Crystals song, like he's running out of girl groups. Nikki knows this song. Hates this song. One of Rossi's clients, some finance bro with a nasty reputation, worse than most, made Nikki perform every time he came in. That was usually once a month, twice if his wife ran out again. She would dance in one of those too-small rooms with a metal-framed bed that he sat leaning forward on and squeezing his knees, shaking her shoulders and hips (*it's in the fucking HIPS, baby!*), while he put the Crystals on repeat. Always the same song, every time. She looks at the song link, thumb hovering over it. She clicks it and hears it for the first time in three years. The Crystals with "He Hit Me (And It Felt Like a Kiss)." She thinks about that client, how he would pay Rossi an extra grand for thirty more minutes with Nikki. Those thirty minutes felt like a year lost in the Sahara. She lets it play to the end. She doesn't dance. The envelope of money stabs at her belly and she pulls it out, throws it on the kitchen table.

She screams at the phone. She is reflected in the phone screen, her wide-open mouth looming open like a gaping maw ready to consume everything in her path. Her screams make the Crystals disappear into the void until her throat catches her yelling and burns. She stares at the song and does the only thing she can think off. In the music app, she types out a song and sends it to Rossi, feels like a fool again for playing his fucking game but he asked for it. In the chat,

Lesley Gore stares at Nikki with hair that would catch fire from a spark. She raises him a "You Don't Own Me," anything to throw him off, to shut him up, and this time Rossi doesn't have a ready-made reply. Nikki feels the blood flow out from her cheeks. She closes her eyes, breathes, tries centering herself, and feels the phone vibrate after a couple minutes.

The Dixie Cups with "I'm Gonna Get You Yet," followed by a smiley face with cool shades on.

Nikki thinks, fuck it. Looks at the envelope and back to the phone. She hits the number and brings the phone to her ear. It only rings once.

"Hey there, baby," Rossi says.

***

When Nikki gets to the Blarney Stone, "Leader of the Pack" plays through the haze of the cigarette smoke from the regular drunks. There's the bartender, a weathered veteran of this watering hole, skin like a fast-food napkin left roasting in the sun for years, and two or three regulars. She called her boss at the Taproom, put on the tears about a dead grandmother that is as real as trickle-down economics. Nikki's a good worker, her boss says, take the day. Nikki told Rossi over the phone about this place, out of the way on the Kansas state line, no chance she'd run into anyone she knows. And if things get rough, she knows the Blarney Stone is the kind of dive where situations like that get put down as quick as the bartender can load a round of buckshot. Told him to meet her here around six, the rest of her day running the cracked sidewalks of the neighborhood until the lactic acid in her leg muscles twisted every fiber into hitch knots. She ran through that. Thinking.

She's unarmed, doesn't have a gun, Johnny doesn't believe in guns, and Nikki's fine with that. Only piece she's carrying is the envelope of Rossi's leftover cash.

The cigarette smoke is so heavy it filters the neon lights of beer advertisements like eclipse glasses. Rossi sits in a table in the back of the joint, facing away from the door. Like he knows Nikki's no threat. Mary Weiss whines on the speakers and if the morning drunks hate this sort of music, they aren't saying anything. They barely acknowledge anything except what's in front of them. The bartender gives Nikki a short nod when she walks in, then goes back to the *Garden and Gun* he's reading. Mary Weiss sings how goddamn sorry she is for hurting the leader of the pack.

Nikki walks over to Rossi slow, listens to the song. Memories from her on stage at Rossi's club flood back to her. Spotlights in red and blue and pink cascading on her. So hot it made her mascara drip down her cheeks that made her looked like she was crying. She never cried in those days. Not even with the meaner clients. Not even because of Rossi. She promised herself they would never see her like that. Not even the other girls she played Big Sister to. It's a promise she intends to keep.

The leader of the pack crashes on the speakers, his soul going where all teenaged bad-boys go: in the hearts of the tortured girl. Nikki would stomp those hearts given the chance.

The jukebox is one of those touch ones. They have every song, it seems. Nikki walks over to it, slips in a Lincoln. There are four songs ahead of whatever she will pick. Rossi's picks, she's sure. More beehive hairdo music. He doesn't care if he drives these drunks crazy. Nikki punches in letters, finds Hole. Needs something with edge. Something with bark and bite. She selects "Asking For It" and uses an extra two credits to skip the next song and play this. She doesn't mind the extra cost. It could cost an arm and a leg and she'd still pay it.

Rossi looks up when Nikki stands in front of his table. A half-full glass of whiskey is in his left hand. His right hand is bandaged, the pinky and ring finger splinted in a way that doesn't look like the nurses did it. Short, greasy black hair slicked back, like he's trying to look like he stepped out of a Scorsese flick. A too-loose Hawaiian shirt hangs from him. That was Rossi, Nikki thinks, never able to play it subtle. But it's his face that Nikki notices the most. What she remembers, it used to be full, the beginnings of an extra chin starting to form. Now it looks like someone threw putty over a skull and wrapped it around as tight as they could. She can see every curve of bone on his face, and his nose is broken and his right eye looks like a picture of space. The voice inside her head screams she hopes it's cancer, but the universe probably isn't that kind. He smiles when he gets a good look at her. Yellowed teeth ready to bite.

"You go to a salon or a butcher?"

Nikki runs fingers through her pixie cut. "Been like this for years."

"Tragic," he says. "Women with short hair, like getting rid of an umbrella after one storm."

"Grow your own out, then."

"It's slicked back for a reason, baby. Wrong genes."

"How did you find me?"

"Did you skip over my songs?" he says. "I had the Chordettes coming up."

"Yeah," she says. "Duh."

"What's this?"

"Hole."

"Isn't that the chick who killed Cobain?"

"Some boring white dudes started that rumor."

"She sounds angry," he says.

Nikki pulls out the envelope from her back pocket, throws it at Rossi's chest. He lets it stay there, his bandaged hand scratching his face. He stops, points at his bad eye.

"Should see the other guy."

"Probably better looking," she says.

He smiles wider and Nikki notices a black gap in his mouth, like it wants to swallow her whole.

"What's this? A letter of apology?"

"It's all I have to say."

Rossi opens the envelope, working his bad hand carefully. Nikki sees him wince. He hides it fast. She goes for a power move, something learned from her past, and turns to leave. End the conversation with the last word and before the other party gets the frog out of their throat.

"Sit your ass down," is all Rossi says, not looking up from the envelope. Nikki turns and the barrel of a pistol pokes out from under the table next to Rossi's thigh, the black hole at the end pointing right at her forehead. "Don't think I won't shoot everyone here. I'll be gone so fast, cops will be kept awake twenty years from now fat off their crap pensions wondering what happened. Sit. I'm not asking."

Nikki moves her eyes around the bar; no one notices a thing. Everyone is stuck in the bottom of the bottle of their lives. She sits, feels the gun staring at her like a threatened snake. Rossi licks his finger and counts through the cash. Takes his time doing it, lets Nikki know he's in no rush. He was always a deliberate counter.

"This a joke?" he says, without looking up from the money. Not that he needs to, Nikki thinks. The gun acts like his third eye. "Twelve Gs when you ripped off sixty. Been what, three years? This wouldn't even cover the vig's ass."

He tosses the envelope on the table like it's a piece of trash, sips his whiskey, grabs his broken finger and holds it like it'll make the pain disappear.

"This doesn't begin to cover the damages you left me," he says. Nikki sits there gripping her knees, digs her fingernails like she's digging for cartilage. "After you pulled your little, *stunt,* couple the other girls thought they could do the same. Pretty soon I was left with just some backup singers and no Ronnie. Regulars stopped coming in. Hell, even folks just wanting to hear some stupid girl group song. Some of the boys from Brooklyn had a slice of my ass so fast I didn't know what to do. All this time I've been thinking about you and where the costliest piece of ass in New York would run to."

Nikki notices sweat falling down Rossi's forehead. His face seems to sink in deeper and deeper every second. He doesn't even bother hiding the gun anymore. It shakes in his hand like it has a dirty little secret to tell.

"I never told them to run ," Nikki starts.

"Stop talking," Rossi says. "Doesn't matter if you did or not. You set a, what do they call it, a precedent. One by one. I managed to get people off my back for a few years, had to sell a few things. Had to work whoever was left extra hard. That's on you. But this," he held up his bandaged hand and pointed to his eye, "is my last warning."

"So what," Nikki says. "Take what's left. Go somewhere."

Rossi smiles like Nikki's the stupidest girl in the world. He always did have a knack for that. Nikki hasn't missed it. "They'd find me," he says. "This is pocket change to me, but just a penny to guys like them."

He brings the gun up from out of view, puts it on the table. It never leaves his hand, and when Nikki sees his finger on the trigger, pinpricks stab her spine.

"I don't want to hurt you, Nikki," he says, then moves his bandaged hand so that it covers hers. The pinpricks shoot their way up to Nikki's brain, severing synapses. "But you owe me."

Her hand freezes to the table. "That's all I have."

Rossi smiles like the bully who looks back when the teacher doesn't believe you. His fingers tighten on Nikki's hand. If the broken pinky hurts him, he doesn't show it, and that makes Nikki glued to her seat. He's a man who really doesn't have anything to lose, and men like that had a way of behaving like mousetraps wound too tight. Nikki knew her fair share of them, like the finance bro. You never knew when the coin would flip inside their heads. Neither would they.

Nikki looks around the bar. The fading sunlight through the thick glass windows makes everything look like a sad sepia filter. The bartender absorbed in his magazine. The regulars slumped over their Hamm's and Old Crow. She and Rossi might as well be the water stains on the ceiling. The Chordettes come over the cheap speakers, begging Mr. Sandman for that dream. She looks into Rossi's eyes and nothing can pinch her from this nightmare.

"What do you want."

Rossi leans back, placing the gun back on his lap. "I had to close up shop earlier this year," he says. "This business, it's ruined. You got OnlyFans and scam girls taking all the clients. Everything's at home these days. No one wants a show anymore."

"You can always collect unemployment," Nikki says. "If you're going to cry about it."

"Always the funny one," Rossi says. "One reason why I liked you so much." He pockets the envelope and Nikki still feels the gun staring at her. It must be starving. "I'll take this, see what it gets me with the boys back home. But you-," he points towards the speakers, now playing Nancy Sinatra's "These Boots Are Made for Walkin'," "owe me a show."

"No," she says. "Anything else, Rossi. I'm not doing that."

That bully smile again and Rossi leans forward. Off-brand cologne slam into Nikki's nose. "That's fine," he says. "That's fine. Why don't we take a little trip to that funeral home over in Brookside? Heard the guy who runs that is as sweet as can be."

Nikki looks down at her hands. Her nails have broken the skin on her knees and beads of blood pool and dry. Nancy's voice fills the bar, tears through the dense specter of menthol smoke, buzzes right into the center of Nikki's brain. And Nikki, looking back up at Rossi and his pathetic black eye and broken finger and pothole face, thinks, yeah, I'll give you a show.

Nikki smiles and thinks, *I'll show you how these boots walk.*


***

In the bathroom mirror of Rossi's short-term rental, Nikki stares at a knock-off Lesley Gore type. Rossi came prepared, she thinks, like the freak he is. One suitcase of Sixties-styled dresses and heels, and another one that was only big enough for a beehive wig that feels like it could sink a cruise liner. One wrong move and she thinks her neck will snap. She applies mascara, draws the green cat-eyes sharp enough to slice a diamond. She is a blast from her own past.

Through the closed door and drone of the fan, Nikki hears Rossi's playlist. Shangri-Las to Angels to Supremes to Ronettes. She feels stuck in a vacuum of humidity, her stupid dress ugly and hot. An inch taller in heels that she would pour acid on if she had any. She's the leader of all girl groups, the queen of them all. The thought of going out in that room and put on her show for Rossi, him watching her with eyes that crave like scavengers, makes her esophagus burn with bile. She hears him sing along, his voice shrill, like how he thinks a woman really sounds. She grips the edge of the sink and pushes her head into the mirror.

She thinks, if she does this right, she will do a piece of her show just like old times, do everything Rossi taught her, and he make him leave with his tail tucked between his legs and more broken fingers. Tell him this is what you get when you fuck with the queen of dead girl groups resurrected against her will.

Rossi bangs on the bathroom door like an annoyed Big Bad Wolf. Any harder and his fist would break through.

"Hurry up, baby," he says over the music. He goes back to that shrill fake singing with Lesley Gore. "You Don't Own Me," this time. Nikki thinks, the goddamn audacity.

Nikki applies the last bit of makeup, takes a final look at what used to be herself in the dirty mirror. She closes her eyes and thinks of the broken fingers she will give Rossi and walks out into the room.

Rossi sits on a twin bed. The rest of the place looks like a hotel room in purgatory: a single small TV next to the bathroom door, a sad overhead light, a chair that no one uses in the corner. Place must have been cheap, and Nikki knows that it tracks for Rossi. When Nikki walks out, Rossi looks at her and gives her that bully smile one more time. It turns the bile caught in her throat into cyanide.

"That's it," he says. "Don't you feel at home?"

Nikki bites her cheek again, tastes that sweet rusty blood and lets it stay in her mouth.

"Before you start," he says, getting up and walking to a small portable speaker next to the TV stand, "I want you to do it to this song." He fumbles with his phone, types with one good finger. He puts the phone down and sits back on the bed while the song queues up.

Nikki doesn't need a psychic. She knows what song he picked. Deep down, she had to know he would. Guys like Rossi just can't help themselves to seconds, even when they feel bloated. The thought of letting him off with just a few more broken fingers flies out the window as soon as the Crystals start up with that fucking song of theirs. "He Hit Me," and Nikki stares Rossi down with her sharp as razorblades cat-eyes.

And before either she or Rossi can understand what's happening, Nikki pounces on him. Takes Rossi by complete surprise, and she thanks her lucky stars. She sees his good hand going for the gun somewhere on the bed but she manages to whack it on the floor, a dull thud as it hits the cheap carpeting. Now they're a mangled and twisted bunch of limbs, Rossi trying to grab at her hair, only to realize that of course she put on that goddamn beehive wig like he told her to, and Nikki uses that moment to wrap her hands around Rossi's pencil neck, headbutting him in the nose. Her vision flashes white like stage lights, must have hit him hard, because he's yelling and blood gushes from his nose and she hears him call her names with a helium voice.

The Crystals keep singing, and over Rossi's muffled voice she can hear it clearer than she wants. She looks into Rossi's eyes while the Crystals sing about how the girl's lover hit him and how it meant he loved her. Her grip tightens and she leans closer to Rossi's face, so close she thinks any closer and she could see the molecular structure of the blood caking on his upper lip.

"Why'd you stop singing?" she says. She thinks it's a whisper but for a second she can't hear the music anymore. "I want you to sing."

Her hands loosen and Rossi coughs, a few blood specks land on Nikki's face. She doesn't mind. Let it mix with the mascara she feels running down her cheeks. They will both wash off.

"Sing."

He starts to, and in his eyes Nikki sees something. Behind that black eye, she sees that Rossi is thinking that maybe he won't get out of this. That maybe he should have let his queen of dead girl groups alone. That maybe he knew better than to come all this way just to prove a point. That maybe the coin inside her head flipped before his got a chance to. His voice cracks. The bandaged hand reaches up to Nikki and she bites the broken pinky, remembers something Johnny told her about how easy it is to bite through a finger. Nikki bites just hard enough to make Rossi squirm.

"Keep going," she says. She has his arms pinned now with her knees, pushing the bone in.

"'He h-h-hit me,'" he starts again.

And something goes off in Nikki's brain. It might be the song, it might be Rossi's broken voice, it might be the stupid too-heavy-too-hot beehive wig on her head that she throws off. It might be just the memory of everything Rossi put her through, and something other than self-preservation pumps through her heart.

Her arms shake and tighten their grip before she lets one hand go and slowly make its way down to one of her heels. She pulls it off and flashing in her mind is Ronnie Spector and Lesley Gore and Mary Weiss and how the leader of the pack crashes his motorcycle and mama said there were going to be days like this but how could they tell just how awful some of them could be and how the way to tell if a man loves you is in his kiss shoop-shoop didn't you know and all those girl groups singers with hair as big as skyscrapers are right there in Nikki's head and before Rossi can let out a puny pathetic "please," she brings the stiletto of the heel down on his black eye and it goes in so much easier than she thinks, like a fork piercing Jell-O, and she doesn't even think about doing it again she just does it and she hopes it felt like a kiss to him and for some reason she hears the crash of metal and realizes that his phone is still playing golden hits from an era long gone.

***

She drives slow through the empty Kansas City streets and gets to Brookside in ten minutes, her arms feeling like she just tried out for a body-building competition. If the camera adds ten pounds, then Nikki thinks dead weight adds about one-hundred. Rossi is rolled in three layers of sheets in the trunk, along with the beehive wig, his gun, and the dress. Self-preservation kicked in again, and he was loaded up and the rental cleaned the best it could within two hours.

The lights of Brookside Funeral Services are off except for the one at the bottom, where Johnny keeps the crematorium. She remembers when he bought a new building with room to put that in there, provide grieving families with a cheaper option without having to send their loved one to the staties where they don't give a shit. She pulls up to the back door, puts Rossi's car in park, checks the streets for any movement. Nothing but Kansas City still-life.

Johnny told her the code to the back door in case of emergencies. Nikki thinks this could count as one, even if Johnny doesn't need to know about it. She punches in the code and opens the door. Cold air makes a wall and she stuffs a wedge to keep the door open. This has to be quick, she says to herself.

Rossi is harder to move the second time around. Her lumbar curses at her but she tells it to get over it. She tells Rossi c'mon, let's go. There you go. He flops on the asphalt with a thud that makes Nikki's stomach turn but also makes her laugh. She drags him by the feet into the cold basement. The sheets slip off at the top and she gets one last look at his face. She lets the image burn into her head.

The crematorium isn't rocket science. She opens a draw big enough for a body and hits a button, amazed at how fast flames appear. It's like looking into the depths of Hell, the heat of the flames overtakes the cold, clinical air, and she thinks it's about a fitting resting place for Rossi as any. She hoists him up, doesn't worry about being delicate, until she hears a bone or two snap and is forced to swallow down bile. She goes back into the car, grabs what's left in the trunk, and tosses them on Rossi. Then she closes the drawer and swears she can hear something inside there. Screams or someone singing. She ignores it and waits. She fidgets and paces for an hour and opens the drawer again. Nothing but a pile of ashes that look like an anti-smoking ad. There's a little shovel on the wall and she scrapes the ashes off the drawer, figures if Johnny sees anything he'll think it was just something leftover.

She wipes away a layer of sweat off her forehead and locks the door behind her. Rossi's car is easy to drive and she takes it all the way to Broadway, parks it on some quiet residential street behind a CVS. As she's getting out, she remembers the heels left in the trunk. She grabs them and places the keys on the hood of the car. Figures, what the hell, it's Kansas City. Someone's going to come along, see a free car and take-off. No questions asked.

It's a two mile walk back to the Blarney Stone where her car is parked. The night is clear and through the screen of light pollution she can see a handful of stars, glimmering and shining like singers on a stage. After a mile, she doesn't even notice the burn of concrete through her cheap sneakers. She stops and throws the heels in a trashcan after a mile. Somewhere deep inside her head she hears a teenage girl crying over the death of a motorcycle loving bad-boy. The queen of dead girl groups smiles as she buries that girl in some forgotten cluster of fast-food bags and runs away.

# THE RECLUSE

## BY KAREN HARRINGTON

Looking out across the lake, Hopkins wondered why he'd kept renting the cottage next to his house. First, there was the constant risk that his secret would be discovered. And second, he didn't need the money. He didn't like people so it wasn't the company or conversation. Renters tended to be loud and untidy. And when they realized who he was, they were overly familiar.

"Maybe I'll close it up this year," he said, chucking a stone into the water.

In a back file of his mind, he discovered the true reason for the cottage: relevance. Hopkins enjoyed the flicker of being recognized by strangers for his work. He remained part of the literary canon, an ambition he'd pursued without success for years. Brutal rejections once dogged him.

Then came *Mudleaf,* his acclaimed masterpiece. Apart from the fact he'd stolen it, the work still brought him joy.

Hopkins walked the property in search of left behind items and trash. The fire pit, circled by six Adirondack chairs had a collection of amber and green beer bottles. He could have hired a caretaker to clean the property, but he preferred to inspect the grounds himself. He had relented to a cleaning staff who turned over the interior of the cottage following each guest's departure. He kept up with his own housekeeping. No one could ever discover the secret he kept there, behind the heavy upstairs door with the deadbolt. He'd taken a lot of pains to keep his life private. All his events, virtual. All his interviews, done by phone. It had garnered him a reputation as a recluse. It added to his mystique. It cost a high price, though. You had to live and have experiences to be a writer.

So, he had to rely on spying on the renters for new inspiration. The second reason for keeping the cottage open.

When the new guests arrived, he was tucked into his house, standing at the long window with a view of the lake. He heard the metal clunk of car doors and moved to the north-facing window. It afforded him a discrete view of his guests. A couple, set to stay just a few days. But three adults traipsed to and from the vehicle.

Hopkins heard a woman's voice shout. It was a tone he couldn't classify as happiness or distress. He observed the trio making trips up the cottage steps. All similar in shape and age. Two women and one man.

Something heavy thudded against the floor of the upstairs room. Hopkins jerked his head upward. It was time to feed Frank, the man behind the locked door. The original author of *Mudleaf.*

He prepared the tray and balanced it on one hand, using the other to lean into the stair railing. His right knee gave him trouble and the stairs pained him with each step. It was increasingly problematic, though nothing could be done about it. Hopkins couldn't leave the property and Frank couldn't be left alone.

By the time Hopkins ascended the landing, his knee screamed. He knocked four times then plucked the keys from the wall and unlocked the deadbolt.

"Hello, Frank," he said. "Bouncing around today?"

Frank paced the floor in socks with holes. His writing desk was overturned.

"Frustrated," Frank said.

Hopkins placed the tray on a large round table. The room was more of a suite, it being the combination of two rooms with a bathroom in the center. Hopkins never knew how he'd find Frank's room. It depended on Frank's moods and headaches. That day, there was a composition book brimming with Frank's maniacal handwriting and drawings. Frank's bed was unmade.

"Grilled ham and cheese, just like you like it, Frank."

"My favorite," Frank said, seizing upon the sandwich. He ate with the elegance and chomp of a goat, the same as the day before when he'd dined on the same sandwich. Each new day, the memories of previous hours erased and Frank was able to delight in his sandwich anew. Since the brutal car accident had deformed a side of Frank's face, it was something they both had to endure. Liquids were a worse sight. Sometimes Frank used a straw at other times he gulped. In all, he was a hideous creature.

"Take your medicine, Frank."

"Middle, middle. If I can get it right." Frank popped two pills into his mouth and jerked his head back so they would stay. He clutched his head. "Pain. Hopkins. Words are fuzzy. Will you help?"

"Yes, Frank. I'll help." Hopkins bent to upright the overturned desk.

"Good brother, Hopkins. My head hurts all day."

"It will feel better soon."

"Dessert cartoon," Frank tapped the table with each syllable as if typing out the words.

"Of course, Frank."

They sat in silence and watched cartoons, a ritual that calmed Frank and brought out his grotesque smile. Hopkins wriggled in his seat. Of all his daily chores, this one discomfited him the most. He studied Frank's damaged profile. Frank, too, once swam in the literary seas. For a time, Frank's reputation ran far ahead of his older brother's. How far the accident had taken him, stolen his brilliance. So much so that he worked on the same passage each day, failing to move even a paragraph forward. His brain had gnawed on the same unresolved plot point for twenty years.

Frank giggled and pointed at the television. He was now satisfied with the tragedy of an underwater fry cook and his thin nemesis. Hopkins didn't mind this next part of the night. The clearing away of the tray. The locking of Frank's door. The half-tumbler of Scotch that beckoned like a faithful friend who told pretty lies.

"Brush your teeth and rinse your mouth, Frank," Hopkins said.

Hopkins took the tray, locked the door, and crab-walked his damaged knee down the stairs. With his dessert drink in hand, he opened the patio door and stepped out into the night. A thin fog hummed over the lake. Screech owls sang a night song. A square of ice chimed inside his heavy glass tumbler.

Leaves crunched beneath Hopkins' perch. He saw a slim woman with bright white sneakers. She was heading toward the dock. He watched the white footsteps descend the slope until she disappeared into the fog.

He settled into his chair and nursed his drink.

"Oh, hello there!" The voice rose up from the ground. He'd been spotted.

"Yes, who's there?"

"Lorna, from next door. I seem to have lost my sister."

"On the dock," Hopkins said.

"Thank you," Lorna said. She aimed for the lake, then turned back. "I'm sorry to disturb you, but you're the owner, right?"

"Guilty."

"So you're...Hopkins Hawke?" Her saying it as a question grated.

"A fact buried on the website."

"Yes, well, I'm excited to meet you," Lorna said. "I'm also a writer."

She hadn't asked a question so he let her declaration go unanswered.

She fidgeted with her hair. "I'm hoping to get some writing done at the cottage. How long have you lived here?"

A question.

"Many years." He had to stay vague. Details put together by the wrong nosy person might lead to questions about Frank.

"I imagine you get a great deal of inspiration here," she said.

Hopkins saw the bright white shoe steps approaching. "Well, there I believe is your missing sister. Good night," he said. He rose and went inside. The two women's voices teemed with debate. Neither one seemed happy to find the other. He recognized the tone of quarreling siblings. He and Frank had frequent squabbles in the past. Before the accident, Frank could be moody and unpredictable.

*Your music is too loud, Hop.*

*Why did you move my pen?*

*That woman isn't right for you.*

The biggest fight was over the Farlon Anthology. Big names were attached to it. Hopkins finally had an acceptance. Then news got out that the co-editor was a man with a concerning reputation born from nasty encounters at writing conferences. Hopkins didn't publicly call out the editor's behavior.

Frank had. The others had.

Hopkins hoped it would blow over, but he was shamed by the community.

In the end, the whole project was canceled, muddying his reputation and taking with it Hopkins' first chance to shine. The day that news was announced, Hopkins had picked up Frank for lunch, and they'd had a horrible fight. It was an angry, rain-soaked drive with Hopkins clutching the wheel, white-knuckled with rage.

*You don't know how to play the game, Hop. You'll never make it until you do.*

These were Frank's last cogent words. They were cut off in traffic. The car careened off the road and into a fiery rollover. The passenger side wrapped around a tree.

The following day at the lake, Hopkins rose at dawn and completed his 500-word regimen. Then, he greeted Frank with a breakfast tray.

"Someday? Someday I will finish it, Hop,"

"It's a new day, Frank."

"The middle of *Mudleaf.* Middle, middle." Frank seized on a piece of paper and scratched out a note.

He sat down with Frank to make sure he ate. He excused himself, locked the deadbolt, and returned the tray to the kitchen. A gentle rain tapped at the roof. Today, the groceries would be delivered and he hoped the rain wouldn't make them late. The man arrived just after ten with two large cardboard boxes and a sack.

"Morning," the man said. "New guests at the cottage?"

"Indeed."

"Mind if I offer them my services?"

"Do as you wish." Once, a grocer had sold Hopkins' grocery list online. You couldn't deter the curious.

"You're missing the tomatoes and a rosemary plant," Hopkins said.

The man hurried back to his car and retrieved the items. "Need help carrying these inside?"

Hopkins frowned at the man. *No one enters my house.*

"Sorry, sorry, I remember now. Your rule."

The rain fell in sheets. The delivery man abandoned the jaunt next door and drove away. Hopkins lifted a dampening box and hurried inside. The slant of rain coated all his goods. On his second trip to the porch, he lifted the box and his knee gave out. He fell into a prayer posture and shouted as several canned goods spiraled away.

"Let me!" a woman's voice called. Hopkins eyed the woman named Lorna as she scrambled to retrieve spiced peaches. She hurried to the porch and without asking, began pulling Hopkins up. He grumbled but relented as his knee fired shots of flaming pain. She ushered him inside and sat him in a club chair near the fireplace. His heart raced as he protested.

"I'll take it from here," Hopkins said. He was terrified.

But she was unfazed as she made more trips to the porch and dragged in the rain-soaked goods. Thunder cracked and rattled the windows.

"I'll put the cold things away," she insisted, zooming about his kitchen. "You just rest. You need to get back to writing and get your 500 words. Rainy days produce the best words."

She winked at him. So she'd read his interviews.

"No, no," he said, hobbling toward the kitchen. "You'll sell the story of my kitchen. You must leave."

"Whoever did that with your grocery list was a jerk. Me? I'm going to say you sexually harassed me." Her face was blank.

Hopkins froze and recalibrated.

"Or I could say the same about you," Hopkins said, pressing his lips into a grin.

Something passed between them.

"Oh, well, I guess you could!" she said. "But I would end up internet famous." She had an easy smile and wide, deep eyes, a hint of cherry color in her hair. Altogether lovely, if not wicked.

Hopkins said. "That's what you want? To be famous for some tawdry lie?"

She let out a laugh. "You haven't heard a joke in a while, have you? I'm teasing."

The thunder cracked a second time, trembling the house. He heard Frank's pained yelp cut through. His gaze fell on the line of amber pill bottles on the counter. She had to leave.

"What was that?" she asked.

"The woods make all kinds of noises," he said. "You could catalog them in your writing. Do you write about nature?"

He knew that this question, coming from him, lauded Hopkins Hawke, could pull a dreamy writer from any distraction. Lorna fell into the trap.

"Well, yes, I do. A couple of novels so far. One self-published and a new one got me an agent, believe it or not."

"Impressive," Hopkins said. He wondered how long it would be before Frank began scratching at the door or knocking out his rat-tat-tat taps. "Tell you what. We'll talk more about it later. You must be eager to get back."

The rain let up a degree.

"Can I be honest?" she asked.

"Of course."

"That's why I begged my sister and her husband to let me come with them to the lake," she said. "I'd hoped…"

The house shook. Frank scratched at his door. Hopkins trained ear could hear the pawing.

"Oh, that's it. I've just realized what comes next," he said, shifting his eyes toward the desk. A thick manuscript sat there, neat and sentinel.

"That looks pristine," Lorna said. 'Is it ready to read?"

Hopkins walked to the desk. "Indeed. Now, the muse calls. Please let me work."

"Maybe you'll join us by the fire for a drink. I've read that you have done that a handful of times."

It was true. Hopkins had succumbed to the edge of his reclusive loneliness once or twice.

"Perhaps," Hopkins said. Lorna refused to move. He needed to get the pushy woman out before nature stopped concealing the sounds of a madman.

He walked to the door and opened it. He jutted his chin toward the porch.  A thunderclap boomed followed by pounding fists. Lorna was unaware and beaming. She stepped outside and Hopkins closed the door. Lorna remained on the porch and looked back into the thin warp of glass. He locked the door and headed for the stairs. His ascent was painful and fraught.

"Hop! Hop!" Frank screamed behind the pulsing door.

"Just a minute, Frank, just a minute," Hopkins said. "It's all right."

"All right. Write. Write. Must write *Mudleaf.*" Frank said.

Hopkins opened the door. Frank was drenched with sweat, blood dripping from a single broken fingernail. He'd clawed a deep notch into the door, another dent in a line of scratches. Hopkins eased Frank into his chair and fired up the TV.

"Frank, you've got to watch your cartoons when you get anxious."

"Read Hop."

"Let's watch TV."

"No, read. The story. The path."

Hopkins took a deep breath. He hated this game. The one where he had to read from *Mudleaf,* old pages of it inside a manilla folder on Frank's desk. He'd tried to remove the folder from Frank's possession, but that had failed. It was one of the few things Frank's brain clung to day after day.

"Settle down now and I'll read."

Hopkins began to read from the draft pages. Frank mouthed the old words. Words Hopkins had altered.

"The van gave a sudden lurch that knocked Franny's head into the side wall," Hopkins read.

Frank rose. "But the middle, can't get it right, Hop."

"You struggled with that," Hopkins admitted. "You'd landed the ending with brilliance, but couldn't build a bridge to get there. And now you suffer from eternal writer's block, unable to break free."

Frank's eyes softened.

"Maybe a cartoon now," he said.

The afternoon was claimed by the two brothers watching television until Frank grew tired and crawled into his bed. Hopkins covered him with a quilt their mother had sewn. He left, securing the lock behind him. It had to be done. In those first years after the accident, Frank had wandered off and forgotten his way back.

Arriving downstairs, Hopkins was reminded of the woman. Lorna. He tried to see his house through her eyes.

The sink was full of two of everything. That could be attributed to laziness. But the row of pill bottles? Would Lorna gossip about an untidy writer who took numerous prescriptions? How could he have been so careless as to let her inside?

He'd have to charm her and give her a better story, a better anecdote. Could he sound interested in her writing and ambitions? Maybe he hadn't played the game right in the past, but now he had years of experience shifting the conversation away from himself and onto others.

He'd have to nurture Lorna's belief in herself. Not that she seemed to be in doubt.

The following night was clear and cool and the very advertisement for October. He lay in wait for the guests at the cottage to visit the firepit. There, from his spy window, Hopkins watched as the male guest, Lorna's presumed brother-in-law, built a fire. The sister with the white shoes carried forth a cutting board, stacked with all manner of snacks. And Lorna in tow with a wine bottle and stemware. The window was cracked open and Hopkins could hear snatches of conversation.

"Oh, gosh, I forgot the bottle opener," Lorna said. Her phone buzzed. "Oh, let me take this." She settled the phone to her ear and wandered toward the cottage, up the steps, and through the door.

The man muttered something that annoyed his wife. "You know how Lorna is," she said.

"Why did we let her push in?" the man asked. So it was one of her traits, Hopkins thought.

"Because she's crazy enough to think this Hawke guy is going to help her."

He filled in the gaps of what was being said as the pair talked. Lorna was an annoying third wheel.

Lorna returned to the firepit, in full conversation mode. "My writing group loves the first draft and they are so jelly that I met THE Hawke and saw the inside of his house. He's sort of a slob."

"That's sort of rude," the sister shot back.

"Whatever," Lorna said.


Hopkins made Frank's tray and performed the routine. Frank seemed tired and listless. For good measure, Hopkins added an additional sleeping pill to the menu.

"Good night, Frank. Sleep well."

"Good night, Hop."

Hopkins gathered the tray and locked the door. He had to pull on it a second time to close it securely. The foundation of the house shifted in the fall. Some doors loosened, some stuck.

Downstairs, he made his cocktail and prepared to move to the porch where he was certain an invitation would be proffered. He'd mock protest, but relent.

The scheme worked. Hopkins joined them around the circle.

"You have a beautiful property," said the wife. "Have you used this as a setting?"

"Yes," Lorna answered. "I'm sorry, I've read every article about you."

Hopkins took a sip of his drink. "You've done your homework."

"Like a true fan would," Lorna said.

The husband poked at the fire. "Fine line between a fan and a fanatic."

"Hush, Josh, you don't understand true brilliance. His writing is transcendent. The Hemingway of our time."

"Just without all the wives," Hopkins laughed.

"I thought Hemingway was controversial, now," Josh said. "What do you think Hopkins?"

Lorna seethed. This was supposed to be her conversation. "Josh, what do you care?"

The trio sat in silence, concentrating on the flickering light. Hopkins was ready to get done what he'd come there to do.

"Now Lorna," he said. "Every writer has a country. Themes they play with. Tell me, what is *your* country?" Hopkins stood his elbow on the wide arm of the chair and propped his head beneath his chin, his eyes fixed on her. She relaxed into herself and gazed at the sky. Lightning flashed in the distance.

"Relationships, I think."

It was as banal an answer as he'd ever heard.

"Yes, the quagmire of the human condition. Tell me more about your work. Just a nugget."

Here, Hopkins slung his ice cube around his heavy glass and waited for the response, aware that husband and wife were feeling left out.

"My agent says it's about love and loss," she said. "She loves it, but wants a complete rewrite." She went on in some detail. "....and so then, Marty, the main character is redeemed. His father has given him grace."

"Your country is familial relationships," Hopkins said, leaning toward Lorna and almost whispering. "Did your father ignore you?"

Lorna's sister let out a laugh.

"Lorna refused to be ignored," she said.

Lorna deflated by half, sinking into the back of her chair. Then she poured another glass of wine. Josh excused himself and went back into the cottage.

"That was rude," Lorna said.

Hopkins let the silence settle between them. "Great artists are often cursed to be misunderstood, my dear." He held his glass aloft, beckoning her to clink her wine stem in agreement, cementing their bond. She did. *There,* Hopkins thought. *I've brought her on my side.*

Josh returned with two amber bottles. "What's your pleasure, Hopkins? You need topping off before the weather turns."

Hopkins knew he should resist.

"Why not," he said, offering his tumbler to Josh.

"Now Josh's family, that's a story," Lorna said.

"Lorna, don't," her sister said.

"It's true, though. They put the fun in dysfunctional," Lorna said. "Hopkins, I've based a character on his mother. Classic borderline."

"Lorna!"

Josh took a drink. "Told you we shouldn't bring her," he said, then turning to Hopkins. "She always does this, Hopkins."

"Always does what?" Lorna asked.

"People's lives aren't for your consumption and entertainment, which is why no one wants to share with you anymore," Josh said.

The discomfort was delicious to Hopkins.

"Hopkins, you drew inspiration from your life, didn't you?" Lorna asked.

"Of course, you've studied my life and know the answer," Hopkins replied. "My current work in progress lives in the same country, yet is a departure. And speaking of work, I must take my leave."

Hopkins pushed up from the wide Adirondack armrests but fell back into the seat. His face reddened. He lifted himself again with some effort and felt his head grow dizzy.

"Thank you for the enchanting conversation," he said. He took a wobbly step forward. The bad knee quaked and he had to rebalance himself against the back of the chair.

"Here, let me help," Lorna said.

His heart thundered as his mind sent up a barrage of red warning lights.

"Why thank you," he heard himself say. Despite his misgivings, he had to continue giving her grace. A helpful arm might save him from further embarrassment or some rumor she'd write online. The pair ambled toward the house, up the steps and at the threshold, where he intended to part ways and return to the spy window and listen to the guests gossip.

"I want to see you settled," she said.

He blocked the doorway with his body.

"It's fine," he said. "I forgot to eat. I get so immersed in my writing that I forget. You get swept up, you know? I imagine that happens to you, dear Lorna."

Her eyes brightened at being compared to a literary genius. "Yes, all the time."

She persisted in standing there. He fantasized about pushing her, sending her tumbling down the steps, cracking her neck, such was his revulsion. A loud thud boomed from above. Lorna looked up.

"That old tree branch might snap with the winds," he said. "Now, I must say goodnight. Afraid I will earn my reclusive title for the next several days as I stay locked in with my editing."

"Of course," Lorna said. "Could I ask you a huge favor? Will you sign my copy of *Mudleaf?* I'll go grab it and be out of your hair."

He sensed she'd hound him if he refused. And of course, if he wrote a worthy inscription, she'd be more generous with her gossipy posts and forget all about his sloppy kitchen or watching him stumble walk to his house.

"I'd be honored, but be quick," he said. She dashed out. He moved to the kitchen and poured a huge glass of water. He heard another great thud from upstairs. It was followed by a peal of thunder. This had to go fast.

He went to his desk and selected a pen. There she was, sashaying through the door, sidling up to him at his desk. He glanced at the sharp letter opener. He imagined it dripping with her blood. Then, he pushed aside the thick, printed-out tome.

"Bespoke," she said, reading from the top page. "What an interesting title."

"Indeed."

She held a hardback of *Mudleaf,* a sharp black and white photo covered the entire back jacket. The book club edition. And she'd called herself a true fan.

Hopkins took the book into his hands.

Silver streaks of lightning flashed through the windows. The house rattled. "The strangest October," Hopkins remarked as he put the book on the desk, leaned over, opened the title page, and began writing. He clapped the book shut and pivoted upright to face Lorna. She wasn't there.

She was at the foot of the stairs, gazing into Frank's deformed face. How had he escaped? Had the shifting foundation loosened the door so much that it opened?

"Hop," Frank said. "Hop will be mad."

"Hopkins, who is this?" Lorna asked.

Hopkins quickened his steps toward the stairs and thrust the copy of *Mudleaf* into her chest. "Time to go."

"*Mudleaf*," Frank pointed to the book.

"Yes."

"My book. My story. The middle," Frank said.

"What is this?" Lorna asked.

Hopkins turned to Lorna. "My brother, he gets confused. He suffered a great injury."

"Middle, middle, must finish the middle," Frank stammered. "Must finish *Mudleaf.*"

"But Frank, here it is. *Mudleaf* is finished," Lorna said.

Not for the first time, he regretted keeping Frank's original book title.

"The middle part, we will work on tomorrow. Right Hop? Finish *Mudleaf.*"

"You're upsetting him, Lorna, now please go," Hopkins said.

Lorna's eyes darted from Hopkins to Frank and back again. "Frank, did you write *Mudleaf?*"

"This is absurd," Hopkins said.

"Frank writes. Hop helps," Frank said.

"I insist you leave now!" Hopkins shouted.

Lorna smirked as she connected the dots. "Who doesn't love those twisty stories about authors and plagiarism and faux writers? But here...it happened."

"Those are baseless claims," Hopkins said, taking Lorna by the elbow. She wormed out of his grasp.

"Hop helps," Frank said.

"What else, Frank? What did Hopkins do?"

Thunder shook the cabin. The boom made Frank sit on the stairs and rock back and forth, a string of drool hanging from his disfigured mouth.

Hopkins felt his face redden. "I demand you leave now or I will call the police?"

The two of them had a stare-down. It ended when Lorna said, "I don't think you will. You might say I have control now."

Rain pelted the windows. Pea-sized hail tapped at the glass.

"Tap tap tap. Hop typed. Rat tat tat. Frank wrote on yellow paper. Hop typed." The flash of memory caused Frank to grin. "The idiot editor, Hop, didn't like you. Rat tat tat."

"That's not what happened, Frank. Your memories are flimsy."

"I think there's more to this story," Lorna said. "People might like to talk to Frank about his writing. I seem to recall old articles about the writing brothers, one who had an accident."

"Frank. Frank lives behind the locked door. Lock the door and write and finish *Mudleaf* and don't get lost. Don't get lost."

Lorna glared at Hopkins.

"It's for his safety. His short-term memory is lost. Every day, he forgets the previous day."

"For his safety or to keep him quiet? You took his words."

"Frank's book," Frank said.

"No, Hopkin's book," Hopkins shouted. "Now, Lorna. You must leave!"

Lorna let out a laugh and plunked down on the sofa. "What a rumor this could be, true or not?"

He thought of six ways to kill her, starting with the iron poker by the fireplace. He searched his desperate mind and there, in his misery, found a Faustian bargain. She wanted fame. Big fame. But she lacked the talent. "I can help you, Lorna. If you are silent about Frank, I can help you a great deal. Elevate your career."

"I doubt that," Lorna said. "Not once the truth is revealed."

He took deep breaths, wondering if this would work.

Part of Hopkins had always known someone might pull the strings of the *Mudleaf* problem. Someone who wouldn't understand the obsession to be published, best his detractors, and not let the sheer genius of Frank's unfinished story lay dormant. In the end, it was only stolen valor by half, he'd rationalized. He had to be respected and lauded. He was once ravenous for it.

And here, inside his shaking cabin in the woods, appeared to be his fame-thirsty, female equal. He wondered if she would keep her silence if she got something for it.

His eyes stayed trained on hers. He tipped his head toward his writing desk. The crisp white pages of the *Bespoke* manuscript seemed to vibrate.

"A gift," Hopkins said.

"A gift?"

"My manuscript for your silence."

Lorna turned toward the glowing stack. "Is this proposal what I think it is?"

"It's perfect. It fits your country. It will take your finessing with your agent, you can't skip that step. But it's so complete, you'll get to cut in line. And you said yourself, that your novel needs a complete rewrite. That could take months. Years. Why wait?"

Lorna rose from the sofa and went to the desk, where she picked up the first pages of *Bespoke*. A brilliant, finished Hopkins Hawke manuscript would, with hope, allow her to achieve her goals.

"How do I know you won't wreck this? Come out accusing me of stealing? Or worse, rush ahead and get it published?"

"I won't."

"You are willing to sacrifice all of your efforts for this?"

"I would and I will," Hopkins said. "It's yours. I wish to protect my brother. He's fragile."

Lorna beamed. "You'll delete all the copies?"

"You researched my methods. I print out the draft and delete the electronic file and begin again by hand. There's no verifiable trace of my hand on that story. To protect my brother," I'll make sure of it."

"You mean to protect yourself," she said. "But this could work."

"This is the best work I've done in years. I hate to sacrifice it, but sacrifice I must."

Hopkins went to the kitchen and fetched a brown paper grocery sack. He took the pages from Lorna's hands, set them flush with the others, and slid the whole manuscript into the paper bag.

"You'll be on your way. Josh and your sister and your family will eat their words. Think of it!"

She grasped the paper bag. He felt the key click into the lock of the bargain. The deal complete. Hopkins guided her to the door. She went easy now, lost in her dreams. She left as if by floating, forgetting her signed copy of *Mudleaf.* Good, Hopkins thought. No trace, no connection.

Hopkins turned his attention to Frank.

"What about a cartoon, Frank?"

"Cartoon,' Frank said.

"What if we moved someplace new," Hopkins asked, as they journeyed up to Frank's room. "Someplace without stairs."

"No storms," Frank said.

"Yes," Hopkins said. "No storms."

Now that he'd escaped her trap, he'd make sure Lorna would never find him.

\#

It was two years later when Hopkins was cleaning the lunch dishes and Frank was sleeping behind the locked door in a separate wing of the sprawling home he now owned by the sea. He refused to compromise on being near a body of water. Instead of guests to spy on, Hopkins walked the beach and eavesdropped on couples and families. The TV was on in the background because the grocery delivery was due to arrive soon. A string of chimes hanging from the eaves. The noises provided cover for any unusual sounds echoing through the house. Hopkins didn't take chances now.

Hopkins ignored the TV news, but on this day, a story caught his attention, owing to the name Lorna.

*"Debut-author Lorna Lane faces fresh charges of plagiarism for her novel, BESPOKE, published earlier this year."*

Hopkins dove toward the remote and pressed record.

*A claim came forward through Ms. Lane's publisher after a writer claimed her work was nearly identical to a manuscript he'd completed three years ago while vacationing at a cottage near the home of acclaimed author Hopkins Hawke. The man told authorities he'd left his manuscript behind in hopes Mr. Hawke would read it.*

*Ms. Lane's representatives were not available for comment. However, we can reveal through Ms. Lane's social media posts that she did once stay at the same cottage near Hawke's home.*

Hopkins stared into the file photo of Lorna, a rictus grin beaming from her author photo.

"Gotcha!"

It was true that one September day the author of *Bespoke* had thrust a manuscript upon Hopkins with such force it resembled a reverse mugging. One solitary night, he'd read the first chapter and it found the writer had aped his style. Frank's style.

"You thought you had control, Lorna," Hopkins said to the TV. "Who knows how to play the game now?"

Any wild stories about Frank and *Mudleaf* Lorna concocted to get out of her plagiarism scandal would work to discredit her, Hopkins thought. She'd appear foolish with zero proof.

A knock at the door pulled Hopkins from his schadenfreude. Hopkins put on a pair of glasses, pulled down a ball cap, and stepped out onto his porch.

A delivery woman checked her clipboard. "Delivery for Mr. Monk?"

"That's me."

Lorna would never find him. No one would.

# CLICKER HILL

## BY ERIC O'NEAL

I was immediately set upon by the very sweaty mayor when I stepped off my train. His fingers had moistened and creased about a third of the brim of his hat, which he was holding at about thorax-level. He didn't spare any pleasantries. He didn't look like he had the nerve to delay any longer.

"I'm so glad your train was on time," he spewed. "Now, we are dealing with a very delicate situation. As you know – I assume you were able to read the wire?"

I let that one go. He looked about one frayed nerve away from complete loss of bowel control. I told him I was caught up on the details.

"We'll be going to the edge of our territory, but first we'll pick up the sheriff. He may ... I don't want you to think you aren't appreciated ..."

"Wouldn't be the first time one of us was brought into hostile negotiations," I replied. I knew exactly what the sheriff would think of my trespassing there.

"No, not hostile but …." He knew he couldn't in good conscience finish that sentence, so he changed tack. "Things are sensitive and I felt it wise to incorporate an Investigator." After the trip I'd made to get to Clicker Hill, I was anticipating to agree. It's always a shame to be dragged across land and sea just to be told my presence is no longer necessary.

I climbed into the back of the automobile and listened as my train whistled away down the tracks. The next chance I had to leave was well off – the one I actually used, in fact. Mayor Chisham and I rode in relative silence for the short journey over to the jail. When we pulled to a stop, I laid eyes on the sheriff. It wasn't that he had a handsome face, by any means, but he made no attempt to disguise his disgust at seeing me. Chisham was sitting beside me, opposite the sheriff, and so had to totter around the auto in order to make proper contact with the sheriff. In the time it took to do so, the sheriff had already begun voicing his displeasure. I recall hearing a very clear "fuckin' Investigator," amongst other, lesser whining. I watched Chisham and his sweaty, crinkly hat beg and plead the sheriff to put aside his obvious distaste for working alongside myself. It was reminiscent of arguing with an outhouse to not reek so obscenely. At least it was good to know exactly where I stood in the matter I was undertaking, as well as who I could trust to make honest decisions.

Somewhere in the middle of the arguing, the deputy emerged from the jail, smearing his hands on his pants to rid them of some unpleasant substance. He intervened and managed to drag Chisham and the sheriff apart, eventually hauling the latter off to their own auto. Chisham floundered in the air for a moment, then returned to the seat beside me.  He made some poor attempt to excuse the sheriff's behavior, but I had none of it.

"We Investigators are tools to be used for specific situations," I said. "Some people prefer to work with their hands, alone.  You clearly prefer a more pointed approach, hence my being here.  You really don't have to pardon any shortcomings."

Chisham seemed moderately consoled by my plainness.


Our two-unit convoy arrived at the edge of human land after a lengthy, dusty trip across loose dirt and brush.  A collection of self-important men was gathered on our side of a very simple-looking fence.  We climbed out of the auto and joined them.  Most of them, when they caught sight of me, silently declared allegiance with their sheriff.  I followed Chisham through the lot of them to the fence.  On the other side of the fence, another human stood just in front of a tricondylanth.  Chisham addressed the non-human.

"As arranged, we've come to have a look at the body.  May we cross?"

Its three-hinged mandible opened as it made a series of sounds not unlike the ticking of a clock, but much faster, and less percussive.  It evoked memory of a stone skipping across the ice of a small, frozen pond, just more clipped.  The tricondylanth's human – an interpreter – responded.

"This gathering is received as a threat."

I didn't need an interpreter to know that. The sheriff threw up his hands and muttered something about this being a "waste of time." The deputy approached the mayor.

"I'll keep the boys here if you two want to go in. Sheriff, too."

"I think that would be appropriate." Then, to the tricondylanth, Chisham made an addendum: "I'm sorry for the affront. Only three of us would like to enter. The rest will wait here."

Again, the tricondylanth responded, in its own way.

"This is amenable," the interpreter said, opening the wide gate a little. The space was just wide enough for a person to pass through, although the gate was only about waist-high. Chisham and I proceeded through, followed by the sheriff, who again mumbled, this time something about "fuckin' clicker."

Mirroring the congregation of men by the fence, the body was surrounded by several tricondylanths and fewer interpreters. From what knowledge I had of the creatures, it was not uncommon for humans to be accepted into the fold as interpreters. Outside of duties, these humans were segregated into their own small reservations within tricondylanth land. This irony was pointedly ignored by the sheriff, whose surname was Myrl, I gleaned from Chisham. When we made contact with the group of tricondylanths, I glanced over to see Myrl pretending not to fiddle with the catch on his holster but to simply hold his hands on his hips. Tricondylanths' eyesight is markedly better than that of humans, I feel it necessary to add.

"The body is just here," said one interpreter.

"We can see that," Myrl shot back. He eyed the group, not making any moves to inspect the body.

Chisham was holding his hat again, careful to crease a new part of the brim. "If I may, I'd like my – the Investigator takes a closer look."

The tricondylanths acquiesced via interpretation.

I knelt down by the body, taking in the most obvious information. By the attire, it appeared to be a prostitute. I hadn't been in town long enough to visualize it, but my research told me it contained a brothel. I hardly expected Chisham to be forthright with such information, partly from his nervous demeanor and partly from common decorum. Still, I'd imagined Myrl would have told him at least as much as what kind of person the victim was. I looked the body up and down from a short distance. Before disturbing the scene, I requested permission.

"We know where she is, if that's what you mean," grumbled Myrl. "Do your fancy in-ves-tig-a-tion."

Firstly, I tilted the face toward my own. The head was askew, laying on its left side, facing toward deeper tricondylanth territory. I brushed aside the curls and studied what was left of the face. Even without its skin, the sharp jawline caught my attention. It made me wonder how stupid the killer was. Next, I held up the hands, perhaps looking for a sign of struggle. Blood under the fingernails can completely turn an investigation, under the right circumstances. I collected no such evidence. There were several healing cuts on the arms, however.  I skipped over the trunk of the body before I confirmed my

suspicions.  I knew doing so would cause a fuss.  I ran a hand down the inner line

of each leg, looking for a stowed weapon of any kind.  I turned up nothing, aside

from more healing cuts, none more than a centimeter in width, if that.  The

tightly laced boots were worn, the leather cracked along natural seams and both

the sole and toe were dusty as the ground.  The only other disturbance to the

body, as far as I could see, was the abdominal puncture wound.  No blood was

apparent under the body, despite the significant blood loss the victim should

have sustained.  It was time for me to complete my inspection.  I turned to

Chisham and Myrl.

"You have my assurance that I would never improperly handle a

woman, living or dead."

Chisham's brow furrowed, tilting his head.  "I don't follow."

Myrl just snorted.  "Didn't think you could touch a woman, at all."

These were both suitable statements of permission for me.  Laying a

heavy hand upon the right breast, I looked squarely at Myrl.  "I take it you did

not want to look further than the garb.  If you had, you would have known this

is not a woman."  Under my hand, the corset's bosom crumpled flat against the

chest.  The left side did the same under similar pressure.  I knew I had Myrl'

attention when he got in for a closer look.  He made no sound, just stared.

"My God," Chisham whispered.  He looked about ready to collapse.

"Care to explain why someone murdered a man, shaved his limbs, curled his hair, dressed him up, and skinned his face, sheriff?" I inquired as plainly as pie. "Or at least who this is, since you seem to know."

Myrl refused to look at me. "Son of a *bitch*," he hissed, turning around. "Mayor, we gotta talk." Though Myrl was beckoning Chisham, the latter refused to budge. I don't think he was listening. The tricondylanths started talking to each other, in his stead. "Stop all that goddamn clicking!"

That got their attention, and squarely on the one person who was armed, no less.

"They prefer 'trilling,' sheriff," one of the interpreters said. It looked like they were all saying the same thing at once. "Using that word is considered derision."

"I don't give a shit –" Myrl started.

I intervened with trilling of my own. It was not perfect, I knew, but it was enough to draw heat away from the blowhard and onto someone more sensible.

<Ignore,> I said. <Wrongdoing. Wait. Help.>

"Of course you can," I heard Myrl say over the response.

<Remove person. You: authority. Less trespass.>

Their language cuts straight to the point, much to my satisfaction. I interpreted the message from the tricondylanth who spoke to mean that Myrl was no longer welcome, and that I was allowed to conduct the investigation as long as I did not bother them too much.  I said as much to Chisham.  One of the interpreters nodded, but loosely, indicating that I had missed some subtlety.

Myrl cursed all the way back to the fence, and a bit more back to his auto, where the deputy and his posse awaited news.


Chisham had told me who he had suspected the victim was, on the way back from the site.

"We'd heard of a wanted criminal in the area.  The wire said his name was Ibrin, Ward Ibrin.  He was about the same build as the ... as the body, and he had long hair.  He was on the run for some time."

All that explained was why the corpse didn't need a hairpiece.  Before we returned to town, I asked about Myrl's inspection, or apparent lack thereof.

"To be honest, I'm ashamed," Chisham whimpered.  "I'd hoped my sheriff would have taken the murder of a girl more seriously.  Now that it's likely Ibrin, he really should have been more thorough.  I know it's on their land, but ..."

I let Chisham stew in his own feelings for the rest of the ride.  I had no need for his crumbling confidence, nor for Myrl's self-important air.  It was a disappointment to know a lawman neglected to collect the details, whether or not the body was in his jurisdiction.  Even worse, the tricondylanths deferred the investigation to me, underwritten by Myrl, so he definitely should have taken more than a cursory glance at the report.  His deputy, Urban, told me as much.

"I was the one who got the message," Urban said once we disembarked from our vehicles. He was watching the sheriff stomp back into the jailhouse. "One of the folk who live with the clickers told me there was a dead body that looked like a whore, so I relayed that to him. He just sorta huffed about it and said he'd ask the whorehouse about it at some point." Urban looked me up and down. "I didn't think Mayor Chisham would've called in an Investigator for this. He really must be cracking."

"It would appear so," I replied. It didn't take an Investigator – or even a deputy – to reach that conclusion. "Any reason why?"

"Well, I think it has something to do with Mama Hooch. She's the hostess what runs the whorehouse. She's been toeing the line, looking for more money to flow in through ... she's been looking for ways to get her hands on hallucinatory herbs."

I became even less excited to inspect the brothel.

"Ibrin." Urban held his hands on his hips and stared incredulously at the dirt. "Goddamn. He really came through here."

"That seems to be the case."

"We'd got a warning, sure, but we never really thought we'd see such a slippery bastard. You know he held up the bank in West Thormosa? Big fuckin' bank. That was ... some two or three years back."

"Good to know." Urban was proving to be a regular fountain of information, almost entirely unprovoked.

Urban looked around idly, again wiping his hands on his pants. "Well," he said, for no particular reason, before following in Myrl's footsteps.

I scanned the town from beside the mayor's auto before making my own move. It was as basic a desert town as any other. The limited passenger train schedule only served to isolate it further. I began to walk. I had no interest in dirtying my hands in the affairs of the town, especially if it altered the political balance. That is not an Investigator's job. I hoped I would be able to exit on time with a solved murder to report.

Finding the brothel was not a difficult task. As if to reflect Urban's words, it was painted a garish color, the color of wine and burst blood vessels. The windows were closed and no one was around. I decided to wait until night.

When the sun sank low, the brothel's windows and doors opened in response. Hooch was all but declaring war on Chisham's authority. Sound and smoke poured out of every opening, polluting the sky. I entered through the front doors. I ignored the eyes that tracked me from every staircase and doorway.

"Can I ... help you?" The voice came from a short woman with dark brown hair, like that of Ibrin. Her tone was not of surprise but of amusement.

"I'd like to talk to the management about an investigation I am conducting."

She smiled in the least friendly way a person could before saying, "Sweet stuff, I'm sure I don't need to tell an Investigator that good information is never free. And definitely not in here. Besides, Mama Hooch is unavailable."

"One of the prostitutes will do fine."

I don't know what terminology she was expecting, but I don't believe any word I chose would've satisfied her. "Mister Investigator, I'm a good judge of people. I take pride in that. So you can take it as fact that you ain't the type to go askin' for 'prostitutes.'"

"I assure you, all I need is one." For good measure, I added, "I won't be long."

The look on her face told me she couldn't begin to fathom what I could want with a prostitute, nor did she want to be in the room with us when I was able to do as such, at least as far as she could imagine. She bid me stay put while she dove into the back of the establishment. Every second she made me wait was an intense displeasure. Finally, she returned with another woman, the first dark-skinned person I'd seen since before I climbed aboard the train. I was surprised to find her in the brothel.

"She'll do fine for you," the first woman said. I noticed her fingers wrapped several degrees too tightly to the second woman's arm. I held my hand out, supine, as an offer that she take it with the hand that wasn't being restrained by the boorish maître d'.

"Name?" It only seemed right I have this woman's name. I stood by what I said to Chisham and Myrl by the dead body.

The first woman cut in, unfortunately. "We don't do names here. It's for the girls' safety." She looked at the prostitute she brought me. "You can call her Heyou. Everyone else does." Finally, she let her go.

"I've heard of many people changing names," I said to the dark-skinned woman. I'd had enough of the impudent, short thing. "Show me to a private room, if you will."

The woman barely waited to speak after closing the bedroom door.

"How in the hell did you find me?"

"You don't strike me as the prostitute type."

"You're here on an investigation."

"And that, I hope, is where it ends. I have a train to catch."

She sighed, shaking her head. "Always on topic. Always on schedule."

"Could you be so kind as to remind me how I know you?" Truthfully, I couldn't recall, but she was confident about who I was.

"Calveston," she said. "Do you remember the embezzlement case? With the holdout on the pier? Warehouse full of dynamite?"

Her questions fully triggered my memory. Though I didn't know her before I started that Investigation, we had ended up working together on that one. I didn't know where she was going after I caught my train.

"Meuriam Lange. I remember. You would make an excellent Investigator."

She screwed up her face. "I haven't the stomach for it."

"It's not much different from what you do."

"It's very different," she said, waving away the compliment. "Besides, I couldn't moonlight in a place like this if I were."

"Which again raises my point: you don't look like the prostitute type."

Lange chuckled. "You may be factually correct, but I'd go to all lengths to avoid referencing the girls' line of work with any word. You wouldn't like it much if I called you a clue-sniffer."

We were wasting time, so I pressed forward. Lange was reliable the last time we'd been together. I considered myself lucky to be questioning her about the murder, as opposed to another prostitute in the brothel.

"What can you tell me about Ward Ibrin?"

"As much as anyone else. Slimy son of a bitch. Wanted for more things I care to count. I heard he had several hidey-holes out in the dirt, but he was trekking east, for some reason. Why?"

"Any accomplices?"

Lange squinted at me. "You're digging for gold, but you don't know how far down it is."

I repeated my inquiry. Trustworthy though she was, I had no time to be resisted.

"We think he has friends all around, but no one he travels with," she said after releasing a sigh. "He's something of a loner." She leaned on the door. "Are you gonna tell me how this connects to a dead whore on tricondylanth soil?"

It was my fault for forgetting how good Lange was as a detective.

"The person to whom you refer is most likely Ibrin."

Lange let out a brief whistle, then flicked her head as an admission of understanding. "We all have our predilections."

I shook my head. "I do not believe he was made up to look like he worked here as some sort of pastime. His arms and legs were shaved badly and his hair was curled."

"Who am I to judge," Lange interrupted.

"And his face was skinned."

"Ah."

"But it was the abdominal wound that killed him."

"I see." Lange started to pace around the bed, beside which I still stood. "Do you think the bugs got him?"

"Tricondylanths used to be a more violent species," I said, "but not anymore. And certainly not when corralled into unnatural communities."

"Could be these here are testy, didn't take kindly to a wanderer."

Again, I denied her positing. "Unlikely. Additional evidence suggests Ibrin was murdered elsewhere and dragged into the reservation. The ground beneath him was dry."

"I see." Lange looked in a mirror. She bounced a curl of hair in her hand. "So Ibrin was killed in his get-up and dumped out by the bugs in a pretty picture frame. Which means someone identified him ... now I get it." She looked at me. "You're trying to get at Mama Hooch."

I wanted nothing more than for her to be off the mark, but she proved capable, even still. "It would appear so, yes."

"Well, she doesn't like me, I can tell you that much."

"I would wager no one here does."

She shot me a look, then dropped it. She knew I was the only ally in town.

"Let me put it another way: you'll have to find someone else to open that door. Does that work for you?"

I nodded, then asked my only remaining question: "Why are you here?"

"I told you, I'm on downtime. I'm allowed to."

"I don't think it's that simple."

"It is," Lange said, turning back from the mirror.

We looked at each other for a moment. She would not tell me anything more, I knew. I hoped I would not need the secrets she hid. I left the brothel.


When day broke, I returned to the jailhouse to await Myrl's arrival. At some time later in the day than I would have returned to my place of work if I were sheriff, Myrl appeared. He grimaced at me, then pushed through the doors to enter. I followed suit. As was my intention, Urban was nowhere to be found. Being new to Clicker Hill, I did not know when he was to show up for his duties, if he even stayed at the jailhouse as I expected he did. I took advantage of our time alone to probe the sheriff's mind.

"I'm told you did not inspect the body before we all went together."

Myrl dropped his holster, gun inside, heavily onto the table. He eyed me like he was having a staring contest with the sun.

"Look here, you. You might be the mayor's guest, but I authorized no such intervention. To me, you're an interloper. It won't matter to me if that train you're waitin' to catch rides off without you. Just give me a reason to put you behind these bars – I know they can hold you."

I did at least appreciate the sheriff's consistent nature, if nothing else. Perhaps I knew then that if I pushed him, he might prove proficient enough to help.

"I can assure you I will cause no such issue for you. My objective is not to interfere with your daily duties, but rather to uncover the murderer. After that, I will depart."

"I'd ask you to spit'n'shake, but ..."

"I agree. Quite unnecessary." I gave him a moment to process my olive branch. Then: "Please tell me what you know of the victim."

Myrl rubbed his chin, one hand resting on his holster. I could tell he was still sizing me up, but he spoke. "We'd received word over wire that Ward Ibrin, a wanted criminal, was creepin' around these parts. The Man told us he was movin' east. Probably had hopes for hitchin' a ride across the water."

"You believe the victim was Ibrin? Even without his face?"

"I might not mean much to you," he said, "but even I could tell that was no girly. He sure fit the bill, alright."

"If you had inspected the body before my arrival, you would not have needed me to illuminate this fact."

"Look here, freak," he started, jabbing a finger at me.

I held up my hands and replied before he could continue. "It is a point I only make because, had you reached that conclusion before my arrival, I might have been able to accelerate my investigation."

He glared at me. I had to sweeten the point.

"Which would have shortened my tenure here. It also would have reduced the tense scene between us and the tricondylanths."

"I really don't give a shit what those clickers have to say."

"Duly noted. Still, your problem has extended onto their property, which means that my problem involves them."

Myrl huffed. He turned away to start polishing the cell bars. It was amusing.

"What does Urban think of your suspicion of who the deceased was?"

"What do you mean?"

"When we left the site, did you discuss this with him?"

"I didn't say much of anything on the drive back." He looked at me. "I wasn't exactly in the mood."

"What about with Chisham? Did you discuss this with him last night?"

"I keep about as far away from that tinderbox as I can, these days."

I dropped a breadcrumb for him. "Because of Hooch, I presume."

He stopped his pointless task and turned back around.

"You've got your thumbs in more pies than I think you should, Investigator."

"I assure you, I want nothing to do with the political affairs of this town. Happenstance brought her name to me. Unfortunately, I believe she may be entangled in this affair."

"You're sayin'," Myrl said, sauntering up to me, "that because Ibrin was wearin' a dress and all that you think we need to start pokin' around Mama Hooch's lovenest?"

"Odds are good the two were connected. The prostitute guise was likely his means of protection in this town. If that were true, Ibrin would have been as hard to catch as I believe he was."

Myrl leaned back on one foot. "You think she was helpin' him hide out?"

"It wouldn't be beneath her. I am also told she wants to pressure Chisham with the sale of recreational hallucinogens."

"Who in the hell told you that?"

"That is irrelevant. I believe this to be true, therefore it is pertinent."

The sheriff shook his head, then moved toward his desk. He fixed his holster to himself before turning back to me.

"I think we may just need to pay Mama Hooch a visit."

I held up a finger. "While I agree, I believe it may be more important that we return to the tricondylanths."

"How d'you figure?"

"For one thing, the body is still on their land. For another, there may have been a witness when the body was dropped there."

"He was stabbed and skinned there, wasn't he?"

I reminded him of the dry ground. He considered this for a moment, then agreed to accompany me back to the site. I promised him I would convince the tricondylanths to allow him back on their property. Now that I had two allies, I didn't want to lose track of them.


Dust still billowed behind our auto while we stood at the fence. Myrl told me they never need a signal of any kind to beckon the tricondylanths to the barrier, but said it was a mystery he'd just as soon not solve. I already knew how adept they were at sensing vibrations in the ground. Soon enough, a tricondylanth and an interpreter appeared in the distance. Once again, I urged the sheriff not to speak. He needed no words to express how uncomfortable that made him.

When the pair finally reached the fence, they spoke.

<Investigation: continue. Solo,> became, "You've returned to see the body, we see. But the agreement was that only you may pass," the interpreter said to me.

"I recall the agreement. However, conditions have changed. I require the sheriff as a partner in this investigation. I request that you reconsider." For good measure, I added, <Apology. Desire. Help. Think. Two.> It was not the content of my trilling I hoped to communicate, but the attempt at a bilingual

connection.

The sheriff kicked at the ground while the tricondylanth thought.

Finally: "Your request undermines your authority.  As a result, you are allowed

one visit.  After this, they will dispose of the body."

"God– ..." Myrl grumbled to himself.

"One visit is enough," I said.  "Additionally, we will be removing the

body, ourselves, as a show of goodwill."  <Yes. Take. Me. Person. Apology.>

The tricondylanth approved of the rewritten agreement and dictated

the interpreter open the fence once more.  Even without the posse present, the

fence was still opened only enough for one person to pass at a time.


The body laid undisturbed.  The bosom had rebounded to its original

shape.  Insects had begun to flit about the open wounds.  Removing the body

would be unpleasant, but I felt it was a necessary offer to make.  Plus, it put

Myrl to work, hopefully to teach him something.

Myrl knelt by the body, looking for additional details.  Despite a

thorough palpation of the entire costume, we found no tools, notes, or messages.

Ibrin was running from meal to meal, we concluded.  Myrl suggested that he

may have been hiding something internally, but immediately rescinded the idea.

If he had hidden any contraband thusly, it would be laid to rest with him.

I set about searching for a tricondylanth with whom I could discuss the

murder.  The group was spending time beneath the surface, it seemed, in burrows they had dug in the dry ground. The burrows were well-formed with moistened soil. Either they had happened upon an underground spring, or they had been given water by the humans who had pushed them out. It seemed more likely that the former was true, seeing as how they required water to survive. Regardless, it felt improper to descend into their homes without requesting access, so I instead moved over to the interpreters' pen. They had constructed themselves reasonable frontier homes, sturdy enough to withstand the weather, but simple enough that most people would consider living in them downright barbaric. One of the interpreters, a man clearly not native to Clicker Hill, was closest.

"Do you know if any of the tricondylanths witnessed anything pertaining to the murder?"

He looked disturbed at my calling, as if it were unnatural to be asked a question. I supposed he wasn't used to being spoken to without a tricondylanth at his back.

"They didn't say anything, if they did, but I doubt they did."

"Would you be willing to confirm that for me?"

The man left his yard and came to the fence where I stood.

"You misunderstand me. They recently came out of a comatose state. You see, once every season, they enter into a kind of hibernation. It's complicated, but I can explain it."

"No need. When did they emerge?"

"It was a couple days ago."

The dried blood on the body and the lack of rigor mortis suggested Ibrin had been dead for longer than that.  The tricondylanths offered no information.  I thanked the interpreter and returned to Myrl.  He was still inspecting the body.  I told him what I had learned.

"Of course the clickers had nothing to say."

"I imagine you might have kept them from talking, had they anything to share."

He squinted up at me.  "What are you gettin' at?"

I met his gaze.  "I only proprose that a small dose of cooperation can prove fruitful, in the long run.  You could have come assess the scene when you were first told, as well."

Myrl smirked.  I don't think he found what I said to be humorous.  He looked back down at Ibrin and cast a hand at the boots.  "Even my boots don't get this dusty, just walking around.  I think he was dragged."

"I would agree.  But where is the track?  There is nothing to be found."

The sheriff stood up and scanned the area.  "Son of a bitch covered his tracks.  But I bet ...."  He trotted off in one direction, looked, then trotted in another.  He did that two more times before sweeping a hand to me, asking that I follow.  When I got close, he thrust a finger toward the space between a couple of bushes.  We both walked over to it.  "I was right.  He only wiped the track so far.  Fucker didn't think we'd find it."

"Or he was waylaid."

"By what, a clicker?  They were in the dirt."

We followed the track all the way to the fence. We agreed to continue following the track after we left tricondylanth territory. But before we could, unfortunately, we had to move Ibrin. By the time we finished the latter task, Myrl was sweating almost as much as Chisham was when we met.

I asked Myrl what he planned on doing with Ibrin once we returned.

"Far as I know," he said, squinting at the dirt road ahead of us, "only a few of us know it's him. I'd like to keep it that way, for now."

"You don't want the public to know?"

"Won't do them a lick o' good until we figure out who gutted him."

"So you and Urban will retain his body for the time being?"

Myrl nodded. "I got an ice box he can rest in until we can dump him in some government 'mobile. Yeah ... not lookin' forward to that wire."

I inquired as to what he meant.

"Big Man's gonna be wonderin' why their wanted boy is dressed up like a girlie. They may just ignore his missin' face."

"We all have our proclivities, sheriff."

He looked at me. "Sure. But I don't think that was on Ibrin's list."

I climbed out of the auto once we returned to Clicker Hill proper. Myrl asked me where I was staying. I said it wasn't relevant information, so he blinked once and then motored off to the jailhouse. I passed the nighttime wondering how best to approach Hooch.

Once the sun crested the horizon, I decided it was time to make the next move. I considered returning to the brothel. There was a chance it was just closing for the day, or perhaps it was already closed. Either way, I had not spoken with Chisham for a time, and I wanted to probe his mind for possible murderers. Failing that, I would ask him about Hooch.

I entered town hall with no difficulty. Clicker Hill was a small town with a brothel; I shouldn't have expected many locked doors. I weaved through the sunrise-lit corridors and ascended the stairs to the mayor's office. Just as I was walking toward it, the door opened. Looking as put-together as when I had last seen her, Lange exited the office as blasé as could be, careful to close the door behind her. She saw me and a proud smile crept across her lips. She looked as if she had something to hold over my head.

"He'll need a moment to get dressed," she whispered once she got close to me.

"This is all strictly within protocol, I assume."

"It is if I say it is. Besides, all they care about is results."

"So this was in progress toward your primary objective?"

She frowned. "This was for me," she snapped, then started to walk away.

I caught her arm as gently as I could. "You know you can trust me, Lange. We may be working on two different cases, but we are not at cross purposes."

"As long as I am undercover at the whorehouse, you will pay Mama Hooch what she's owed if you touch me."

I released her. I hadn't intended to upset her, truly.

"And that may be," she said, rubbing her arm where I had gripped it, "but I was sent solo, so solo I will work. We don't use Investigators as contacts."

"Would that you could be one, Agent."

Unfortunately, Lange departed in a foul mood.

I waited for the sun to rise a little higher before calling on Chisham. It turned out I had to do no such thing. Once again, the door opened, and he was the one making eye contact with me in the hallway.

"Oh! Investigator! I hope I ... were you looking for me at home?"

"I haven't tried to figure out which house is yours. I simply assumed you would arrive at your office in the morning. I was correct."

"Um ... yes."

He looked less sweaty than when I first met him, but that was not to say he was bone-dry. I marked the ring on his finger and the bruises on his wrists. I asked if we could speak in private. He glanced out the window at the cool colors of the dusty land in the morning light.

"Yes. Yes, we can ... actually, can we postpone this? I really should be going home. I had a late night worrying about ..."

"You could say Ibrin, but I think you mean Hooch." As long as he was going to lie, I supposed I could use it to my advantage.

Chisham sweated into his widely opened eyes, forcing him to blot them with his sleeve before he replied. "I was going to say that. Yes, Mama Hooch. And Ibrin."

"A question, then: does Hooch have any true means of importing her illicit herbs?"

The mayor's mouth hung open, but without airflow. Clearly, he was not expecting his hired hand to dip its fingers into more embarrassing matters.

"I, uh, I don't ... I thought we were going to reschedule this."

"Just one question, mayor. Then you can go home to your wife."

I hadn't meant it to come across as a threat, but whatever delivered me the information I sought was acceptable to me. It wasn't as if his life was in danger.

"Damn you Investigators." Chisham sighed, then turned back to his office, opened the door, and entered. It remained open for me, as well. I made sure to close it behind me.

"I don't know," he said, leaning on his desk. "I hear bits and pieces from the townsfolk. The sheriff and deputy don't know a thing."

"About Hooch's venture or her means of achieving success?"

"The latter. They know she's itching to make more money. Has all the girls whispering to the folk that it's coming, the recreational medicine."

Hooch seemed too big for Clicker Hill. I asked Chisham from where she hailed.

"She and a bunch of the girls came from Iydenton, up north. It was just her, at first, but she sent for the lot of them. They had that whorehouse set up faster than you could blink. More girls rolled into town as they pleased. I don't think a one of them is from here."

"Your law enforcement allowed them to stay?"

"Myrl doesn't think it's an issue. He says it helps reduce crime when the men have their fill of skirts what can't run away. And Urban's honey works there."

"Interesting."

"I know. I mean, I wouldn't want *my* wife –"

I considered hinting at Lange's work, but thought better of it. Operatives should work as one. "But you don't know if Hooch has any way of manifesting her plans?"

"I figure she does, but I have no proof. Neither sheriff nor deputy would support me if I marched in there, demanding answers."

"Is she able to send wire communications from within the brothel?"

Chisham stood up from the desk. "You don't think ...?"

"Mayor, I must be honest. Your problem with Hooch was not the reason you hired me. Rightly, I should have no business with it, at all. However, the Ibrin matter has swelled in size and forced me to become tangentially entangled with Hooch and her brothel. I will be making all future efforts to become disentangled from it as an endeavor to stay true to task. If you have gained any insight as to the Hooch dilemma from this conversation, kindly

333

do not report it to my overseers. I would not appreciate the implication that I stray from within my boundaries. Good day."

I left Chisham to sweat and caress his bruises. I had one more item on the steadily lengthening itinerary to attend to before knocking on Hooch's door.


"Urban," Myrl called. "You have a visitor."

The sheriff had not risen from his post behind his desk when I appeared to call after the deputy. The cells were as polished as he had left them from yesterday. Urban appeared through the back door. In hindsight, I could have circled the jailhouse and found him, myself, but I thought it proper to use the front door. If it made Myrl trust me any more than what little he did, I was for it.

"Oh, Investigator. You wanna talk to me?" Urban briefly lifted his hat to adjust his hair.

"Indeed. May we speak in private?"

Urban looked to Myrl who gave a noncommittal shrug. I took that as a sign that the sheriff did not altogether mind our jaunt to the tricondylanths. The deputy looked back at me.

"Where d'you have in mind?"

"We can walk the town, actually. As long as just the two of us can converse."

Urban followed me out into the road. I chose a random direction and started walking.

"I presume Myrl updated you on the body."

He nodded. "Yeah, Ibrin's corpse." He whistled. "Son of a bitch got his. And in Clicker Hill, no less. Still tryin' to find the killer? Or maybe you think it ain't worth it."

"What I think is irrelevant, deputy. You should know that Investigators complete whatever task is assigned to them unless explicitly unassigned by their overseers or by the citizen who requested their aid."

"And you haven't got neither."

"No. Not as of yet. So, until that time —"

"I getcha, I getcha. Man's got a job to do. Er ... you get what I mean."

Urban had a way of talking that greatly displeased me. It was no wonder he had a direct tie to the brothel, the only other thing in Clicker Hill that had made me feel as such. I decided to change the subject.

"Myrl says the brothel is not a problem for the town. Do you agree?"

"The brothel? You mean the whorehouse? Naw, it's no problem. What good city doesn't have one? And if that's the case, why not us? Mama Hooch has some good girls there. They know what they's doin'."

"You partake?"

"Ah ...." He looked unsure of how to escape his own insinuation. "Not really. I mean, no. I don't ... I don't pay to fuck, if that's what you mean."

"I suppose you have a different vice, then. One of intoxication, perhaps?"

"No, sir. I don't touch the stuff. Tastes like rat piss and makes you feel like it, too."

Urban, a teetotaler? That surprised me. I changed the subject again.

"What do you make of Chisham?"

Urban spat in the dirt. "That flimsy scarecrow doesn't know runnin' a town from his ass."

"Is that the popular opinion in town?"

"I don't really talk much politics with the people. Mostly just pleasantries, you know. That's my own thoughts."

"How did he enter office?"

We had walked a decent distance, already. Urban took a moment to lean one hand against the post of the general store, that it could better support his regaling me of Chisham's tale.

"Last mayor was Mayor Koppel. She was a good mayor. We didn't mind her bein' a woman. She had a good head and she used it. We had some trouble with the bugs, once, and she had it handled fast. Hoo-ee, she got the army in here but quick! Yeah, we liked her." He readjusted, leaning his full back on the post. He paused to spit again. "Then she got sick. She got sick so fast, we hadn't time to hold a new election. Sure, the town constitution says there's an order to these things, but we were thinkin' about who was gonna run next year. She only had the one year left, see? Well, she up and died 'fore all that could happen and Chisham was there. We never could figure out why Koppel had put him in a seat, in the first place." Urban shook a finger at me.

"I'll go to my grave swearing he had somethin' on her. Anyway, he was supposed to be next up, so up he went. And he was only supposed to finish her term, but the folks voted to give him his own, full term, startin' the day Koppel died. I think that's mighty disrespectful to her memory. But what can you do with these Clicker Hill people?"

I processed the largely unimportant story and developed one question I wanted answered.

"You're not from here?"

"Oh, no. I moved here from far off."

"Where?"

Urban chuckled. "So small, it don't even have a name. Good riddance."

I decided that was enough information gathered from the deputy, so I bid him a good day and we parted ways. It was time to find Hooch.


The brothel sat rather unimpressively in the midday sun. Without the sounds of debauchery peeling from within, it had no strengths but its gaudily painted exterior. If the town hall was any indication, I anticipated this front door to be unlocked, as well. But with all I'd heard about Hooch by that point, I should have been less surprised to find that it was, indeed, locked. Undeterred, I cut to the back of the building to search for any opening to use or person to talk to. The rear entrance also proved resistant to my mild efforts toward ingress, unfortunately. The windows were all shut. No one was around. I'm not too proud to admit the thought of breaking in crossed my mind, but Investigators have protocols for a reason. Instead, I decided to retreat into the shadow of the abutting building and wait for someone to enter.


It was before sunset that someone approached, likely even before the brothel was supposed to open. A plump girl with brown hair in common clothes slipped between the buildings and produced a key to unlock the brothel's back door. She cast a quick glance around before disappearing inside. I gave it a moment before entering, myself.

The interior was as thoroughly decorated as I remembered. The design suggested nothing of the sort related to what actually happened within those walls, save for the connotations of such rich décor. It was surprisingly clean for what one might have expected. Furthermore, it was entirely empty of customers and workers. The girl left no trace of where she'd been or went after entering the building. I had no choice but to start hunting.

I climbed the first flight of stairs I could find and encountered nothing but private rooms. I descended to the ground level and tried another flight. Those were more productive. I could hear, through the floor above me, someone speaking. In fact, I could hear two voices, both feminine, sharing a dialogue. While I could not discern words, I gathered two things. First, the conversation was short, at least as much as I heard after taking the wrong set of steps. Second, one of the speakers was the girl, the other was Hooch. No wonder it was so difficult to contact the brothel madame; she didn't seem to ever leave her parapet.

The conversation ended quickly, as I said, and the younger voice retreated a short ways on small, clomping footsteps to the staircase beside me. I made a silent decision before slipping backward into the darkness of a private room's alcove. The brown-haired girl walked right past me and descended to the ground floor. I counted my stealthy build a boon. Carefully, I crept to the stairs leading up to Hooch. I inched upward, taking precautions to avoid creaks in the woodwork. What I found at the top of the stairs precluded further hunting, as there was naught but a single door on the landing. I knocked twice. A voice from within drew close.

"Harah, I thought we –"

The door opened. Hooch was surprised to see me.

"An Investigator!"

Hooch turned and ran into the room. I'm not one for physical challenges, but I found it necessary, at the time, to overtake her. It was not difficult. She wore her years of life poorly, and below her natural center of gravity. Inside her abode, I found the thing she was running for was a small signal emitter, a simple pin on a lever which would transmit code through finger taps. I could only imagine her plan was to tap on it in rapid succession or in one prolonged press to signal someone on the other end of her apparent danger.

"Hooch, I believe we need to discuss some things."

"We've got nothing of the kind," she huffed, before racing back to the open door.

Again, I overtook her, closing the door in her path. She took this as a chance to dart back to the signal emitter. I could see how this was devolving quickly into a game of cat and very desperate, very inept mouse. I decided to dip ever so slightly into the force clause of my protocols. Hooch did not take kindly to being shoved sideways onto her bed.

"I'll scream if you do anything to me, you copper bastard!"

"You recognized me as an Investigator. You should know we do not make acts of violence with wanton abandon. You were evading my inquiry and wasting my valuable time. I have a train to catch. Now that you're in a more favorable state, I wanted to talk to you about Ward Ibrin."

The shift in topic made Hooch a little less uneasy, but she was still quite wary of me. I could tell this by the way she hovered a hand between her face and mine, as if she were able to protect herself from anything but a pestering insect.

"Ibrin? The little snot they say comin' through here? What about him?"

"Have you seen him?"

"No I haven't fuckin' seen him. Are we done?"

Hooch somehow managed the impossible, sinking below Urban on my list of people I desired to talk to.

"Do you hire all of your prostitutes?"

"They're my *girls*, jackass. And, yes, I do. They all have contracts with me."

"That's very professional of you."

"I run a business."

"Is it profitable?"

"I think we're done."

Hooch stood up. I remained stock-still, evenly between her and both the door and her emitter. Unless she had a firearm stowed beneath her bed, which was unlikely, at that point, she had no true option. I was going to get the information I needed.

"You're making strong pushes to infiltrate Clicker Hill with hallucinatory herbs. You're having your prostitutes talk to your clients about it. Chisham is worried sick that you'll run this town into the ground with your supply of vices. Myrl and Urban have no interest in stopping you. Have I got that all correct, so far?"

"You've been busy. You haven't been here more than a couple days and you've already stuck your nose into my business."

"I take that as confirmation. Hooch, I have no interest in anything you are doing in this town. I was hired for one reason. I see you are no longer directly connected to that reason. So as a show of indifference, I will depart after one more question."

"What?"

"Which prostitute belongs to Urban?"

"Which *girl?* Which girl is the deputy's? She's the redhead. Tall and bosomless. Not the most popular of the crowd, but she pulls her weight. That all?"

"Thank you for your hospitality, Hooch."

I turned and left her room. I heard her scuffle over to the emitter.

I paid a quick visit to the jailhouse before planning to return to the brothel. Myrl and Urban were both present. The former had his boots up on his desk while the latter was fiddling with his badge on a chair in the corner. Urban called out.

"All good, Investigator?"

I ignored it.

"Sheriff," I said, "how were wire communications established in Clicker Hill?"

"They dug long lines and laid down a crap-ton of wire, same as anywhere. Why?"

"And what about short-range emitters? How are they established?"

Myrl lowered his feet to the ground.

"You mean them things people to flick like this –" he demonstrated with one finger "– to send messages?"

I nodded.

"They'd be a lot like wires," he said, rubbing his chin, "but more ... smaller, more discrete."

"Above ground or below?"

"Could be either.  What's this about?"

"Hooch established an emitter in her room atop the brothel.  I did not yet take time to inspect the line or to where it goes.  Thank you for the information."

Myrl stood up.  "I should probably check this out, too."

"Who cares what she does, sheriff," complained Urban.  "She's practically a cripple.  She don't go nowhere on her own.  It's probably how she calls for food and the like."

"I can assure you, deputy," I said, finally addressing him, "the way she ran to it when I approached her was not to call for light refreshments.  I suspect she has been dealing with someone by way of this transmitter."

Myrl shrugged at Urban.  "We really should know about this sort of thing."

Urban groaned and stood up.  "Alright.  I guess we're goin'."

"I didn't say y'had to come with, deputy."

"Naw, it's alright.  You're already goin'," Urban said, waving off the suggestion.

"I don't see anything along the front," Myrl said when we reached the brothel.

"It could be there's a line down the rear," I suggested.

"Deputy, why don't you take a look?"

"Yessir."

Urban trotted off and disappeared between the buildings. I took my opportunity.

"Myrl, I don't trust Urban."

The sheriff squinted at me, surprised. "What? Why not?"

"I have reasons I feel I should not yet disclose. I propose proof, instead."

"What in the – what kind of proof?"

"After Urban returns, I will find an opportunity for you to part from us. You will use that time to closely inspect the rear of the brothel, down to the soil behind it. If you do not find a trace of a line buried under wood or dirt, you can consider this transgression in error. I trust your report."

Myrl looked me up and down. "You Investigators are a strange bunch."

Urban trotted back to us, just then. "Nothin' I wouldn't expect. Building's clean, sheriff. Investigator."

"Disappointing," I said. "Perhaps I was mistaken in my visual read of her device. Or perhaps it was for internal use, alone."

"Hey, how does this relate to finding the killer, anyhow? Aren't you supposed to be working on that, just?"

"I assure you, interrogating Hooch was an integral part of the investigation. Unfortunately, she may have led to more questions than answers. In times like this, I often prefer to check off smaller tasks so that I may better process information and recoup efforts. Myrl, have you told Chisham that we confirmed it was Ibrin who was killed?"

"No ... I haven't."

"Do you think now would be an appropriate time?"

"I wasn't plannin' on it just yet."

"How long would it take for officials to come collect his body after being notified by Chisham, if you were to notify him?"

I watched Myrl think about it. I believed he understood my point, even if it did twist his arm some.

"Yeah, I guess it would be a while. You think you're close to findin' the killer?"

"How long," I repeated.

"Prob'ly a couple days, if I had to guess. We've maybe got one visit in as long as I've been sheriff."

"Plus the army for Koppel," Urban interjected.

I ignored the deputy. "That should be plenty. Yes, I think now is an appropriate time to update Chisham, before the body decomposes too much more."

"If you think so," mumbled Urban.

"Yeah, I agree. Deputy," directed Myrl, "go with the Investigator and tell Chisham we've got a wanted criminal in our ice box, ready for transportation to whatever royal hole in the ground they want him in."

"You're not comin'?"

"I'll meet y'back at the jailhouse. I don't wanna leave it alone for too long."

Before Urban could protest, Myrl left us alone.  Urban looked at me.

"Lead the way."


"So it really was Ibrin, huh," mused Chisham, after we told him.  "Myrl guessed it, straightaway.  Strange circumstances, indeed."

"That's right, sir.  Sheriff and the Investigator picked him up from bugland.  He's in our ice box, ready for ... ready to go."

"Alright, I'll wire them back, let them know he's here.  They'll want to confirm it, I'm sure.  Could you maybe do away with the whore dress?"

"I would argue the difference made would be minimal.  His face was removed, after all.  Their need to be certain beyond all doubt will make it moderately more difficult for them to confirm the identity, either way, despite whatever assurances you offer that it is truly Ibrin.  And in one scenario, the corpse remains clothed."

"Good point," Chisham remarked.  "Well, thanks for letting me know.  Honestly, it's a weight off my shoulders, knowing a wanted criminal is done away with."  Chisham picked up the receiver of the phone on his desk, dialed it, and spoke.  "Yes, honey, if you could wire the government men who called us about Ward Ibrin, tell them to come as they can ... the number should be on the notice.  ... On your desk, that's right.  Thank you, sugar."  He replaced the receiver and looked up at us.  "Anything else?"

"Not as far as I know," Urban said, looking to me.

"I believe that is all. I should have a resolution to the murder before they arrive."

Chisham's face relieved just a little of its tension.

I dropped off Urban with Myrl. The deputy shortly mentioned that the job was done, and then he disappeared out the back door once more. I looked at Myrl. He gave me a curt nod with an intense look in his eyes. He traced two fingers together through the air and then split them, wide. I left.

I had nowhere I needed to be until the brothel opened. I wasn't excited about wasting more hours, but I could think of nothing else that needed to be done until I could get inside to see Urban's partner. I waited on the edge of town and stared out into tricondylanth territory. A voice ended my isolation.

"Do you have any idea what you've done?"

I turned to see Lange storming up to me, wearing plain clothes. She shoved me, knocking me, ashamedly, into the dirt.

"Tin can *fucker!*"

"Lange, I don't know why you're upset. I have tried to share everything with you –"

"All of you, brains in jars," she ranted, "and not a one of you has any ounce of subtlety or concept of nuance! No *wonder* no one likes you!"

I shook dust out of my joints and stood up.

"Lange, I can see you are upset, but I desire more clarity. I would wager you are implying I have unknowingly interfered with your own investigation."

"You're goddamn right, you have. You went to see Mama Hooch, didn't you?"

"I did. She was greatly unhelpful."

"Did you mention me?"

"I would never." Lange did not need to know I considered confiding to Chisham about her presence.

"That's something, at least. But did you happen to notice her little ticker tool, probably set on a counter of some kind?"

"The signal emitter, yes. I allowed her to send a message when I left. It would have been improper to destroy it. I assumed it was simply a message to bar me from reentry, a problem I would have dealt with."

Lange suppressed a scream. "You have *no* idea what you did. You weren't supposed to talk to her. She's a flighty bitch. She called for help."

"To whom?"

"To the man she's asking set her up with the herbs, you moron!"

I shook my head. "You mean to say they already have a working relationship?"

"I didn't think they did, but they sure as hell do, now. He's coming with a lot of support to just take over Clicker Hill, never mind set up a trade point here. This was exactly what I was trying to prevent. Or damn near it! You *idiot!*"

Myrl's silent message suddenly clicked.

"You created a connection to Hooch's emitter. You have been intercepting messages for some time."

"Look at you go, Investigator. Really catching on, now."

"How long do we have?"

"Two days, maximum."

"That could be very convenient."

Lange stared at me with the most baffled of looks. It was as if she'd just witnessed an earthbound animal fly.

"How do you figure that?"

"Chisham just wired the government to collect Ibrin's corpse. They, too, will be here in two days' time."

I let her calculate the course of events. Her rage subsided.

"There'd be a shootout."

"But it could make your mission a success."

Lange looked at me, long and hard. "We need to round up help. How many blues are coming?"

"I don't know for certain," I said, shaking my head. "Likely too few to survive without help. Myrl will assist."

"What about the deputy?"

An idea sprang to mind. "The deputy is useless. I have a better thought." I braced Lange's shoulder. "Would you do me a favor?"

"Why would I?"

"All is not yet lost."

She sighed. "What?"

"Can you arrange a meeting between the tall, red-haired prostitute and myself for this evening?"

Lange snorted. "There's nothing she could do to get you off."

"I need to talk with her outside of the brothel."

A moment passed. I suspected Lange was wondering if I was worth the trouble. If she didn't accept, I would find my own solution, scarce though I was on time. At last, she pushed my hand off her shoulder.

"Fine."


Later that night, I spied the red-haired woman standing behind a bush, just beyond the edificial edge of town. I approached carefully from my position until I was near enough. I signaled her with the clicking of my fingers. Her head snapped around to spot me, her hand jumping to her chest. I heard her whisper obscenities.

"I did not mean to frighten you."

"There was no way not to," she admitted. "What do you want from me, Investigator?"

"Have you ever met Hooch?"

"Mama Hooch, y'mean? No. I heard tell she'd moved here from Iydenton, and she had a good reputation of carin' for her girls, so I came down this way, myself. But I never seen her, no."

"How did you meet Urban?"

The shift in questions caught her off-guard, I could see. I had no interest in her connection with Hooch, unless it was significant enough to change the course of the interrogation. I was more concerned about whether she would tell the truth on the latter point.

"Uh, he was already deputy when I –"

"I have no interest in lies, miss. How did you meet Urban?"

She fiddled with the trim on her shawl. They had that habit in common.

"It was a while back. We grew up in the same town. It was a small town."

"West of here?"

"Far west, yes. How did you know?"

"A suspicion. Continue."

The woman shifted her weight between each foot as she told me the story.

"When we were old enough, he joined the army. He said he was built for bigger things. He was gonna send for me after a year. I never got a message. Nothing. I gave up on him. I probably shouldn't have, but ... well, I got myself partnered up with another boy from town. He was older than we were, showed up after Arkis left – that's Urban's first name. Older boy treated me bad. I ran away. Last thing he said, he made it sound like he was gonna find me, one day, so I kept runnin'. You know how it is with boys, these days. Then I got to

Iydenton and I heard of Mama Hooch.  She made it sound like honest work, so I took it.  Truth be told, I like it."

It was exactly as I was beginning to expect.

"You reunited with Urban here."

"Yes, I did.  He said he *had* sent for me.  I don't know why I didn't get it.  But we're together, now.  And he doesn't mind what I do.  It makes me happy."

I took the final stab, not completely in the dark.

"The older boy.  What was his name?"

The woman averted her gaze.  "I don't really remember, now ...."

"Unlikely.  Incredibly unlikely.  You just said you were running for your safety.  You would remember such an antagonist's name."

She clutched at the corners of her shawl with both hands and bent at the knees.

"Please don't ask me again!  I don't want none of it!"

I had no time to waste.  Rather than the one I had taken with Hooch, I chose a more empathetic path with the woman.  "What's your name?"

"If I tell you, it'll just make things worse!"

"I have no way of formally addressing you without a name.  It's all I ask."

She squeezed both ends of the shawl into both hands and did her best to shrink inside it.  "Maribee."

"Maribee. I need you to confirm the name of the boy from whom you ran so that I may conclude my time in Clicker Hill. What's more, I do not have time to waste. Please, do me the kindness of telling me the name so I may put an end to this investigation."

Truly, it looked as though Maribee thought she was hidden under her shawl, even though her red hair was still entirely visible, as was every other square inch of her tall body.

"Please, Maribee. We both know it. I only need to hear you say it."

And in a tiny voice, the sacred words were uttered: "Ward Ibrin."


In the morning, I trekked once more to town hall. I caught Chisham coming out of a latrine. He was very startled, which gave me small satisfaction, I admit.

"Investigator! What – what do you need?"

"Let's go to your office. We have people to call."

He did as he was told. I commanded him to call Myrl and Urban to his office. Once that was done, I told him to call Hooch.

"I don't have her number," he cried. "And why do I want her here, anyway? What's going on?"

"We don't have the time for questions to be answered before we all have gathered. You can call the brothel and they will send her over, I assure you. Or, if not her, a representative will do."

He called the brothel. Partway through, he suggested a representative be sent. I corrected him loudly, forcing him to revert to my original demand. After an agonizingly long wait, the sheriff and his deputy arrived. Before anyone from the brothel arrived, Lange appeared at the door. That gave Chisham quite the fright.

"I figured you would be here," she said to me.

"Everyone of note will be here soon."

"There goes my cover." She looked at Chisham. "I had fun."

The mayor nearly fell to his knees.

"Looks like you're putting a bow on things, Investigator," Myrl said. "Got a name for the killer yet?"

I nodded, but told him it was not yet time to divulge. We had one more person to wait for.


While I was not expecting Hooch to be timely, I did not think she would wait until midday to grace us with her presence. I should not have thought stalling beneath her.

"I see everyone's present," Hooch wheezed. "Time to formally declare a truce, Chisham? Or perhaps a surrender?" She noticed Lange standing behind me. "Aren't you ... Chisham, you fucking devil. She was working for you, wasn't she? I knew there was a reason I didn't trust her."

"That's not why, and you know it." Lange glared a volley of gunfire at the brothel madame. "I'm an Agent."

Hooch threw up her hands. "They'll hire anyone."

I addressed the group.

"Clicker Hill is soon to be under siege. Hooch has alerted a band of ne'er-do-wells to take the town for themselves, likely to become a bastion for criminals and a regular trading post for illicit goods." I added a line to Hooch: "Please correct anything you know to be untrue." When she refused to speak, I continued. "At about the same time, some government officials are coming to collect the body of the now deceased Ward Ibrin. He was found in a prostitute's clothing, killed by an abdominal puncture. The killer removed his face so as to prevent or delay identification. Ibrin was killed somewhere close by and then dragged out to tricondylanth territory to either obfuscate the crime or to allow the other species to dispose of the body. The killer betrayed his fundamental misunderstanding that tricondylanths are essentially a peaceful species and have no need for corpses." I paused, only to measure the amount of eye contact I still had. To no one's surprise, Hooch was looking anywhere but at me. "Myrl. Though I hold no authority in Clicker Hill, I recommend you detain Hooch on the grounds of conspiracy to do damage to the town. Chisham, I suspect you would agree."

Chisham nodded. His head vibrated in small bursts, then large bursts, then small again. He had no idea what kind of power he truly had as mayor. Myrl gave me another curt nod, withdrawing a pair of handcuffs and proceeding to haul off the brothel madame with the help of Urban. Through her smoke-stained throat, her offensive protestations could be heard even after they rolled her into their auto and pulled away to the jailhouse.

"I ... I thought you wanted ... n-nothing to do with Mama Hooch," Chisham stuttered.

"I don't," I replied. "She was an unfortunate obstacle which cropped up in the course of finding Ibrin's killer, which I have done."

He looked at me, still reeling from the arrest of his rival.

"Who ... who is it?"

"I will answer – if you follow me."


Chisham, Lange, and I walked out of town hall, across Clicker Hill, and over to stop by my train tracks.

"Lange, it was a pleasure to encounter you again, circumstances being what they were."

"You're not awful for a brain in a jar," she acquiesced. "Let's not do this again too soon."

I nodded at her.

"You would still make an excellent Investigator."

"I told you, I don't have the stomach for it. I'd miss my skin."

I looked at Chisham and said the final words of my investigation.

"Mayor Chisham, I have solved your case. Ibrin was using Clicker Hill as another point in his journey to freedom, nothing more. If you ask all of the prostitutes, I'm certain you'll find one will confess to helping him blend in as a prostitute. I can't say which one, as I don't truly know. It was bad luck for him he came here, because he discovered Maribee, the red-haired prostitute who was once his partner."

"Use a different word! Please," Lange interrupted.

I continued: "Urban, Maribee's first lover, caught wind of Ibrin's reappearance and killed him. I don't know what possessed Urban to then remove the wanted criminal's face, seeing as how little time it took for us to informally deduce his identity, but – and I do not say this lightly – Urban is a vapid man who does not deserve authority. But that is a superfluous detail. So, Mayor Chisham, have I completed my investigation as you detailed it to my overseers?"

Weakly, he nodded.

"I need verbal confirmation, please."

"Y-yes. Yes, that's right."

"Excellent."

I felt the train coming to pick me up. Lange stepped forward.

"That's it? You're going?"

"My train is coming."

"What about Hooch's men coming? And the blues for Ibrin?"

"I made an arrangement with the tricondylanths. They'll handle the threat."

Chisham spoke up. "I ... I thought you said they were peaceful."

"They are, largely.  You should know this for the rest of your term, Chisham.  If someone were to convince tricondylanths that their way of life is once more at stake, perhaps threatened by men of ill repute with no shred of dignity, they will – albeit reluctantly – give in to their violent instincts.  For a short time, anyway.  They are currently digging tunnels underneath Clicker Hill to facilitate an ambush."

Both humans stood in complete awe.

"So that's why you had me fetch Maribee, put her way out in the brush," Lange marveled.

"Indeed."

My train pulled up behind me and beckoned me within.  Before I climbed aboard, I had one last thought for my client.

"Chisham.  I have every reason to believe that the town will survive thanks to the tricondylanths.  If I may suggest your next executive action as mayor: change the town's name.  They don't like that word."

I heard Lange laughing as the train took me home.

*Anything more to report?*

No.

*Investigation closed.  Good work, Investigator.*

Thank you.

## ABOUT THE AUTHORS

**CHARLES ARDAI** is co-founder and editor of Hard Case Crime as well as an award-winning author. His five novels include the Shamus Award-winning *Songs of Innocence*, which the *Washington Post* called "an instant classic." In addition to the Shamus, Ardai has received the Edgar Allan Poe, Ellery Queen, and Inkpot Awards. He was a writer and producer for six years on the television series *Haven*, inspired by Stephen King's first Hard Case Crime novel, *The Colorado Kid*. King has called him "a true renaissance man" and "a master of the short story." Ardai lives in New York.

**ROBERT J. BINNEY** has written about Joe Strummer, James Bond, joyriding with the Salt Lake City police, and his relationships with Peter Frampton and President Jimmy Carter (though not together) for the *Los Angeles Times*, AtwoodMagazine.com, and other fine publications. His "Sasquatch, PI" series recently debuted in Down & Out Books' anthology *The*

*Killing Rain.* Binney is a member of the Northwest Screenwriters Guild and the Mystery Writers of America. He holds an MBA from Emory University and an MFA from University of California, Riverside. For more, see www.ThirdActMedia.com.

**CONNOR BOYLE** saw *Creature from the Black Lagoon* at a young age and has been fascinated with monsters ever since. His work has appeared in the aquatic horror anthology *Rampage on the Reef,* the mall horror anthology *Escalators to Hell*, and the yardsale horror anthology *Curbside Curses.* His favorite authors include Harlan Ellison, Joe Lansdale, Owl Goingback, and Brian Keene. In addition to writing fiction, he serves as the editor and publisher of *The Orbit Drive-In Zine.* He lives in Santa Fe, NM.

**CHRIS BRADY** writes historical pulp and crime fiction. He lives in Nebraska where he teaches history at a small college. He's also the historian for *Everything I Know I Learned from A Gold Medal Paperback*, a blog dedicated to Fawcett Gold Medal books and other topics. (goldmedalbookblog.com)

**COLIN BRIGHTWELL** is a Kansas City, Missouri, native. His work has appeared in Reckon Review, Flyover Country Literary Magazine, Bull, past-ten years, Dark Yonder, and Rock and a Hard Place. His debut collection,

*Nothing Good Ever Happens in a Flyover State*, is forthcoming from Cowboy Jamboree next spring.

**RON CLYBURN** lives in Dayton, Ohio, where he grew up reading comic books and watching The Three Stooges. As he grew older, he discovered novels, such as Doc Savage, Tarzan, and Mack Bolen the Executioner. His introduction to comedy was NBC's Saturday Night Live and the Not Ready for Prime Time Players. In college, he tried his hand at journalism, but the editor kept cutting out his jokes. So, he was given a weekly humor column to satisfy his thirst for parody and satire. He is a veteran of the U.S. Army Reserve, a sports fan, a family man, and former stand-up comedian. He still lives in Ohio, where he works as an "IT Professional," and looks forward to retirement so he can focus on writing. Ron is currently working on his first novel featuring his character Joe Cooper, the Dayton, Ohio, based private eye from his short story, "Domesticated."

**P.N. HARRISON** is a writer and professor living in Western Kansas. He studied creative writing as a student in West Texas. While he has written numerous academic articles on topics such as H.P. Lovecraft, J.R.R. Tolkien, and books bound in human skin, his contribution to *Starlite Pulp Review* is his first published short story. When not muttering in dead languages, he enjoys watching baseball, traveling to historic sites, and watching horror movies with his wife, Ashley.

**KAREN HARRINGTON** is the award-winning Texas author of numerous short stories and four novels, including SURE SIGNS OF CRAZY (Little, Brown) and JANEOLOGY (Shotgun Honey Books). She won the 2021 Ellery Queen Mystery Magazine Readers Choice Award for "Boo Radley College Prep." She received the 2023 Derringer Award for Flash Fiction. Her story "The Mysterious Disappearance of Jason Whetstone" appears in Best American Mystery and Suspense 2024. A feature of her writing space is the unicycle she got for her eleventh birthday. Say hello at www.karenharringtonbooks.com.

**GABRIEL HART** is an author and journalist from California's high desert. His debut novel *On High at Red Tide* is out now from Pig Roast Publishing. Hart is also the editor-in-chief/publisher of *Beyond the Last Estate*, an arts/literature magazine launched in 2024. Other works can be found at Expat Press, Punk Noir, Rock and A Hard Place, Apocalypse Confidential, and Hobart Pulp. In collaboration with local veteran outreach organization Mil-Tree, he hosts the Mojave Noir reading series. On the air, he reports daily for Z1077fm.

**DAVID SCOTT HAY** makes a mean Old Fashioned and the best ribs on the block. He is a former award-winning Chicago playwright and screenwriter. As a novelist he is a two-time Kirkus Prize Nominee for the literary satire *The Fountain* and techno horror/romance *[NSFW]*. Both are in multiple printings and have been picked up for translation. *[NSFW]* was listed by Tor.com as one of the most anticipated novels of 2023 and made Dennis Cooper's Top Fiction of 2023 and was recently named a Top 100 Indie Book of the 21$^{st}$ Century by *Genrepunk Magazine*. He is a member and volunteer for the SFWA and HWA. When not city hopping to sell books, DSH now lives in a valley between the ocean, the mountains, and the desert with his wife, son, dog, library, and a dozen typewriters.

**PAIGE JOHNSON** is EIC of Outcast Press, which has published some past Starlite authors like Nevada McPherson and Manny Torres. Likewise, she designed and featured in Craig Clevenger's *Diner Noir*. Johnson is author of the illustrated poetry books Percocet Summer and Citrus Springs. The characters featured in the story here will be in novellas one day, and appear in short stories featured in Cowboy Jamboree's MOTEL anthology, Punk Noir Magazine's Hellton Towers, and Urban Pigs Press Unintended Consequences.

**ANDREW MILLER** has previously published short stories in the Jacked Anthology from Run Amok Crime, Apocalypse Confidential, Close to the Bone, Pulp Modern, Switchblade, Broadswords and Blasters, and Starlite Pulp Review. He had a novella, *Lady Tomahawk*, in *LA Stories*, and his first novel, *Namaste Mart Confidential*, was released by Run Amok Crime in 2024, and has been shortlisted for Best Independent Novel by Crime Fiction Lover.

**ERIC O'NEAL** is a second time-Starlite Pulp-published author. He writes in the very scant time he has between working as a new Women's Health Nurse Practitioner, rehearsing a play in the local theater, hawking his play for said theater, teaching himself Yiddish, and building a TTRPG with his friends based on one of his other short stories. His wife, inspiration, and fellow (read: superior) actor, Maureen, is his biggest fan and editor, followed by their toddler, Arthur, and three cats. Eric really truly planned on getting back to reading the H. P. Lovecraft, Dashiell Hammett, and Zane Grey stories he previously started when he was still a nightshift nurse, but, wouldn't you know it, there are still only 24 hours in a day. Eric loves to write about everyone's favorite topics: cosmic horror, private investigators, Old West dialects, and being Jewish. Y'know. The classics.

**FRANK REARDON** was born in 1974 in Boston, Massachusetts, and currently lives in Charlotte, NC. He's published short stories and poetry in many reviews, journals and online zines. He published five collections of poetry with Punk Hostage, Blue Horse, and NeoPoesis. Frank is currently working on a nonfiction column for Hobart; more short fiction, and a short story collection, will be completed later in 2025.

# Also from Starlite Pulp:

## Starlite Pulp Reviews #1-4

Praise for the Review:

"Pulp fiction in all its glory."

"An excellent first Review!"

"Starlite Pulp is the most exciting new publisher on the block."

## *Outlaw Ballads* by Brian Townsley
A Sonny Haynes collection

Praise for *Outlaw Ballads*:

"Sonny Haynes deserves a seat at the bar next to Marlowe and Spade."

"Townsley takes readers on a film noir-style tour to the early '50's in Palm Springs, California, that bears little resemblance to the Los Angeles many of us know so well. The Sonny Haynes series acts as a mental time machine, and is worth every minute of the trip."

"Sonny Haynes did what other men boasted of."

Visit **Starlitepulp.com** for your pulp books, hoodies, tees, decals, submission guidelines, & so much more!